MURDER STALKED
IN THE SUNSHINE

Up in her bedroom, Ellen wept into her pillow. Down in the woodland, Philip and Claire kissed and clung and could not keep the thought of a dead man's money from their minds. Up and down the gravelled drive Peta walked with her love and would not speak kindly to him because he had brought all this trouble upon them "instead of just letting poor Grandfather be buried and not making any fuss." On the marble terrace Bella sat listlessly, her pretty face swollen with tears of pity and loneliness and grief; and down on the lawn among the buttercups and daisies Edward grew weary of Rosy-Posy's artless prattle and suddenly wondered what it would be like to stick a hypodermic needle into her; and whether it was himself, the real Edward, just thinking it to frighten himself, or whether it was his other self who had put the thought into his head—and whether he was mad, whether he was dangerous, whether he was already once a murderer . . .

Bantam Books offers the finest in classic and modern English murder mysteries. Ask your bookseller for the books you have missed.

Christianna Brand

SUDDENLY

AT HIS

RESIDENCE

BANTAM BOOKS

TORONTO · NEW YORK · LONDON · SYDNEY · AUCKLAND

*This edition contains the complete text
of the original hardcover edition.
NOT ONE WORD HAS BEEN OMITTED.*

SUDDENLY AT HIS RESIDENCE

A Bantam Book / published by arrangement with the author

*PRINTING HISTORY
First published in Great Britain in 1947
Bantam edition / March 1988*

ISBN 0-553-25465-0

Published simultaneously in the United States and Canada

---

*Bantam Books are published by Bantam Books, a division of
Bantam Doubleday Dell Publishing Group, Inc. Its trademark,
consisting of the words ''Bantam Books'' and the portrayal of
a rooster, is Registered in U.S. Patent and Trademark Office
and in other countries. Marca Registrada. Bantam Books, 666
Fifth Avenue, New York, New York 10103*

PRINTED IN THE UNITED STATES OF AMERICA

KR 0 9 8 7 6 5 4 3 2 1

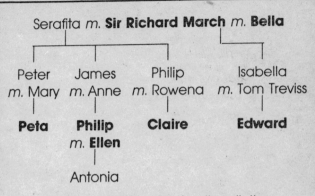

Serafita *m.* **Sir Richard March** *m.* **Bella**

Peter	James	Philip	Isabella
m. Mary	*m.* Anne	*m.* Rowena	*m.* Tom Treviss
Peta	**Philip**	**Claire**	**Edward**
	m. **Ellen**		
	Antonia		

Stephen Garde, the family solicitor.
Brough, the gardener, and **Mrs. Brough,** his wife.

Among the ten people whose names are here given prominence
were found two victims and a murderer.

CHAPTER I

Edward Treviss sat in a darkened room blissfully pouring out his soul to the latest new psychoanalyst —dramatically escaped (some fifteen years ago) from enemy-occupied Austria. 'Yes, I'm nearly eighteen, doctor. I've come to see you quite secretly because usually my grandmother *will* insist on coming with me, and she goes and tells a lot of stupid details which aren't in the least interesting. . . . My grandmother? Oh, she's Lady March, my grandfather's Sir Richard March. Only, you see, their daughter, that's my mother, was an illegit. Of course, she and my father were quite properly married and all that. . . .'

'Nevertheless, this stain of illegitimacy you haf brooooded over, my poor boy?'

'Oh, good lord, yes, I suppose I have,' said Edward, who had hardly ever thought of it as affecting himself. 'And then, you see, the frightful thing was that my parents were drowned in a boating accident, and I saw it happen. . . .'

This was not strictly true, for he had been busily occupied with a sand-castle at the time: but later in the day a nursemaid had kindly given him a graphic description of the disaster, adding that reely it was enough to make the pore kid turn queer in the head. The next time he was due for a spanking, therefore, he had put his little hand to his forehead and declared that it felt queer; and, to his delighted astonishment, punishment had been deferred and it was apparent that he was an object of interest and discussion. He had been taken to see a succession of grave-faced men who had let fall—usually in thickly guttural accents —some such comfortable phrases as 'not to be overworked', 'allowed to go his own way', 'better not to thwart the child': and since Grandmama had regularly

1

employed these catchwords from then on, he had come to cling to them as a species of nursery lifebelt whenever a storm blew up. They had seen him through odd terms at different preparatory schools and later a series of headmasters had written tactful letters suggesting that their various establishments were perhaps too rough and rude for so delicate a plant. In time, banishment from home had become an impossibility for the darling little psychopath, and even Edward himself could no longer distinguish between his real and his self-induced manifestations of abnormality. A minor accident a couple of years ago had greatly aggravated at least the imaginary side of his condition; and now, from this new alienist, came the joyful tidings that he might be liable to lapses into unconsciousness, fugues, automatism, heaven only knew what. . . . 'You mean I could sort of walk about and do things and not know what I was doing, doctor?'

'Thiss iss possible, my boy.'

'Good *lord*!' said Edward, enormously impressed.

'Also you shall not looking *up* too quick! Thiss iss dangerous to you and may bring on the fugue. Perhaps you are dropping somesings that you have in your hand. Carefully, therefore, not to look *up* too quick!'

It was extraordinary how often one was tempted to looking up too quick, when one got out of the dim room and into the street. Edward marched along cautiously, his eyes glued to the ground and when he came to a telephone booth could hardly persuade himself to raise them sufficiently to enable him to insert his tuppence and dial his cousin Philip's number. The adventure was finally accomplished, however, without mishap. 'Hallo? Ellen? It's me, Edward. Are you and Philip coming down to Swanswater today all right? Because, if you are, I'm in London, and I wondered if you could find room for me in the car?'

At the other end of the line, Ellen stood considering, receiver in hand. 'Well, there's me and Philip and the baby—and all the baby's things, Edward, that's

the trouble; and we're taking down Peta and Claire.'
However the more people there were, the less tension
would there be between herself and Philip and Claire.
She said at last: 'I don't know about finding room,
Teddy, but I daresay we can make it.'

'Could you? Thanks awfully. Are the others there
yet?'

'Claire's here,' said Ellen.

'Oh, well, I expect Peta's on her way. See you in
half an hour, then . . . .' He rang off and collected
his hat; a slim, dark nervous boy, picking his way,
with his rather charming smile, along the street—not
looking *up*!

Peta, however, was not only not on her way, but
still hopping with impatience while Matron, with maddening deliberation and obviously just to spite her,
counted over pillow cases. 'Twenty-seven, twenty-eight,
twenty-nine—where's thirty?'

'Under Sergeant Robert's knees, Matron, in number four bed . . . .'

Sergeant Roberts, with Peta's imploring eye upon
him, hunched up his knees to look as much as possible
as though there were a pillow there. 'Good. Thirty,
then,' said Matron, completing the heap with a sat-
isfied little thump. 'I hope *that* will satisfy the quar-
termaster; he'll be round to-morrow.' She bowed
majestically to Sister, ignored a mere V.A.D., and
marched away with her little retinue. Outside the door,
however, she said to the lady commonly known as
Ass. Mat., 'Who is that tall pretty child with the fair
hair and too much of it showing?'

'Nurse March, Matron—quite a good nurse. Her
grandfather,' added Ass. Mat. reverently, as though
that explained everything, 'is a Sir.'

'Her uniform is not regulation,' said Matron. 'It fits
too well. She's had it made privately, the little minx.'

Peta took formal farewell of Sister, sent Sergeant
Roberts' temperature soaring with the warmth of her
gratitude, waved a goodbye to the rest of the patients,
smiling indulgently from their beds, and sped off along

the corridor, tearing off her cap and apron as she went, a thing she was strictly forbidden to do. 'Soon, soon, soon, I shall see Stephen!' Scrambling out of her uniform, feverishly buttoning up her frock, perching her foolish straw hat on her shining head, all the time she thought, 'Soon I shall see Stephen! . . .' And all the way to St. John's Wood, jogging along in the dear red London 'bus, she prayed, 'Dear God, this time *don't* let me go all silly and wave my hands and make Stephen despise me for ever. . . .' From the days of their childhood together, Stephen had teased her about her fluttering hands.

And in the little house in St. John's Wood, Ellen adjured the solitary maid-servant to keep the brass plate polished, and if anyone rang up be sure to tell them that the doctor would be back a week from to-day, and meanwhile would they telephone Dr. Blair. She said, as her husband came slowly down the stairs, 'Oh, Philip—Edward's rung up and says can we take him down: I suppose we can?'

Philip was not unlike his younger cousin: dark too, and with the same air of nervous breeding, the same rather humorous charm; but he was irritable now and did not disguise it. 'It'll be a hell of a squash; and it'll look bad if we're stopped on the way.'

'You've got a perfectly good excuse: you're a doctor going down to see a case.'

'Well, thank goodness for Grandfather's dickey heart.' There was an uncomfortable pause. He said: 'Did you put my medical bag in the car?'

'You put it in yourself,' said Ellen.

Philip knew quite well that he had put it in himself. He knew quite well that he was playing for time, that both of them were playing for time, that neither of them wanted to go back to the drawing-room where Claire was supposed to be 'keeping the baby out of the way' while they got on with the packing. Claire had got away early from her newspaper office because she thought they all ought to 'have a talk' before this holiday together. 'There's no use shutting our eyes to

the inevitable, Ellen. . . . We may as well be honest,
Philip . . . .' She would sit there nervously twisting her
hands, her head bent, staring down at her little feet:
that glorious corn-coloured head, with its great twisted
bun of hair, low down on the nape of her neck. Philip
would think how expressive her mouth was, Ellen
would think that she spoilt herself, making such faces
when she talked. Earnest, passionate, nervous, uncertainly seeking, she would plunge them all into drama.
'You must know, you must have known for months,
Ellen, that Philip and I were in love . . . '

Ellen lifted one dark, eloquent eyebrow. 'My dear
Claire—*sheer* Home Chat!'

Philip, standing with his back to the mantelpiece,
shifted wretchedly from his toes to his heels. Life had
been very dull in the past six years. He had come
home from America, picked up his English degrees
and settled down into a promising practice: and all in
five minutes war had come upon them, and he, kept
back from the army from the sheer necessity of one
doctor remaining in a practice that had carried four,
had slaved ten and twelve hours a day—dull, routine,
unprofitable work among the panel patients who for
much of the time were the only ones who remained
in London. Paying back the cost of the partnership,
keeping up the shares due to his partners, hard-up,
overworked, bored, irritable, and consequently increasingly disagreeable to his wife. Ellen—small, dark,
plump, vivacious—had not played up. She had not
petted and sympathized, she had maintained intact
that standard of insouciant laughter which once had
carried so much of her charm for him: but a man
needed more than laughter, and now it was often too
quick, too relentless, too unkind. By contrast, Claire
had seemed understanding and tender. It was typical
of Ellen that she should meet this very real crisis in
their lives by calling it sheer Home Chat.

'This is something you can't meet by just laughing
at it, Ellen,' said Claire resentfully.

'Well, then, what do you *want* me to do?' said Ellen.
'We must all try and think of some way out.'

'There *is* no way out,' said Ellen reasonably. 'If Philip's in love with someone else, I can assure you I haven't the slightest desire to go on being his wife; but there's no money for a divorce and meanwhile the baby and I have got to live. Incidentally, Philip, I must say I think you might have told me why you were making all this fuss about sleeping in the spare room, instead of just letting me think I was losing my sex appeal. I was getting quite worried!'

Claire cast Philip a look of appreciation and gratitude, Philip looked self-conscious and miserable. He said, reverting to Ellen's casual bombshell as to a divorce: 'I couldn't possibly have a "scandal"; it would absolutely do me in. I've got a chance now of specializing, and that sort of thing's fatal, especially in genæ work.'

'Well, it's all very depressing, Philip. I mean, who *is* your wife, I who live with you and *don't* live with you, as it were, or Claire who lives with you but doesn't live with you? If you see what I mean,' said Ellen, with her head on one side.

Claire made indignant denials. Ellen, who was evidently only too ready to part with her husband, asked with her usual practicality, 'Couldn't you borrow on your expectations from your grandfather? Both of you have got something coming to you.'

'No we couldn't,' said Philip firmly. 'Grandfather changes his will at least twice a year, and neither of us can possibly be sure what we'll get. He always changes it back again; but his heart's so dickey that he may pop off at any minute in the meantime, and then we'd be properly in the soup.'

'Anyway, I shouldn't think we get more than about ten thousand between us, Philip?'

'About that,' said Philip.

'I must say I think it's very unfair,' said Claire. 'You, the only male in the family and yet the property and all the money goes to Peta, who's a girl.'

'Her father was the eldest son, and she's his heir. It's perfectly reasonable. I've always known things were fixed that way.'

'Not when you first came home from America. Grandfather was all for making you his heir then, only Stephen Garde went and interfered.'

'I feel that Home Chat is degenerating into the Fat Stock Prices,' said Ellen, ironically amused. 'However, here are the others coming up the path, so this delightful discussion must now cease or be continued in the car.' She went out into the hall to meet them. 'Hallo, Edward. Hallo, Peta—you got off all right from your frightful hospital?'

Peta enlarged plaintively upon the iniquities of Matron which culminated in *al*ways starting off stock-taking the *min*ute anybody wanted to go off on their seven days' leave. Edward embarked upon his experiences with the new psycho-analyst. 'He's most frightfully good, he knits all the time, and he says I may have fugues—*you* know, I sort of wander about and do things and then quite forget what I've done . . .'

'What does he knit for?' asked Ellen practically, bundling Antonia, the baby, into a state of helplessness in woolly coats and shawls.

'Well, it's most frightfully soothing to the nerves and encourages people to talk about themselves——'

'Then for heaven's sake, Ellen, don't bring any wool down to Swanswater with you. We don't want to spend the whole week hearing about Edward's fugues . . .'

As they all went down the steps together, Peta said, putting her hand on Ellen's arm, 'Your first real holiday in years, Nell; you must be quite excited.'

'Deliriously,' said Ellen dryly. 'Bella will drive me crazy the entire time telling me how to manage the baby, and your grandfather will spend the rare intervals telling me that I ought to have lots more— babies, I mean. Which, anyway, I can't, because Philip and Claire have fallen madly in love, and Philip has moved into the spare room out of loyalty to her.'

They climbed into the car: three cousins, Philip and Peta and Claire March; and Ellen, Philip's wife; and Edward Treviss, their half-cousin, whose grandmother, Bella, had in the naughty 'nineties been Sir

Richard's mistress and was now his wife. Philip sat
gloomily at the wheel, in the shamefaced despair of
a man over whom two women are quarrelling, Claire
beside him regretted the exposure of their love to
Ellen's earthy mockery; Peta, her own long legs wound
round the packed legs of the baby's cot, prayed earnestly for strength not to appear silly and affected in
front of darling Stephen, and Edward practised not
looking *up*, with complete success. Ellen, pointing out
trees and moo-cows to her daughter, fought with all
her hardy spirit against the pain and humiliation of
henceforward depending for her everyday bread and
butter upon a man who no longer wanted her. 'All
the same, Ellen,' said Peta, attracted for a moment
out of her self-absorption, 'I do believe you're crying!'

'Antonia hit me on the nose with her wicked fist,'
said Ellen. The baby, a helpless cocoon of woolly shawls,
looked up at her mother with what well might be
reproach.

CHAPTER II

Grandmama Serafita had kept her husband's love
for twenty-five years by the simple expedient of being
everything to him that she fancied his mistress was
not. 'Tsimple? But of course,' she would insist in her
charming broken English when her sons protested,
laughing, against this qualification. 'What is this Bella,
after all? Not so very preeety. Not at all weeety. And,
enfin, an intellectual. To be a woman and to be an
intellectual, my dear boys—thiss is not compatible. Le
bon Dieu did not intend men to fly; and he did not
intend women to think. Nobody could call *me* an intellectual,' Serafita would declare proudly and with

profound truth, 'and it is a comfort to your poor father to come home to me from time to time and listen to a little feminine nonsense. She is very well, this poor Bella, but she is a bore. Let her remain peacefully at Yarmouth, and I, Serafita, shall remain here at Swanswater; and when I die, she will marry your father and console him for my loss. And *then* we shall see who will win!'

'Perhaps you may outlive her, Maman,' the sons would suggest, laughing again.

'No, no, I am too tactful to grow old,' Serafita would say complacently. 'You shall see. I shall die, still young and beautiful,' (she was at this time well over forty), 'and your father will never forgive himself. He will bring her here, this Yarmouth Belle, with her illegitimate brat, and she shall live in my home and listen to nothing but "Serafita", "Serafita", "Serafita" till she is sick of the very sound of my name—'

This was exactly what happened. Still young and beautiful at fifty, Serafita died; and Sir Richard married his mistress and with her continued at Swanswater—a magnificent old man with his great jutting nose and gentle, deep grey eyes—brilliant, stupid, ruthless, sentimental, splendid, pathetic, a living monument to the memory of the little hybrid ballerina who, in the merry days of the eighteen-nineties had danced her enchanting way into his heart; and Bella, entering diffidently upon her inheritance, had struggled henceforward beneath the heavy burden of Serafita's posthumous spell. The three gay sons had been killed long ago in the days of the only war that counted for anything with Sir Richard; their wives were dead, too, or remarried and disappeared from the family ken. Only the third generation was left, but mercifully there they were—the grandchildren! Peta, the heiress, Philip returned from that heathen America where in his childhood his mother had taken him, Claire who insisted upon working in some dreadful newspaper office, full of nonsense about independence and a career. Not that Sir Richard cared two hoots about Claire; she could do as she liked with her life and so far that had not amounted to much! Peta was the darling, Peta the child of the eldest, Peta with her pretty ways and her fluttering hands, whose charm could knock all Claire's blonde beauty into a cocked-hat. And Philip and Peta and Claire were all coming down to-day to Swanswater to take part in the little ceremony that Sir Richard always held on the anniversary of Serafita's death. Serafita had loved fêtes and anniversaries, and all the trivial ceremonial of well-conducted family life; and nowadays everything that Serafita had cared about had grown to be the law. Sir Richard stormed through the great house. 'Bella! Is everything ready for those children? Is everything prepared for to-morrow? Has that old crone dusted the portraits? Has Brough done the geraniums? Has he sanded the paths?'

'I'm seeing to it all, Richard,' said Bella patiently.

He stood teetering on the front terrace looking down across the drive and towards the lodge; and in the bright sunshine, all the air was heavy with the scent of Serafita's roses. Swanswater lay two miles out of the small town of Heronsford, in Kent, on the other side of the downs, from Heron's Park, and just across the Tenfold Ridge, from Pigeonsford. It had been a beautiful house in its day and the hall and principal rooms still wore the distinction of their Georgian elegance; but it had been much added to, and on either side of its plain brick front sprawled whole wings of glass-houses, squash-courts, orangeries and a swimming bath, with a nightmare of marble terraces and balconies. To the east, the house fronted on flowered terraces, running down to the river's edge; to the west, the gravelled arms of the drive enclosing a wide green lawn, opened out through magnificent wrought iron gates on to the main road. Serafita's influence had clotted the grounds with little bowers and temples, each quite charming in itself, but utterly ruining the character of the park; and on either side of the gates stood two of them, highly ornamental lodges in pseudo-

Grecian style. In one of these tiny houses lived Brough, the gardener and his wife; and in the other, Serafita had died.

The chauffeur had lived there then. Serafita had been fond of this man; he had shared her passion for roses and between them they had ringed his little home with magnificent beds of Ophelias, to which, in jealous competition with Brough, he had given devoted care. On the day of her death, she had stood with him for a long time in the hot sunshine, discussing the blooms which were then at the height of their beauty; and there she had been taken suddenly ill, carried into his sitting-room as being the nearest shelter, and so had died. Sir Richard, in his passion for memorial building, had swept the chauffeur into other quarters, and built a shrine about the room in which she had breathed her last. One of the innumerable portraits had been moved in and hung upon the wall, a few pieces of furniture of which she had been particularly fond were placed in the room, and the roses were henceforward to be considered sacrosanct; never picked but to decorate her memory. During all her fêtes he haunted the place, increasingly fussy as the years went by over every small detail of ceremonial; but the anniversary of the night she had died, he invariably spent alone in the lodge. His original sentiments had long ago sunk into the dunderheaded obstinacy of, 'I've always done it and I'm not going to stop now!' There would be a little ceremony in the morning at the actual hour of her death, and after dinner he would march solemnly off and finally settle himself on a specially arranged divan bed underneath her picture, for a night of vigil; often holding out for as much as twenty minutes before falling off into his customary untroubled slumber. This year again, Bella and his doctor protested and with increasing vehemence, but in vain. 'My heart's perfectly all right, and if it isn't, I've got this stuff in my pocket, I'll keep it by the bed. There's the telephone extension to the house, and Brough and Mrs. Brough in the lodge just across the gates. Leave me alone Bella! I will not be dictated to! And where are those children? It's nearly a quarter to.'

'They're coming, Richard. They've all had to go upstairs and change.'

'I should think so,' said Sir Richard angrily. 'The idea of thinking that just because it's a hot day again, they can come down here in bits of nonsense not fit to be seen in, at the best of times. I tell you, Bella, these modern young people are more than I can understand.' He started off down towards the lodge, pausing on the lawn to stand and roar up at the bed-room windows on the first floor. Ellen appeared on her balcony like a cuckoo from its clock. 'Hallo? Were you calling us?'

'What do you think I'm doing, girl? A variety turn? Hurry up, the whole pack of you! It's a quarter to eleven.' He stumped on towards the gates and there vented some more of his irritability on the gardener. 'I thought I told you to sand these paths, Brough? They're a disgrace, and to-day of all days!'

Three narrow, sanded paths ran up through the rose-beds to the lodge; one to the front door, one to the back door, and one to the french window of the sitting-room, which faced towards the big house. 'The old woman's been back and forth cleaning the place,' said Brough, giving a perfunctory tug to the peak of his cap. 'She's got the path all scuffed up; and her ladyship, doing the flowers and such . . . ' He jerked his thumb over his shoulder towards his own domain where were his tool-sheds and rubbish dumps, neatly hedged in. 'I've got enough sand there for one more coat—and not a grain more; that'll be the end of it.'

'Well, let it be the end of it. Get the paths done before lunch.'

'I've got the geraniums on the front terrace to do,' said Brough. 'You always want those picked off special, in her ladyship's week. Her *first* ladyship,' he amended with a sly glance at Bella, whose fair, rather foolish, round face flushed a little, uncontrollably, and stiffened into self-conscious unawareness.

Sir Richard marched forward on his journey. 'You'll get those paths done before the day's out, Brough, or I'll know the reason why.' He paused before the french window, always the mode of entry used when going to the lodge from the house. 'Well—this doesn't look so bad. The flowers are very nice, Bella.' His brow darkened, however. 'What's all this rubbish doing here?'

The aged charwoman had evidently been called away suddenly near the completion of her task of cleaning up the lodge for to-day's ceremony; her vacuum cleaner stood abandoned in the middle of the room, its various attachments writhing about it in chromium coils. Bella, tchking, opened the door of the tiny hall between the sitting-room and the front door, and pushed the whole lot in. 'Nobody will see it there; we always use the french window. I told her not even to bother to clean it.' With the toe of her shoe she made a little squirl in the dust on the tiled floor of the hall. 'Where on earth does dust come from out here in the country? It's absolutely *thick* . . . '

'Where are those children?' said Sir Richard fretfully.

'They're coming, dear, they're coming.'

He stood at the window looking up towards the house, and at the roses ringing the little lodge. 'The Ophelias are at their loveliest—one day more and their petals would be falling. A breath of wind would disturb them, even now.'

Bella went and stood by his side, still pink-and-white and pretty, but dumpy and short where Serafita had been so slight and tiny with her little hands and feet. 'I always think it's extraordinary that she should have chosen the ones that would be just right for the anniversary of her death!'

'She was a remarkable woman,' said Sir Richard, evidently accepting this as a tribute to some occult power in his departed wife, rather than a comment on coincidence. 'Ah, here they are at last!' He added indignantly that they were only just in time, though there were several minutes yet to go before the hands of the little gilt clock pointed to the actual moment of Serafita's death. 'Come along now, all of you, hurry *up*! Peta, be careful of those roses!'

Peta's flying hands had brushed a blossom as she came up the narrow path; its pale petals broke away from the ripening calyx and drifting past her brief white skirt lay forlornly on the sand. 'Oh, Grandfather, I'm so sorry!' She squatted on the path to gather them up. 'The very first to fall, and I go and do it! What a clumsy ass!' In the sitting-room of the lodge she laid them out in formal pattern on the table below Serafita's picture. 'There, Grandmama, my pet—a gesture of apology from your graceless granddaughter.' Sir Richard tutted and frowned, but he was secretly touched and pleased. He chivied the rest of them into a semi-circle round the portrait, one eye on the clock. 'All right. Now, Peta!'

Philip and Ellen might be a trifle sheepish, but the others had attended Serafita rites too long to feel any self-consciousness about them at all. In their childhood Peta and Claire had been forced into dancing, hopping about unsteadily with earnest faces, flapping thin, pink, apparently boneless arms; but Sir Richard had abandoned these efforts in disgust. Peta, instead, stepped forward a little and sang in her thin, clear blackbirdy voice a lament over which Serafita had sentimentalized many years ago. Bella had made a wreath of the Ophelia roses, and this, as Peta sang, Sir Richard hung up over the portrait. Portraits of Serafita were everywhere, all over the great house as well as in the little lodge; and under each stood a gilt casket with pressed flowers, a pair of her tiny ballet shoes, and a pair of long, elbow-length gloves. The gloves had been her means to such little fame as she had ever achieved. She had not been, in fact, a very good dancer; but wise before her age to the value of publicity 'stunts' she had singled herself out from her innumerable sisters by appearing always in elbow-length gloves to match her little shoes. Now the gloves were cherished, laid by in lavender in their caskets all over the house: pink in the big drawing-room, scarlet in the dining-room, white in what was now her succes-

sor's bedroom, and black, of course, in the room where
she had died. At a sign from Sir Richard, Claire stepped
forward and solemnly took them out of the box, laying
them on the table with the faded flowers and the little
shoes. The song died away, and in the silence the old
man stood beneath the portrait looking up at the smiling, painted face with tears in his foolish blue eyes.
'We'll all be quiet for a little while, and think of her.'
After a while he turned towards them. 'A little prayer
now. Edward . . . '

Edward said the little prayer; he was not, in fact,
any relation to the dead Serafita, but he had lived at
Swanswater since his childhood and accepted as natural his inclusion in the celebrations; indeed, in the
absence of his half-cousins, he was much relied upon
to make up the congregation. They all said 'Amen' to
the prayer. Sir Richard took up the black gloves and
the shoes. 'These are the ones she wore on the night
that Dreyfus was convicted. There was a great deal of
excitement about the case in Paris, you know. Her
reception was tremendous; she danced a sort of dirge;
they had been working it out all the week
in the hopes that—in case the verdict went against
him . . . ' He told the story every time the black gloves
were brought out; they listened as respectfully as children to *Cinderella*, knowing every syllable of it, making
it a sort of game among themselves to catch Grandfather out in a word altered from the original, a phrase
misplaced. 'Two of the officers from the tribunal were
there. Everybody knew who they were of course. They
had to get up and leave.' When his voice fell silent,
you knew that in Grandfather's mind was the comfortable certainty that Dreyfus had not suffered in
vain. 'The applause was tremendous, and all the flowers were white, as though it were a funeral.'

The gloves were returned to the casket with the
shoes and the scrap of dusty blossom from that magnificent, far-off day. Peta sang again; and standing in
their half-circle with bent heads they gave themselves
up in their different ways to the mood of the moment.
Bella thought of the exquisite romance of being able

to live on so poignantly, as the newspapers said, in hearts and memories; Claire, that honestly it was like a Chekov short story the way Grandfather's once-tepid love burgeoned with the passing years; Philip, that this might be the last summer that the old boy would be here to pay tribute to his lost darling; and Edward, that it was all very well for the others, but dash it, he wasn't even her grandson and yet it was he who had to put up with most of this stuff. Peta, trilling a little French love-song, reflected that Serafita must have been rather heaven, she supposed, in a maddening way; and Ellen, thunderstruck by the easy emotion with which they all gave themselves over to drama-tization looked up at Serafita's portrait and almost winked—and, for a moment could have sworn that Serafita winked back.

Only Belle, reflected Sir Richard resentfully, would have presented him with a grandson subject to fugues! A thin, jumpy creature, with untidy hair and sloppy grey trousers, not held up at his waist at all, but by the bones of his gaunt young hips and therefore al-ways apparently in imminent danger of falling down. A nice boy, a charming lad, certainly, with that dis-arming smile of his; sweet-tempered, in the ordinary way, good-natured, friendly, kind. But fugues! Au-tomatism! No child of Serafita's, thought Sir Richard, would have given birth to such a weakling; or if they had, she'd have spanked the nonsense out of it, double quick! Look at him now, lounging on the balustrade of the riverside terrace, declaring that he felt ex-hausted 'after all that intensity', fanning himself with a huge straw hat of Peta's while they all sat watching the baby do its dance.

The baby! Concentrating deeply, an animated dumpling in a stitched Viyella smock, gravely, beatif-ically the baby danced. Fat pink hands like Christmas roses flopped at the ends of fat pink arms; soft hair curled up wispily into shining pale tufts of gold. Round and round and round, waddling in unsteady circles to a tune its great-grandmother had danced to fifty

years ago, it teetered on uncertain bare pink feet,
toppled, and finally sat down with a plomp on its
round pink mushroom of a behind, looking about it
with an air of mild surprise. Peta flung herself on her
knees beside it. 'My wonderful, exquisite one! indeed
a *very* good dance, a beautiful, beautiful dance!'

'We'll make a ballerina of her yet,' said Sir Richard,
delighted.

'More than you managed to do with any of us, darling! Oh, those awful mornings at Madame Whatsa-
nameski's! Will you ever forget, Claire?'

'We had all the virtues between us, but we'd got
them mixed. Peta was all supple grace, but she grew
up as leggy as a young colt, and I kept small and neat,
but about as lissom as a bundle of sticks. I'm afraid
there's nothing of Serafita about your granddaugh-
ters, darling!'

'You've got her small feet, Claire,' said Edward.
'Claire got Grandmama Serafita's small feet.'. But he
was bored with all this baby-talk and ancestor worship,
he wanted to bring the family attention back again to
himself and his fugues; he recollected that the psychiatrist had suggested that the stain of illegitimacy
galled him, and so he added in a harsh, sarcastic voice,
'I mean, of course, *your* Grandmama Serafita,' and
marched off into the house.

Bella started to follow him, her pretty face all puck-
ered up with distress. 'There now—you've upset him
again!'

The cousins clamoured indignation. 'Well, I like
that!' '*We* upset him!' ... 'Nobody said a *word*!' ...
'Honestly, Belle ...'

Bella had had a long and trying morning, waiting
upon the memory of Serafita. She subsided into her
chair and said tearfully that she and poor Edward
were always being reminded of their position at
Swanswater. ...

They collapsed in laughter. 'Oh, Bella, *non*sense,
darling! You know we adore your position here!' Peta
said, 'It gives glamour to the whole family, it gives us
a sort of—of cachet, these entrancing glimpses of the

wrong side of the blanket; and anyway, now you've been made-an-honest-woman of, darling!'

'By which you've been done a grave injustice to, Belle,' said Philip, laughing. 'You were our romantic element. You invested Grandfather with an air of naughty-ninetiness which was our pride and joy . . .'

'We could never quite think of him without hearing the pop of champagne corks . . .'

'By gaslight . . .'

'And seeing the thin stream of golden liquid poured into the satin shoe . . .'

Sir Richard stood wrapped in gloom. He had never drunk champagne out of any shoe, but if he had, it would have been Serafita's . . . Bella had stayed quietly in her bijou house in Yarmouth, with frilly net curtains and little pots of geraniums and a couple of nice, woolly dogs . . . it had been Serafita, the wife, who had laughed and sparkled and rushed off with him on wild jaunts to the haunts of gaiety and even, in those first days, a little mild vice. And to-day of all days, to have Serafita's thunder stolen, to have plump comfortable Bella with her pretensions to 'education' being elevated to the throne of a Queen of Glamour. 'Grandfather, do tell us about it—didn't the shoe get all wet and soggy? Didn't it spoil the champagne? Were actresses' shoes sold in threes, one for drinking out of?'

Edward, meanwhile, drooped forgotten in the hall, waiting for someone to follow him in and implore him not to upset himself. Through the front door, however, he espied a figure entering the iron gates and, scenting a new recipient for the tale of his troubles, went down the drive to meet him. 'Hallo, Stephen. You're good and early. Bella said you were coming to lunch.'

'Hallo, Edward,' said Stephen Garde. 'How are you?' He strolled back to the house beside him, a little, slender man whose neat figure would always look slack and untidy because he wore his clothes so carelessly. His hair, ruthlessly brushed flat, was ruffled by his walk up from the village, to ducks' tails of dark gold.

'Is the family safely here? Your cousin Philip? And the famous baby?' With great casualness he added, 'And Peta? Has she turned up all right?'

'Yes, they're all here and Ellen and Claire. I say, Stephen, I went up to London myself, yesterday, and I saw that new psychiatrist, Hartmann. He says I'm pretty bad. I mean, I'm liable to pass out any minute, for hours at a time, and not know what I'd been doing.'

'You wouldn't have been doing anything, if you'd passed out,' said Stephen, practically.

'Well, I don't mean I necessarily faint. I'd just be in a sort of a trance, a fugue it's called, and I could walk about and talk and do things and nobody would know there was anything wrong with me, only *I* wouldn't remember anything about it.'

'Does this man suggest that you've had these attacks, or only that you might?'

Edward was privately convinced that he had never had one in his life, and never would. 'The trouble is, you see, that I wouldn't *know.* I mean, what's to tell me? Nobody would notice anything different, so of course they wouldn't know that I didn't know what I'd been doing.'

'It's very interesting,' said Stephen. They crossed the green lawn and made for the central steps up to the house. 'How's the army?' asked Edward politely, abandoning his own absorbing topic.

'No place for a quiet country solicitor. My lot had a rough time in Normandy.'

Peta ran down the broad steps to meet him. '*Ste*-phen! Darling, how *heav*enly! Stephen, so di*vine* to see you!' Under her affectations and over-emphases her heart beat sickeningly, and the enamelled finger-tips clinging to his arm shook with her nervous effort to control herself. 'Dear Stephen, heavenly Stephen, I *could*n't be more thrilled to see anyone!'

'You talk as though you weren't expecting me, Peta,' said Stephen in his quiet way.

Edward went on into the house. Philip came out and down the steps. 'Hallo, Stephen. How are you? Haven't seen you for ages.'

They shook hands, just a tiny bit awkwardly. Eight years ago Philip had come home from America and presented himself at Swanswater for his grandfather's blessing; and Sir Richard, overjoyed, had immediately summoned his lawyer to alter his will. 'Only man in the family—after all, it's simply sense that he should be my heir.'

Stephen had argued. 'You've always intended to leave everything to Peta, Sir Richard. It would have gone to your eldest son if he'd lived, and Peta's his heir. I think you'll regret it, if you change things now.'

'What do you know about regretting or not regretting—a boy like you?'

'It's the advice my father would have given you,' said Stephen doggedly.

Sir Richard had wavered, new wills had been drafted, initialled, altered, and finally laid aside. 'You're quite right, Garde, the eldest would have had it and through him, Peta. And after all, what do I know of this lad? He's my grandson, of course, but Peta's been with us all her life—I've more or less brought the child up; she knows my ways, she understands what I feel about her grandmother's memory, she's the fitting one to live on at Swanswater . . .' And so Stephen had fought for Peta's inheritance, and won; and in so doing, himself had lost. You do not secure an estate for a young woman, and a hearty fortune, and then fall on your knees and ask her to marry you; not if you are a quiet country lawyer with nothing to offer in return but a steady old practice and no hope of anything more, no desire for anything more. So Peta was an heiress, and Stephen a misogynist, and it was never quite comfortable to shake Philip March by the hand. 'How did you find Sir Richard?' asked Stephen, to cover it.

'No better, no worse. It's a condition; not a case that improves or deteriorates.'

'Philip says his heart may dicker out at any time,' said Peta, 'or he may go on for years.'

'He's in very good hands with your medical man down here,' said Philip politely. 'Brown's prescribed coramine, and, of course, he's right. I've brought a consignment down with me from town; if the old boy always has some by him in case of an attack, we can probably keep him going for ever . . . ' He broke off, bored by this profitless discussion with the laity. 'Well, I believe Grandfather's sent for some sherry.'

Claire, coming downstairs, met them in the hall. 'Stephen, my childhood's friend, how *are* you?' She ran towards him, holding out her pretty hands.

'How lovely to see you, Claire,' said Stephen, kissing her lightly.

Peta drooped in the background, wrapped in gloom. 'Stephen, you kiss Claire, but you didn't kiss *me*, when we met!'

'My dear, you were leaping all round me like a young puppy-dog; I didn't have a chance.' Now that the chance was there, however, not to say offering itself, he did not seem very anxious to avail himself of it. 'How are you, Claire? Still in the same old job?'

'Yes, sweating away to Grandpapa's great fury.'

'Well, I don't see why you stick to it when you know he hates it and so do you.'

Claire became a trifle intense. 'When one *has* writing in one, Stephen, one just has to get it out somehow; of course, journalism isn't regarded as literature and actually I'm rotten at the newspaper stuff, reporting and all that, but still one can do one's little piece trying to raise the standard of decent prose a bit. It's all very mere, of course, but one can't be content, one has to try.' She added, laughing, that anyway, Grandfather having cut her off with a shilling, she had to earn her living and it kept her out of the A.T.S.

'What's that about a shilling?' said Sir Richard coming in from the river-balcony.

'Darling, I was saying that you having cut me off with one, I have to go on interviewing murdered bodies and asking Street Leaders how much they've collected for the Spitfire Fund and things. Look, Grandfather, here's Stephen; oh, and Stephen, here come Bella and Ellen.'

'Time for a glass of sherry,' said Sir Richard, with the naïve pride of one who in 1944 still has Amontillado to offer. 'I sent Edward to fetch the things; no use waiting for that palsied old crone we have now, and anyway it gives the boy something to do, keeps him from brooding over himself. He's been off to town on his own, now, Stephen, would you believe it? and come back filled with a pack of new nonsense, says if he looks up at anything he'll drop whatever he's carrying and go into a fugue or some such nonsense as that.' He pushed open the drawing-room door and stood aside for Bella and the girls to pass through.

Over Serafita's portrait the customary wreath of roses was hanging askew; and Edward stood staring up at it, a silver tray and a heap of broken glasses on the floor at his feet.

CHAPTER III

They stood grouped in the doorway, aghast and staring; and even as they watched Edward moved forward, picked up the decanter of sherry which stood on the table, held it against the light, apparently to see that it was sufficiently full, and, replacing it, sat down in an armchair. As Sir Richard went forward uncertainly into the room he said quite normally: 'I got the sherry for you, Grandfather.'

Bella burst into a pantomime of little signs and twitches, Don't Say Anything—Keep it From Him—Leave it All to Me. Edward asked blinking: 'What on earth's the matter with you, Belle?' Like the rest of the family he called his grandmother by her Christian name.

Peta knelt to pick up the broken glasses. 'She's telling us not to tell you that you've had one of your little passing-outs, darling.'

Edward looked pleased. 'Good lord—have I?' His clenched fists relaxed on the arm of the chair. Bella however, pushed past them all and ran to him. 'My poor boy! How do you feel now, darling? Just keep quiet, don't worry, let yourself go.' Immediately the hands curled again; he went very white and after a moment, sitting staring at her, he suddenly pitched forward fainting on to the parquet floor. Philip forced her aside and kneeling beside him, took the slack wrist. 'Somebody—Ellen—get my bag for me, would you? It's on the top of the wardrobe thing in our room.' He said to Bella: 'Hush, be quiet!' and they were all silent while he counted the pulse beats. 'Nothing wrong with him; just a faint.' When Ellen returned with the black leather medical bag, he selected a bottle, gave an injection and remained sitting on the floor gently massaging the wrist with the ball of his thumb. Sir Richard turned away, staring grimly out of the window as though he could not bear to watch the unconscious boy, the rolled-up eyes and loosely-lolling mouth; it was impossible to tell whether he was distressed or merely disgusted. He broke the silence at last to say abruptly: 'Peta, Claire, go and get more glasses from the pantry. No need to make our guest uncomfortable.'

Stephen was already sufficiently uncomfortable. Edward, however, soon came round and, having asked with some lack of originality where he was, was able to receive with composure the news that it was still the drawing-room at Swanswater. Finding himself the centre of so much attention, he further added that he now felt fine and would like some lunch. 'And I think a glass of sherry would be grand.'

'On the contrary,' said Philip, 'it would be extremely silly.'

Edward looked rebellious. 'Let the boy have it,' whispered Bella, fearful of another attack. 'It couldn't do him any harm, and they say it's better not to thwart them.'

'Rubbish,' said Philip, looking about for a jug of water. He filled the syringe from it and going to the french window squirted the water out in a thin curving arc across the terrace. 'Oh, sorry, Brough—I nearly hit you—I didn't see you were there!' The water finished up in a little pool at the further side of the terrace and in a moment was dried up by the sunshine pouring down. Philip wiped the needle. 'No, Edward, you definitely can't have alcohol after an attack like that, so shut up! Belle must be out of her senses to want to allow it.'

Bella's pretty mouth folded into a stubborn line. 'After all I do *know* about Edward, Philip! I've brought him up! I mean, you don't really specialize in this sort of thing, do you? You're not an alienist. You know nothing about psycho-analysis, *do* you?'

'No, indeed,' said Philip. 'I'm not an Austrian Jew escaped after appalling hardships from a German concentration camp, so how could I? But even a general practitioner may have his poor little pathetic ideas about the suitability of alcohol after a fainting attack of this sort, and I say quite emphatically that I will not let Edward have it.' He flung open his bag and put away the syringe; slightly ashamed of his irritability, he added: 'By the way, here's the coramine I brought down for Grandfather.' Six thin glass phials nested, each in its bed of cotton wool, in a tall cardboard box. 'Everybody'd better have a look. One ampoule during an attack—just shove it into the arm any old where, as long as you get it in. And don't get funny, anyone, and go giving more than one. Bella, Dr. Whatsaname's shown you how to do it?'

Bella was resentful and cross. 'Yes, he has, he's told me all about it, and shown me and the Broughs too, in case your grandfather should be taken ill in the grounds. There's no need, Philip, for you to interfere. And anyway,' said Bella virtuously, 'I don't think it is a conversation to be carried on in front of your grandfather!'

'Nonsense,' said Sir Richard, 'I'm the interested party! You'd better arrange some central place where the stuff can be kept, Bella, and see that everyone knows where it is.' But it maddened him to be subject to such weakness, to have to be fussed over like some silly woman. 'A fine pair we are, Edward, with our faints and our heart attacks!'

A crone so ancient and palsied as to be unacceptable even to the insatiable maw of the new Filling Factory at Heronsford ('except possibly as a filling!' said Ellen) confided in a whining voice that dinner was on the table, Mum, and she'd be glad if they'd get on with it soon, as she and Mrs. Brough wanted to get 'ome—so, in the England of 1944, were Bella's once elegant little luncheons announced. Edward insisted upon coming to the table with them, and the afternoon so inauspiciously begun, continued on what was to prove its disastrous course, till even Serafita, looking down from the canvas upon her peevish family, seemed to have changed her arch painted smile for a little angry frown. Bella was on a high horse, pretending to herself that if Her Shame had not been known to all the family, Philip would not have been so abrupt and snubbing to her in the drawing-room just now. Philip and Ellen had spent a miserable and embarrassing twenty-four hours, for Swanswater hospitality did not extend itself to a 'spare room' and he was sore and angry at Ellen's needling mockery on the subject of their enforced intimacy. Ellen, sick with pain, nevertheless sought stupidly to disguise her humiliation under the cloak of raillery; and Claire, only half deceived but desperately self-deceiving, persuaded herself that Philip was hers by right of their love, that nothing else mattered because Ellen did not care. Edward was greatly excited by his faint in the drawing-room, and talked incessantly of the prognostications of Dr. Hartmann; Peta's affectations were exaggerated almost beyond bearing by her efforts to appear natural and at ease. Stephen, sick with passion and longing, yet could not blind himself to the fact that his love was behaving like an ass. Sir Richard sat with lowering brow, his voice a low rumble of thunder portending storm. 'I don't know why a man ever marries and has a family! Heaven knows he gets no pleasure from it. His children grow up and leave him, or get killed off in some war that does nobody any good and only leaves the world ready for the next war; his grandchildren are like creatures from another world. Look at Peta there—covering her pretty face with make-up, her nails half an inch long, and dipped in ox's blood——'

'Why ox's?' said Peta.

'——and Claire, her hands all spoilt and ugly from typing away like a hooligan in some scrubby Fleet Street office.'

'A very grand office, I assure you, everything artificial right down to the light and air.'

'And Philip—five years married and one puny child to show for it!'

'You talk as though I were a pedigree stallion,' said Philip.

'All unhappy families resemble each other, each unhappy family is unhappy in its own way,' said Bella. She added, ' "War and Peace".'

' "Anna Karenina",' corrected Philip promptly.

'To be a woman and to be an intellectual, my dear children—thiss iss not compatible,' quoted Peta to the table at large, in a mockery of Serafita's broken English.

'Don't you ever marry, Stephen, my boy,' said Sir Richard, sweeping all interruptions aside, helping himself angrily to grilled sausages. 'You take my advice if you want a happy life. Don't marry. And don't have a family.'

Ellen was riled by his earlier reflection upon the physique of her solitary offspring. 'In Sir Richard's experience, the two are not necessarily synonymous!'

It was in tune with the customary banter of the family upon this subject; but Ellen was not really one of them, and it was said, moreover, without laughter or love. Bella was furious. 'How dare you, Ellen, speak so disrespectfully to Philip's grandfather?'

'Well, how dare he speak so disrespectfully about

my child? She's not puny in the least. She's actually over-weight for twenty months.'

'I don't care a tuppenny damn about the weight of your child,' cried Sir Richard, assaulting his sausages as though they had done him an injury. 'What do *I* know about nursery weights and measures? I simply say that one child is not enough. Men are being killed off every day, the birth-rate's going down and down.'

'Actually the birth-rate's rising, Grandfather, since the war.'

'Hail America!' said Philip.

'Up the illegits!' said Peta.

Sir Richard was scandalized. 'Peta, I will not have doubtful jokes of that nature at my lunch table!'

'Well, *I'm* a doubtful joke of that nature, Grandfather,' said Edward; 'and *I'm* at your lunch table.'

The cousins giggled appreciatively, goading each other on to fresh feats of daring. Sir Richard's brow grew increasingly black. 'I apologize for my family, Stephen. I realize more and more that none of the modern generation have any manners, reticence, or good-feeling, and apparently my grandchildren are no exception to the rule.'

'A fine example of manners, reticence, and good-feeling *you* set us,' said Philip. 'Discussing my fertility at the top of your voice in this earthy way. What's it to you how many children I have?'

'And besides,' said Edward, made bold by his earlier success, 'it's no use talking, because he *can't* have any more. He and Claire have fallen in love and now Philip sleeps in the spare room. Don't you, Philip?' In the ensuing silence he clapped his hand to his mouth and regarded his cousin with increasingly genuine dismay. 'Oh, lor! Have I gone too far?'

The clouds broke. The rains came. Faithless, feckless, unstable, unprincipled, irresponsible. Sir Richard rolled out accusation and condemnation and, a little late, demanded explanation. 'Philip—is this true?'

'If you insist upon discussing my marital relations at the luncheon table,' said Philip angrily. 'Yes. It is.'

'You're in love with your cousin, Claire?'

Claire sat proud but trembling, her corn-coloured head held high. 'Yes, Grandfather. We're in love.'

Sir Richard pounded the table. 'Hold your tongue, Miss, I wasn't speaking to you. Now, Philip.'

'What's it got to do with you, anyway?' said Philip.

'What's it got to do with me? What's it got to do with *me*? I'll soon show you what it's got to do with me! You're my family, aren't you? Claire's my family, isn't she? Haven't I brought her up in my own house, given her her education, given her everything she's ever had? Didn't I help you through your studies when you came over here? Didn't I help with the purchase of your practice? Didn't I help you and Ellen when you first set up house? What's it got to do with *me*? Am I to sit back and see my family disgraced? Am I to acknowledge to the world that my only grandson couldn't stick five years by one woman, without going off with his own cousin? Spare bedroom, indeed! One solitary child, because, forsooth, you fall in love with this inky-fingered chit, and sleep in the spare bedroom!'

'What do you expect me to do?' said Philip. 'Set Claire up in a bijou house at Yarmouth?'

Bella dissolved into tears, Claire sat with working face, Ellen rocked on the back legs of her chair and said airily that if *she* didn't mind, she didn't see why Sir Richard should. 'Well, you damn well ought to mind,' said Sir Richard, transferring his wrath to her. 'The whole thing's your fault, Ellen, for letting Philip get tangled up in this ridiculous affair. If you'd had a couple more children, if you'd given Philip a more comfortable home . . .'

'To have three children, and to give your husband a comfortable home, thiss iss not compatible,' said Peta.

'Mind your own business, Peta. A child like you interfering in the affairs of your elders! You ought not even to know what we're talking about!'

'Here we go round the gooseberry bush!' sang

Peta, impudent eyes alert for admiration of her naughtiness.

They relapsed into hysterical laughter. 'I'll disinherit the lot of you,' shouted Sir Richard, standing up suddenly in his place, thumping his fist down upon the table so that the china and glasses leapt on the old, red mahogany. 'I'll cut you all out of my will, the whole ungrateful pack of you! Ill-mannered, irreverent, ungracious, immoral. . . . I'll throw you out on the world without a penny. I'll change my will this day, this very day, you see if I don't. The whole thing can go to Bella and after her to Edward; the poor boy may be feeble-minded, but at least he can't go plunging the family into scandal and disgrace.'

'Just because I have fugues,' protested Edward mildly, 'it doesn't mean that I'm batty.'

Sir Richard marched out of the dining-room, leaving his stewed plums untouched in a sea of Bird's custard, on his plate. 'Come out on the terrace, Stephen, I shall want to discuss this with you.'

'Fish out the old wills, Stephen, and pick a nice one for Grandfather to sign all over again!'

'Oh, *Peta*!' begged Stephen, 'Don't be so—so unkind and silly!' He followed Sir Richard to the little iron garden-table on the terrace. 'Don't take any notice of them, sir. They're only trying to be funny.'

'I don't find it very amusing,' said Sir Richard curtly.

'Well, neither do I, actually, but they've had a rotten time up in London for the past few weeks with the flying-bombs and all that. I mean, it's enough to make them all a bit edgy—you *must* make allowances,' said Stephen, as steady as a rock after the 'rough time' in Normandy.

'*We* have flying-bombs too,' said Sir Richard jealously. He glanced up at the fat silver fish floating lazily against the summer sky. 'The place is a positive nightmare with this balloon barrage they've moved out here, and I believe that the other day they actually brought one down, less than three miles away—the other side of Heronsford. But you don't see *me* getting tetchy and difficult and losing my nerve! The truth is, my boy, that these young people have things too much their own way; they don't know any self-control, and I have only one hold over them, and I must exercise it; I must frighten them.'

'But they never are frightened, sir, *are* they? I mean, you *have* tried it before. And after all, though I couldn't agree more that they've been abominably rude and —and irreverent to-day,' said poor Stephen, feeling a prig, but heartily agreeing with himself, all the same, 'I do think it's been only that—they haven't *done* anything dreadful unless you count this business of Claire and Philip and that'll soon blow over. Claire takes things a bit desperately, always; she's a bit sort of dramatic!'

Sir Richard, however, was a bit sort of dramatic himself, and he had no intention of being done out of all the excitement of altering his will. 'I must have the draft to-day, Stephen, definitely; get it done this afternoon.'

Stephen was a little shattered. 'I'm not really your lawyer actually now sir, am I? I'm only a little tin soldier while the war goes on; and really I've quite lost touch with the office work.'

'Pooh, nonsense,' said Sir Richard firmly. 'You can instruct old Briggs to get it done; he knows all about it, he did it the last time. Anyway, you've got the draft of the one we made out over that business of Claire and the newspaper office, when they were all so obstinate and silly; use that—the whole lot to Bella and after her, the boy. And I want it by this evening; definitely this evening, mind!'

The sun blazed down, and on the front terrace the disinherited family skipped gaily about in brief bathing-dresses all ready for a plunge into the swimming-pool. It was a little hard to be sent off to spend one of his seven precious afternoons, digging about in his office among dusty files. However, somebody must keep in with Sir Richard and be in a position to offer him guidance and advice; and for forty years Stephen, and his father before him, had been guiding

and advising Sir Richard in the matter of his wills.
'All right, sir. I'll see to it.' He trudged off obediently
down the gravelled drive. 'If Peta really does lose her
inheritance . . . If Sir Richard should snuff out before
he changes this will . . . ' But it behoved him the more
to guard against Peta losing her inheritance; because
he so desperately wanted her to. Down by the lodge
the Ophelias filled the air with their heavy scent; he
passed through the gates, and went off alone, along
the road.

CHAPTER IV

The baby was exceedingly busy that afternoon, helping Brough to mow the lawn. Clad in a pair of bright
blue dungarees, with a string of large coloured beads
about her neck, she staggered importantly to and fro,
putting out a starfish hand to save herself from tip-
ping forward and now and again sitting down abruptly
among the daisies. Brough's grandchild, a tiresome
little girl of eight, known as Rosy-Posy, followed her
about with an air of patronage and every time she fell
down, hauled her bossily to her feet again. The family
watched them, idling in deck chairs on the front terrace, sniffing luxuriously at the scent of the new-cut
grass; or bobbed in and out of the swimming-bath,
lying flat on the sun-baked front terrace to dry. Sir
Richard remained sitting at the little iron table, os-
tentatiously working out the terms of his new will and
at intervals sending one or other of his grandchildren
to the telephone in the hall with messages to Stephen
Garde. 'I must say, Grandfather, I think it's in the
worst of taste,' protested Peta, 'keeping us running
about so busily, disinheriting ourselves.'

Peta, his pet, his favourite, with her pretty face and

her pretty hair and her pretty, engaging little ways, who could behave so very unprettily when she liked! His eyes filled with tears of stubborn self-pity. 'I looked to you, Peta, to keep up Swanswater when I was dead and gone . . .'

'Well, *anyway*, I think, darling, that Belle ought to have it, I always have. I mean, it's all wrong to turn her out just because you're dead. If you see what I mean,' added Peta, apologetically.

'Swanswater is a memorial to your Grandmama Serafita,' said Sir Richard firmly. 'It is not suitable that my second wife should be the one to keep it up.' Serafita would not have cared two straws, she had laughed at his infidelities and would have laughed at his present nostalgic sentimentalities, and he knew it; but he had built up this fable of his devotion to her, and in his old age it was very dear to him. 'It's all your fault, Peta, you're not worthy, not *worthy* to have this place. Edward, go and tell Stephen that I shall be at the lodge to-night, tell him to bring the draft will there when he's got it done.'

'Oh, *lor'!*' grumbled Edward, rising for the third time and shambling off crossly to the telephone.

Bella came up the broad steps to the terrace, with Antonia in her arms. She was very pretty still, for all her sixty years, but the rosy glow of the baby robbed her skin of its bloom and took the light from her hair. 'Oh, Richard—you're not going to sign that nasty thing to-night!'

'Go away, Bella,' said Sir Richard. He sent Peta after Edward. 'Tell him I shall be at the lodge from now onwards; I'm fed up with the lot of you. I shall have my supper down there.'

'Oh, Richard, you're *not* going to sleep down there to-night!'

'Leave me alone, Bella,' said Sir Richard irritably. 'Don't go on and on saying, "Oh, Richard, you're *not* . . ."'

'Well, but Richard, your heart, dear! You really ought not to be alone.'

'Get away, get away,' said Sir Richard, flapping the air as though she were a fly.

'But Richard—well, if you're determined, dear, let one of us stay there with you. Suppose, my dear—now seriously—that you had an attack!'

'I'll tell you what, Bella, if you want me to have a heart attack you're going the very best way about bringing it on! I'll hear no more about it. Leave me alone!'

Bella appealed to Philip. 'Do, as a doctor, use your influence with your grandfather. Do tell him he shouldn't spend the night at the lodge.'

Philip, lying on the terrace, opened a cross and sleepy eye. 'He knows that perfectly well; if *I* say it, it'll only make him more obstinate. I think you're very foolish to do it, Grandfather, but having placed my protest on record, I wash my hands of the whole caboosh.' He closed his eyes and apparently went fast asleep at once.

Bella gave it up in despair but could not refrain, as she went on into the house, from a reiteration of her hopes that Richard would at least not bother with that horrid will to-night. 'I don't know why you should worry, Bella,' said Ellen, following her in. 'If Sir Richard does alter his will, you'll be the one to benefit; you'll be sole owner of Swanswater and you can turn us all out bag and baggage just like that!'

'Yes, and I know which baggage I'll begin with,' thought Bella angrily; for if Ellen hadn't gone and told them all about Philip on their way down in the car (as she had now learned from Edward), this trouble need not have happened. She could never remain ill-tempered for long, however, and, when Peta and Edward came out from the hall telephone, her attention was immediately distracted. 'Good gracious, child—what on earth have you done to your nails?'

Peta flapped pale finger-tips. 'Taken off all the ox's blood—don't they look sort of feeble and peculiar?' She stood in her tight green bathing-dress, her wild-rose skin touched to pink by her sunbathing. 'Stephen said I was—was rude and silly to Grandfather, so I thought perhaps this would make up to him—Grandfather, I mean, of course.' She added, laughing, that perhaps if she sucked up to him enough he would reverse his decision after all and she would be an heiress again. 'A fine thing if I'm left a pauper and Stephen's still cross, and nobody'll marry me.'

'You should be a bit barmy like me, darling, and then you would be indifferent to wills and things and could paint your nails all colours of the rainbow. Grandfather has to provide for me, whatever happens, and anyway, whatever I do, people just say I can't help it. Come on,' said Edward, urging her forward with a flip on her tight green behind, 'let's go back to the sunshine while it lasts. Your bathing-dress is still quite damp—ugh!'

Philip and Claire were lying flat on their backs on the terrace, also in bathing-dresses, their hands behind their heads. Peta laid out an elaborate arrangement of manicure accessories and put a coat of colourless varnish over her pallid nails. 'I feel as if I were back on the wards; Matron has fits if your nails aren't absolutely stark *white*! There, Grandpapa, aren't I a polite and unsilly granddaughter? Now you can cancel the stupid old new will and I can be an heiress again.'

A reconciliation with Peta was as exciting and dramatic as a new will, any day. Sir Richard said, almost eagerly, 'Peta, if you will apologize for your disgraceful behaviour to-day . . .'

Claire raised her head, poking it forward to watch them; if only, at this eleventh hour, Peta would say the right thing, would exercise one of those easy little charms of hers that went so deeply to the old man's heart; if only this hateful, unkind, silly row might end! But Peta would not appear to curry favour over the heads of her cousins, and all for the sake of wealth. She stretched herself out on the terrace, closing her eyes against the glare of the sun. 'Well, I *am* sorry I was rude and silly, because I'm slightly ashamed of it

myself, actually, and please witness to Stephen, everybody, that I've made a speech to Grandfather; but I
don't want to be un-disinherited in the least. Bella can
have Swanswater,' said Peta airily, wriggling her toes
against the comfortable heat of the stone, 'and we'll
all come and cadge on her when Grandfather's dead
and gone and sleeps in dull, cold marble, or whatever
that quotation is.'

'I have put a clause in my new will preventing Bella
from giving substantial financial assistance to any of
you,' said Sir Richard, gloomily triumphant.

'Oh, darling, how unco-operative of you! Shan't we
even be able to invite ourselves to Swanswater and
outstay our welcomes, choking ourselves on the bitter
bread of Bella's charity?'

'You will if she'll have you,' said Sir Richard grimly.

'She'll have *me*! Edward, you'll be the little prince
then, *you*'ll see that Bella has me to stay and chokes
me with the bitter bread of her charity, won't you,
darling?'

'She won't have Ellen,' said Edward, stretching his
neck up from his shoulders to look round at Philip.
'Philip, she won't have you and Ellen; she thinks this
is all your fault—and Claire's, of course—whereas it's
really *my* fault, isn't it? for telling what Ellen said in
the car.' He gave a fearful heave to get himself into
a sitting position. 'I say, Grandfather, if *I* apologized,
would it do any good?' But this sounded a trifle intense so he felt compelled to add, 'Or shall I throw a
fugue or something?'

Sir Richard got to his feet and sweeping together
his papers marched angrily to the front steps. Nobody
appearing to notice, he announced loudly that he was
now going down to the lodge and would not come up
to dinner at the house. Peta opened one blue eye.
'Won't you, darling? You'll starve.'

'One of the servants can bring me something down
on a tray.'

'The seventh footman shall see to it,' said Peta. When
Bella appeared from the house half an hour later she
passed on the message. 'I've told the Turtle to prepare

something,' said Bella. 'I'll take it down myself and
try and persuade him to give up this fantastic idea of
sleeping there alone. I shall say to him, "Richard," I
shall say to him . . . '

'Yes, all right, angel, don't rehearse the whole thing
to *us*; we know all about it, and anyway, you'll never
get him to budge.'

'He's as obstinate as a hog on ice,' said Philip. 'It's
the silliest damn thing I ever heard of, but there's no
use *my* saying anything. Peta, you go down with Bella
and try and persuade him; he listens to you—you
nearly had him eating out of your hand just now, if
you hadn't been silly and insisted on remaining a pauper, and us with you.'

The Turtle appeared carrying a large tray laden
with the massive silver dishes which had appeared to
a little ballet-dancer the hall-mark of respectability.
'Here you are, Mum, though I'm shore if I'd known
it was going to be seprit meals I'd never've done it
not even to oblige!'

Peta took the tray from Bella. 'I'll carry it, duck.
Come on!' Tall and slender, she walked with her wil-
lowy grace in the brief green bathing costume across
the lawn at Bella's side. A few minutes later the telephone rang from the lodge. Her voice said: 'Claire?
I say, Grandfather's left his fountain pen on the table
and he wants it.'

'His fountain pen? Which table?' said Claire.

'Well, the little tin table on the terrace, darling, don't
be silly.'

Ellen appeared from the terrace with a fat green
Parker Duofold in her hand. 'Is this it?'

'Is it a green pen, Peta?'

Ellen could hear Peta's voice speaking on the other
end of the line. 'Yes, Claire, he says it's his green one.
What, darling? Well, don't tell me while I'm trying to
tell *her*! Claire, he says he wants it to disinherit us with
this evening!'

'Tell them I'll bring it down to him,' said Ellen,
unexpectedly. Her quick maternal ear caught the sound
of her baby's weeping, and she ran upstairs, the pen

still in her hand. Half an hour later, Bella and Peta, returning from the lodge, met her sauntering across the lawn towards it, the pen a vivid note against her brief red bathing-dress. 'If she thinks she's going to talk Grandfather round,' said Peta a little bitterly, having just failed to do so herself, 'she won't manage it in *that*! There's too much of Ellen to get away with too little of a bathing-dress; it looks as if it had been varnished on, and some of the varnish had chipped.' The futile sacrifice of the ox's blood was still a sore point.

Edward was on the terrace in untidy flannels and a white shirt. 'Will this do for dinner, Bella? Philip's gone in to do likewise. I say, what's Ellen up to? She's gone off to the lodge with a look of grim determination on her face—target for to-night, isn't in it!'

'We think she's going to have a Straight Talk with Grandfather, but she's an idiot to go in a tummy-less bathing-dress.'

'Let's go and make faces outside the window and put her off,' suggested Edward promptly.

Peta thought this a delightful suggestion and would have turned back immediately, but was hustled into the house by Bella with instructions to put on *some*-thing for dinner because her bathing-dress was worse than Ellen's, only Peta was thin. 'Heaven knows what stories the Turtle tells about you all down in the village!' Edward went off down to the lodge by himself. Ellen, however, was already leaving, walking along, a little bouncing in the tummy-less bathing costume, down the sanded path. She said, taking his arm, 'Where are you dashing off to?'

'I was dashing off to this very spot, actually, to jump up and down outside the window and make you giggle in the middle of your Straight Talk with Grandfather.'

Ellen laughed. 'I never felt less like giggling in my life! It's as gloomy as a morgue in there!—he says the sun on the window makes it like an oven, and he's drawn the curtains across and shut out all the light; and he's in a filthy temper, I can tell you! I tried to point out to him that it was all too silly and I didn't

mind in the least if Philip left me for Claire but what
I really couldn't stick was this sort of half-and-half
business, but of course he wouldn't listen. He says it's
our attitude to the whole affair that he minds, and
that we have no sense of decency.'

'He meant your bathing-dress, I expect.'

Ellen glanced down nonchalantly at her well-rounded
diaphragm. 'Can *I* help it if my figure won't stay utility
to fit the rubbish the government sells us now?'

Brough appeared from the sanded path to the front
door, dragging a little garden roller behind him; he
touched his cap to them and went on round to the
back. Edward moved forward to pass her and go up
to the french window, with its drawn curtain. 'As I'm
fully clothed, and practically *sub*-utility as far as fat's
concerned, perhaps I could make more impression!'
But she caught again at his arm. 'I wouldn't go, Teddy,
honestly, I wouldn't. He won't pay the slightest attention to you and you'll only go into an automatic trance
or something and make things worse. Come back to
the house with me; it must be nearly dinner time
anyway.' As he hesitated, she changed the subject and
uttered the magic words, 'How do you feel to-day,
after your faint last night?' He turned back immediately and went with her.

That evening they sat on the terrace looking down
to the river and away from the lodges; tenderly nursing their sunburn and all a little silent after the rather
hysterical unease of the day. Only Ellen kept up a
cheerful insouciance, half maddening, half heart-
breaking; Bella fed biscuits to her dog, a small white
whiskery animal called Bobbin which sat up with a
rock-like steadiness holding its mouth wide open to
receive the fragments which, from a really astonishing
distance, she threw to it. Edward created a diversion
by eating one of the biscuits. 'Rather nice, though a
bit hard. Is this what the poor troops have, called iron
rations?'

'Edward, don't be so *awful*, how *can* you eat it? It's

full of all sorts of strange animals, unfit for human consumption.'

Peta began to neigh horribly; Edward went rather green. 'You don't really think there's horse and guts and things in it, do you?'

'Yes, of course there is,' said Claire. 'It says so on the packet.'

'Horrible squirmy entrails, Teddy, all minced up!'

Edward clapped his hand to his stomach and abruptly rushed off indoors. 'There now, Peta, you've gone and upset him again!' said Bella; but she was too hot and weary to do more than look anxiously towards the house from the depths of her deck chair. 'I hope he'll remember to bring the little wireless out for the news; what time is it?—about twenty past eight?' For the next twenty minutes she fretted and lectured without, however, doing anything constructive, and was then rewarded by the sight of her grandson reappearing, apparently quite well and cheerful, from the house and carrying the portable with him. He put it on the edge of the balustrade, and, as nobody questioned him, said proudly to Peta, 'I was frightfully sick!'

'I *don't* believe you were at all,' said Peta.

'Well, what do you think I've been *do*ing, all this time?'

'Having a fugue, I expect,' said Peta.

Edward turned slightly pale, but after a moment his face cleared. 'Well, I haven't actually, because I can remember perfectly well. I've been putting a film in my camera. I noticed it on the front terrace and it reminded me about taking some photographs of the baby to-morrow, Ellen.'

'Well, so there—you *weren't* being sick!'

'Not all the time,' said Edward. 'Naturally!'

Ellen's interest in the B.B.C. news bulletin was earnest, trustful, and unflagging. She prided herself a little, and not offensively, on taking an intelligent interest (for a woman) in the progress of the war. When, therefore, at this moment, Antonia's voice was lifted in sorrow from her cot she looked in despair at the rest of the family. 'She would! Now I shall miss the news!'

Claire scrambled to her feet. 'I'll go for you, Ellen.'

Ellen would much rather Claire did nothing for any child of hers, but she would not permit herself to have silly 'feelings'. She said as graciously as possible: 'Well, all right—thanks very much, then. I'm afraid this means you'll have to change her, though; but anyway, the little pink potty's under the cot, the one with the Teddy Bear on it.'

'I wonder where Stephen is,' said Peta, as Claire disappeared into the house. 'He said he'd be up before nine. I told him to come over the grass so that Grandfather wouldn't see him from the window and call him in.'

Stephen, passing through the open front door of the hall, stopped at the drawing-room door. Claire was standing in the centre of the parquet floor looking down with dismay at a mass of broken glass, spilt water, and scattered flowers. He said, glancing up at the wreath over the portrait, 'What now? Not Edward this time?'

'Oh, Stephen, I suppose it must have been. He did come in a little while ago. I feel a bit worried—this is the second time. Peta'd been teasing him.'

'It's all an act,' said Stephen. 'He's a little upset like everyone else over this wretched will business, and he just deliberately brings on these attacks.'

Claire shrugged, standing looking down at the mess. 'Oh, well! And Belle's favourite vase, too, not even a Serafita-left-over. I suppose I shall have to clear it up, but I must go and pot the baby first.' She came out with him and shut the door on it. 'Don't say anything to Bella; there's fuss enough for one day. Did you see Grandfather?'

'No, I cheated. My clerk brought the will up on his way home this evening, and handed it in to your grandfather, and I skipped over the lawn so that Sir

Richard shouldn't see me and make me go in and discuss it with him. That'll give him a night to sleep on it; he may have changed his mind by the morning. The trouble is that, if he goes and signs it, I shan't be here to talk him out of it again; I shall be marching about being a soldier boy and meanwhile, with his heart like this, anything might happen.'

He went on through the hall to the back terrace. Claire ran upstairs and, sitting impatiently holding the baby on the pink potty with the Teddy Bear on it, watched, from Ellen's balcony window, Brough come away from the lodge wheeling his barrow with an assortment of rakes and brooms in it. He disappeared behind the hedge surrounding his own little house, and after a minute or two reappeared with his bicycle, mounted, and rode off out of the gates. Brough was on fire-watch duty that night at The Swan, down in the village; and sundown or no sundown, fire-watch for Brough began an hour before closing time.

And so the hot day came to a close and in the cool of the evening hot tempers also were a little cooled, strained war-time nerves relaxed and hearts that were essentially affectionate and kind, recoiled at the recollection of their own unkindliness and vowed for the future, contrition and amendment and all sweet charity. The next day they would all go to Grandfather. The next day they would all say 'sorry' to Grandfather. The next day they would acknowledge to Grandfather that they had all been beastly pigs.

But the next day, it was too late. The next day Claire, walking carefully up the sanded path to the french window of the lodge, carrying Sir Richard's breakfast tray, stopped suddenly and stared; put down the tray in the middle of the path and running up close to the window rattled at the lock and peered in through the glass; and a moment later was running as fast as her legs would carry her, back down the path and across the wide green lawns towards the house.

CHAPTER V

Ellen was standing on the balcony outside her room. 'Good lord, Claire—what on earth's the matter?'

Claire stopped short, her hand to her aching side. 'Oh, Ellen—it's grandfather! He's—I think he's ... He's sitting at his desk and he—he looks terribly peculiar. Is Philip there? Do tell him.'

Ellen turned back and a moment later Philip appeared from the bedroom, settling his collar down over his tie as he came. 'What's all this, Claire?'

'Oh, Philip, do come quickly! I'm sure something's wrong with Grandfather!' She ran back across the lawn, not waiting for him. He disappeared and a minute later was leaping, three at a time, down the front steps; recollecting something he turned back, making a little circle, hardly altering his pace, and reappeared from the house carrying his medical bag. Ahead of him, Claire swerved across the gravel drive and up the path to the french window; he followed her, avoiding the tray which still lay in the middle of the path, and they both paused, breathless at the window, staring in. The heavy velvet curtains were drawn back and just inside Sir Richard sat at his desk, quite motionless, very strange and stiff; his lips were blue and in the crumpled fingers of one thin hand he held a bright green fountain pen.

Philip rattled at the window. When closed it automatically locked, and he wasted no time but kicked in a pane, thrust his arm through the hole, and pushed up the latch from inside. He slung his bag on to the desk, and bending over his grandfather, put his fingers on the still hand, then to the shoulder. 'He's dead, of course ... He's been dead for hours.'

Claire recoiled, wide-eyed. 'Oh, *Phil*ip!'

'He must have had an attack and passed out straight away—no time to do anything. It's *too* frightful,' said Philip, turning aside his head, giving it a little shake as though to rid his brain of the realization slowly being forced in upon it. 'We ought never to have let him come down here at all. He ought not to have been here alone. It's my fault, Claire, that is; I should have made more fuss. But good God, who would have thought he'd pip off like this so soon? And on this one night of all nights, when he was alone! I—I thought—well, I mean, with ordinary luck he ought to have lasted for years.'

'It's all our faults, Philip, not only yours. I suppose after the commotion yesterday . . . ?'

'Yes, it may have affected him. I don't know,' said Philip doubtfully. He took his hand from the old man's shoulder, and the stiff figure tipped gently forward and remained propped up, rigid as a wax dummy, against the desk; the arms spread themselves, brittle and angular, across the polished surface, one blue hand still clutching the gay green fountain pen. Claire closed her eyes against the gruesome pathos of it. 'Oughtn't we to—to *do* something, Philip? He looks so—so dreadful.' She added, 'The others'll be down any minute.'

'No, I told Ellen not to say anything. I thought you were just telling us that Grandfather was ill, and I didn't want Bella rushing down, fussing. Still, we'll have to go and tell them, I suppose, so we'd better just—just lay him down and—and cover him up.' He took hold of the dead man by the shoulders. 'Claire, could you bear it . . . ?'

Claire could hardly bear it, but she helped him carry the poor grotesque stiff figure, set into a sitting position, infinitely pathetic, and to arrange it with some semblance of decency on the divan bed. 'If only he didn't look so—well, rather *fun*ny, Philip.'

Philip opened his medical bag and taking out cotton-wool and a bottle of ether, began to wipe away the dried froth and spittle from the set blue lips. She shuddered away from it, and he said, as though to distract her thoughts from his distressing task, 'I wonder if he'd signed his blessed new will?'

Claire glanced at the desk. There was nothing on it now but a glass, empty except for a few drops of what looked like water; and a half-full bottle of ink. She pulled open the three drawers and closed them again. 'It isn't anywhere here.'

The lodge consisted of two rooms and a tiny kitchen and bathroom. The smaller of the rooms was locked and bare. The little tiled hall, empty of furniture, led from the sitting-room to the front door, facing across the gateway to the opposite lodge, where dwelt Brough and his wife. The kitchen was empty also, uncurtained and without crockery or utensils, and in the bathroom there was none of the usual clutter of bottles and pots, though a cake of soap and clean towels lay beside the basin. The place was used only for the one night in the year when Sir Richard slept there and, except for the sitting-room, was entirely bare. There, there were curtains and an exquisite carpet, to set off the portrait; and a corner cupboard with a few pieces of china Serafita had loved; and the beautiful Sheraton desk and chairs, and the divan bed. Claire opened the doors and glanced into each of the rooms and into the little hall, its tiled floor thick with dust. 'There's no will here.'

'How odd!' Philip looked up from the body for a moment, glancing vaguely about the room. 'What on earth can he have done with it?' As though impelled by curiosity, he left the body for a moment, and went over and opened the drawers of the desk again. 'No, it isn't there!' He crossed to the corner cupboard and felt foolishly in the china bowls and jugs, thrusting two fingers into the vases and feeling about. 'There's nowhere it could be. How extraordinary, Claire!'

'He's not . . . ? It's not . . . ?'

Philip moved the body a little, on the bed. 'No, it's nowhere here. Where on earth can it be?'

'Perhaps he saw Stephen coming down the drive

last night away from the house, and gave it to him then.'

'No, because I walked to the gates with Stephen and saw him off.' He turned his attention back to the corpse; but evidently his mind was still upon the problem, for he burst out after a minute, 'Perhaps he tore it up?'

'Then where are the bits?'

There was no fireplace in the little house, and no fire. 'He put it down the huh-ha.'

'But why? Why not just tear it across and leave the bits. We all knew all about it—there was nothing to hide.' She stood beside the bed looking down at the huddled corpse, the eyes now mercifully closed by Philip's hand. 'Oh, *God*, this is awful! Poor Grandfather dead, and already mystery and fuss about the will!'

'Well, there's not actually a mystery yet, is there?' said Philip. 'I mean, there's probably some perfectly simple explanation, which we haven't thought of, that's all. What's really dreadful, is the old boy dying all alone by himself like this, and I can't help feeling that it's rather my fault.'

Claire moved away and stood at the french window, looking out. Against the sunshine, her hair gleamed in great golden waves, coiled close and smooth at the nape of her neck. The dead man had loved her least of his grandchildren; she was intelligent, much cleverer than Peta, and quite as pretty, though her beauty was more controlled than her cousin's wild-rose grace; but Sir Richard had had no use for 'braininess' in women, he had pooh-poohed her aspirations to intellectuality, and ridden roughshod over many tender spots in her sensitive heart. She knew now that she had always resented it; that in her breast there was no real sorrow for his death or for the manner of it. Since this was so, she would not pretend to a grief she did not feel, and she said, ignoring Philip's last remark: 'It's so terribly important that the will should not have been signed; to all of us, Philip, but especially to you and me.'

For if she and Philip had money, Philip could provide for Ellen and the baby; and she knew that he would never consent to leave his wife without support, without very adequate, comfortable support; he would feel that he must do everything in the world to make up to her for his own defection. 'If we get ten or twelve thousand between us, Philip, we can let Ellen have most of that; after all, you can start up in practice again, somewhere else.'

Philip looked uneasy. 'Yes, well . . . Darling, we can't talk about that now. Never mind about the will—in any event it was only a draft, he wouldn't have signed it, and he'd have to have witnesses and things.'

'Well, then, where is it?'

'I daresay he gave it to Stephen, after all—perhaps Stephen turned back.'

Claire looked out of the window again. 'He can't have; you can see that nobody's been up to the lodge since Brough did the paths last night.'

Philip, his work completed, pulled up the quilt over his grandfather's face. He stood for a moment looking down at the bed; and then, giving himself a little shake, came over to his cousin at the window. 'No, so they haven't. How observant of you!'

Between the rose-bushes, the path ran narrow and golden, up to the window. 'Brough sanded it just before nine o' clock last night,' said Claire. 'I saw him when I went up to pot the baby. You can see my footsteps quite clearly, the ones I made this morning coming up the path with the tray and then turning round and running back again; and then, look, there are yours and mine running up the path; you after me, sort of swishing round the comet from the drive and keeping to that side of the path, dodging the tray.'

Philip shrugged. 'Well, it's very odd. However, we must go up to the house and break the news.' He went slowly back to put back his things into his bag—anything to postpone for a little while the task ahead. As 'Dr. March' he had 'broken the news so often; to so many sorrowing families he had stood as a rock in the midst of a storm of his own creating, and each time he dreaded it anew. Reactions of people bereaved were painfully similar; the words of consolation and support came so glibly to one after a while, that each time he was ashamed to find what comfort they gave, each time he could not believe that the mourners would not catch him out, would not say to him, 'That's what you said to Mrs. So-and-so and to Mrs. So-and-so before *her*, and to a hundred weeping women before them both.' He could imagine Ellen standing mockingly by, while Bella sobbed on his shoulder ('*Sheer* Doctor Kildare!'), and knew that she would have penetrated the defence of his conventional sorrow, would know just how real was his grief and how unreal; would know the depth of his sincerity more clearly than he knew it himself. He screwed up the soiled cotton-wool in a twist of paper and opened his bag to replace the bottle of ether.

And stood suddenly, thunder-stricken, staring down.

Ellen sat uneasily at the breakfast table, wondering what was happening down at the lodge, knowing that Bella would upbraid her for not saying that Philip had been called down there; but he had barked out a 'Don't say anything to Bella!' as he ran off out of their room, and she loyally obeyed. Bella sipped fretfully at her coffee. 'Where on earth are Philip and Claire? It's too bad of them to be late. And imagine, Peta, imagine, Ellen, that Turtle not turning up till eight o'clock this morning! She's done nothing yet but just dust in here and lay the breakfast things . . . '

And suddenly Claire and Philip were there, standing in the doorway with white faces and shaking hands. Bella, gaping at them, cried, terrified: 'Philip—what's the matter? Claire, what is it? What's happened . . . ?' And then, 'It's your grandfather!'

The Turtle appeared at the door leading from the kitchen. Philip took Bella's arm. 'Come into the drawing-room; we can talk there. I'll tell you there.' As he led her across the hall, he said: 'Bella, did you take the box of coramine out of my bag? The one I showed you, the six ampoules, you know?'

Bella was bewildered and frightened. 'The coramine? No, I didn't take it. Richard had some already,
in his pocket.'

Philip looked back over her head at Peta and Ellen
and Edward, following. 'Did anyone take it? Did anyone go to my bag?' As they all disclaimed, Bella caught
at his sleeve as he stood with his fingers on the handle
of the drawing-room door. 'For God's sake, Philip,
what's happened? Is it Richard? Is he ill; has he had
another attack?' At sight of his face she went, if possible, more white than she had been before, and cried
with a sort of desperate comprehension: 'He's dead!
You're trying to tell me that Richard's dead!'

'Yes,' said Philip. 'He's dead. And all that coramine's
disappeared from my bag; and a hypodermic, and a
phial of strychnine.' He stood, also ashy white, looking
back at them in doubt and terror as though astounded
by the implications of what was before them all; and
suddenly blurted out: 'I believe somebody's killed him,'
and so pushed open the door and led the way abruptly
into the drawing-room.

In the centre of the floor, where Claire had left it
last night, shutting the door upon it, was a pool of
spilt water, a mass of broken glass and a heap of dead
flowers; and above Serafita's portrait, the wreath of
roses was hanging askew again.

CHAPTER VI

Inspector Cockrill was at the house before midday.
Small, brown and bright-eyed, a dusty little old spar-
row arrayed in a startlingly clean white panama hat,
he was soon, sparrow-like, at the centre of all interest
and activity, hopping and darting this way and that,
in search of crumbs of information. Stephen Garde

summoned by a tearful Peta, craving sympathy and support, had insisted upon his being sent for. 'Since you know Cockie personally, Lady March, why not get him over and ask his advice? If there's nothing wrong, you can be sure he won't make any fuss; on the other hand, if there is—well, you'll all be in a very bad position if you've made things more difficult for the police.' He had stood there, cold and quiet all of a sudden; such a little man with his childish, fair curly hair, to be steadily opposing the united will of people whom he knew and loved, who should surely, thought Peta resentfully have been his first, his only, thought. 'I *am* thinking of you, it's absolutely for your sakes that I suggest it. You'll be putting yourselves hopelessly in the wrong, if you just go ahead as though there was no question of Sir Richard's having—having died a normal death. Well, yes, Philip, we all hope it was normal, and I quite agree that the disappearance of this coramine and strychnine or whatever it was, doesn't necessarily mean that—that there was anything *wrong*: but with the draft of the will missing—because Briggs definitely handed it in to Sir Richard last night—well, the whole thing looks jolly unsatisfactory to say the least of it, and I simply can't advise you just to let things go . . .'

Peta gazed at his stern face, white and trembling. 'Can't you forget for a moment that you're our lawyer, Stephen? Don't be so—so beastly *pomp*ous!'

'It's for your own sakes,' repeated Stephen, doggedly. 'Anyway, I very much doubt that the doctor will give a certificate, so it's all bound to come out.' He had left them then, and gone straight down to the lodge and there waited quietly for Cockrill to arrive, allowing nobody to come nearer than the rose-beds and the sanded paths. 'All right, if I'm fussing, I'm fussing; Cockrill will decide all that.' Apologetic, but indomitable he had fought them all off till the Inspector arrived. When Cockrill, having glanced over the lodge and allotted tasks to his various henchmen, summoned the family to the drawing-room at the house, he asked, diffidently: 'Can I come along and watch your third-degree methods, on behalf of Lady March?' and without reference to anyone else, perched himself, swinging his short legs, on a table outside the circle and tried to convince himself that Peta would ever speak to him again; and doubted it.

Edward sat in a big arm-chair, very still and frightened. Unconsciousness, fugues, automatism. . . . 'You mean I could sort of walk about and *do* things, Doctor, and not know what I was doing?' The doctor had said that that was possible; and had added that he must be careful about not glancing upwards too quickly, and so bringing on an attack. And only yesterday. . . . He had tried these little experiments for many years now. Unconsciousness was easy; from childhood he had been able to faint almost at will, until at last the thing had become outside his own control and he fainted when it was expected of him, whether he consciously wanted to or not. But had the experiments gone farther than that? For, after all—would he know? Wasn't that the whole point of a fugue, that you passed into and out of this condition and had no idea that anything had been wrong? Yesterday morning, for example, just before lunch, the wreath over the picture had been hanging crooked; it had caught his eye and he had glanced up at it, and it had reminded him of what the doctor had said. He had, accordingly, dropped the tray with the glasses and waited for unconsciousness to follow. Had it in fact followed? He thought definitely not. He had stood staring up at the chandelier, waiting for the family to come in and find him there and make a fuss of him—and a jolly long time they had been about it too; he had got quite tired, and no wonder he had fainted so easily afterwards. But last night? He had not gone into the drawing-room last night. He had come in from the terrace and gone to the ground-floor cloakroom and tried to make himself sick, because Peta had upset him dreadfully about the horse meat in the biscuits and he had felt he owed it to himself to be sick; but he hadn't been able to, and rather than go back and confess that he was less injured, that his nerves and stomach were less delicate than he had supposed, he had wandered out on to the front terrace and had sat there, on the edge of the balustrade, fiddling with his camera, until someone should come and express anxiety about him. He remembered towards the end seeing Brough with a barrow and some tools passing across the drive towards the lodge, though because of a hedge in the way he could not see exactly where he went with them. After a quarter of an hour, during which the family remained most heartlessly undisturbed, he had gone into the drawing-room and fetched the portable radio and taken it out to them, without reproach . . .

Into the drawing-room!

But he had just told himself that he had not been into the drawing-room yesterday evening. He had forgotten, of course, about fetching the radio; anybody might forget a little thing like that. And yet. . . . He had told the family, just now, that he hadn't been into the drawing-room: none of them had noticed that he must have been, to have got the radio—or *had* they noticed, had they said nothing to him, had they only pretended to believe? They had glanced at each other uneasily, wretchedly, and said that a—a vase had been found knocked over in the drawing-room; and asked him if he remembered, if he thought he had had another of his 'little turns'. 'Like yesterday, darling. I mean, before lunch you did—you did drop the tray and the sherry glasses, and you fainted afterwards and didn't—didn't know anything about it all until we told you.' How could he explain to them that of course he remembered, of course he had known all about it, that he had done it all purposely, or sort of purposely, that he had been staging these things for years—staging things until they had become half real, even to him. But were they only half real? Had they not grown quite real, had some of them always been real things that he didn't remember, that he had never known anything about? He knew that the family were afraid, in their hearts, that he had killed Grandfather. At half-past seven, Ellen had seen Grandfather, alive, sitting at his desk in the sitting-room—seen Grandfather, alive and well; by nine o'clock Brough had finished sanding the paths, and the evidence of the footprints showed that nobody had gone near the lodge after that. Between those times the family had been all together—except for him. Between those times, only he, Edward, could possibly have gone down to the lodge; and in the drawing-room was the sign that he had had 'one of his little attacks'. They thought that he had been into the drawing-room to fetch the radio; that he had caught sight of the wreath and looked up at it again, and again lost consciousness; that, unsettled and ill-tempered as he had been all day—as they all had been that day—evil had insinuated itself into his unresistant mind; that he had taken the poisons and gone down to the lodge, before Brough began his sanding, and there had killed Grandfather. He could easily have done it in the time, and he could not say that he had not. Philip and Claire and Peta had whispered together, they had called Bella over and whispered to her, while Ellen sat beside him, talking to him quietly, asking him, as though she believed him, how he had really spent his time. But she did not believe him. She had gone to the others at last and he had seen that, coolly and matter-of-factly, she was acquiescing with all they said. They were going to try to protect him, they were going to lie about him, they were banded together to shield him from the consequences of what he, in his innocence, had done. Stephen, cold, just, quiet, relentless Stephen, had been safely away down by the lodge; Philip had gone out to the terrace and found the camera which had been there on the balustrade all night, and had examined it. There was a new film in it, all right. But Philip, at first rejoicing, had then reluctantly worked out a time schedule. A minute or two in the cloakroom, trying to be sick; a minute or two in the drawing-room, glancing up, losing consciousness, robbing the bag standing unlocked on a chair where he, Philip, had left it after the incident just before lunch; three minutes—two minutes running across the lawn to the lodge; five minutes, if you would, to knock at the window and obtain admittance, to tell Grandfather some hurried tale about an injection ordered by Philip, or, without preamble, to thrust the needle into the arm of an old man utterly unsuspecting and so disarmed. Two minutes more to run back again across the grass. Five, six, seven minutes left to sit, gradually recovering from the trance, out on the balustrade of the front terrace; to notice the camera, to put the new film in, to stroll to the back terrace, unaware and innocent, and yet a murderer! It could have been done; and he knew that this was what, beneath their loyal self-deception, they believed had been done. He sat in the arm-chair, digging with shaking fingers into the padded arms. Cockrill, in the centre of the little group, rolled himself the fourth of a chain of untidy, wispy cigarettes. 'Very well. Thank you for all you've told me. In return, I'm going to tell you something; I must warn you that I don't like the look of this at all. I think it's perfectly conceivable that Sir Richard has been murdered; or, if you want to put it more prettily, assisted out of a world that the killer may have thought he would soon be leaving anyway. And if he was murdered, it seems to me more than likely it was by somebody from this house.'

If he had expected an uproar, thought Edward, he must have been disappointed. They had long ago accustomed themselves to that idea. But oh! why must they allow themselves to glance up at the picture like that, at the wreath of roses now replaced neatly above the gilt frame, at the stain on the parquet where the water had soaked in. Cockie didn't miss those glances—not he! He pointed to the mark on the floor with the toe of his small, shabby shoe. 'What's this?'

'What's what, Cockie?'

'What's this stain?'

'I dropped a vase of flowers in here last night,' said Claire coolly. 'It's the water from the vase.'

But they were not very good at deception. Cockrill watched their eyes travel towards the small rug nearer the fireplace, and then pounced. 'Why has that rug been moved? That's the one that was here, where the water was spilt—you can see that the corner of it's still wet. Why was it changed with the one that's here now?'

'Well, good gracious, Cockie, they got changed when the room was done out, what's wrong with that?'

'Who did the room out?' said Cockrill.

A desperate silence. Then: 'I did,' said Bella and Peta and Claire, all together.

'What time did you do it?' asked Cockrill swiftly.

Nobody answered. 'What time?' insisted Cockrill to Belle.

Belle shrugged her plump shoulders and fluttered her hands. 'Dear Inspector Cockrill, whatever can it matter?'

'Don't "dear Inspector" me, Lady March. You're all keeping something back from me. Now—what time was this room done out?'

'At about ten o'clock,' said Belle, sullenly. 'We only have one woman now, a "help" from the village, and she didn't get here till late, this morning.'

'Oh!' He fished in the pockets of his droopy grey flannel suit and produced a shaggy tin of tobacco and a packet of cigarette-papers. 'So at nine-forty-five you hear the news of Sir Richard's death; and a quarter of an hour later you all turn to and spring-clean the drawing-room.'

Ellen sat on the arm of a sofa in her tight, brief, yellow linen dress, tapping the toe of a neat tan shoe against the parquet. 'What's so extraordinary? We came in here to learn the news, here was this mess of water and broken glass in the middle of the room, and we were all stepping over it and around it and it was in the way. So we cleared it up and dried the floor and moved the wet rug so that it shouldn't get stepped on. That's the way it *is* with death, *isn't* it?—other people have to go on living.'

It would have been more effective if they had not all turned upon her eyes of such passionate gratitude at this timely rescue, this cool return to a sense of proportion and sanity. Cockrill could not quite understand it; but he stored the whole incident away in his mind and returned to matters more obviously connected with the case. 'Now, Dr. March—you told me about these ampoules of coramine missing from your bag. In your grandfather's case, at any rate, these would have been sufficient to cause death?'

'Yes, they would, certainly. His heart was already in a very poor condition and such over-stimulation might easily cause it to peter out altogether.'

'Is his appearance consistent with this having happened?' As Philip paused, looking a trifle taken aback at having this question put to himself, he added: 'Naturally, there will have to be a post-mortem, and all this will be checked; the police surgeon is coming along very shortly, I hope. But meanwhile, it would help me to have your opinion.'

'I see. Well, yes, I think the post-mortem appearance does bear out such a—well, such a possibility. I didn't think of it, when I first saw him, of course; I wasn't looking for unnatural signs; I'd expected him to die one day, just the way he did. None of this would ever have entered my head if I hadn't found the coramine missing. There's certainly no indication that he *did*n't die of an overdose.' He glanced at Bella's tearful face and added sarcastically: 'I suppose you will spare us a more detailed disquisition upon the subject, just at the moment.'

Bella understood him and gave him a tremulous smile of gratitude. Cockrill ignored the entire remark. 'Can you tell me, Doctor, how the fatal dose was administered?'

'Well, the theft of the syringe would suggest that it was injected hypodermically.'

'I'll do the suggesting,' said Cockie tartly. 'Could the dose have been taken by the mouth? Would you know by the post-mortem signs?'

'No, you wouldn't. And what's more, the post-mortem examination isn't likely to reveal that either. Of course, death would follow more slowly, if it was taken orally, and Grandfather was still sitting at his desk, which would seem to show . . . ' He broke off. 'Oh—but I must let you do the suggesting, mustn't I?'

Cockrill acknowledged this thrust with a bleak smile. 'I presume you didn't examine your grandfather for the marks of a hypodermic needle?'

'I tell you, I had no idea he'd died anything but a natural death. In any event he's probably covered with marks of hypodermic needles; he's been having injections from Dr. Brown, down here.'

Cockrill moved from the subject of the coramine. 'I suppose there's no possibility that it was the strychnine that might have been used? There would be indications of that?'

'Just slight indications,' said Philip; he was very weary and anxious, and his voice began to rise and to grow in rapidity as he lost control. 'My grandfather's corpse would have been stiffened into a horrible, convulsive arch, probably supported by the head and the heels, his eyes would have been starting out of his head, his face cyanosed and his hands and feet curved and stiffened into claws.' He knew that he was talking nonsense, that in death the more dreadful symptoms would have passed; but he bitterly piled on the agony, relieving his pent up feelings by the ugliness and violence of his words. It was as good as swearing; and he thus swore at length and with fluency. At the end of it, Cockrill simply said coolly: 'I see. Then you think the strychnine was not used?'

'Precisely,' said Philip. 'How did you guess?'

It seemed so unwise and dangerous to be making an enemy of Inspector Cockrill. Cockie was so quick and acute, he would know that they were all on edge, that they shared some secret, that they were afraid of him—afraid for themselves, or for one of themselves. Edward shrank back in his big chair, looking on helplessly, wishing that Philip wouldn't be so impatient and irritable, wouldn't by his nervousness so clearly show his hand. Cockrill, however, merely said: 'We must all realize that this lethal dose of poison is still missing: whether or not there has been one murder, there is danger all round us here.' He turned away from Philip. 'You have all told me how you spent the evening, and how you went down to the lodge before dinner. What happened there? Peta, you and Lady March went down first?'

'Yes, I carried the tray of supper things.'

'Who prepared this meal?'

'Our old hag did,' said Bella. 'The Turtle we call her; the woman who comes up from the village. I really forget what her name is.'

'Well, I'll enquire into her afterwards. Had you been near this tray or near any of Sir Richard's food, Lady March, before that?'

'No, I hadn't. If you mean to suggest . . . Well, you can ask them in the kitchen,' cried Bella, angrily. 'I never went near the food. You can ask them.'

'I shall,' said Cockrill.

Philip's rage deepened. 'Have you any right, Inspector, to be questioning us like this? You've got no authority here, yet. There's been no—no charge, or anything like that . . . '

'You called me in yourselves,' said Cockrill calmly. 'You do want to get to the bottom of this affair, don't you?'

They all glared at Stephen. This was what came of Cockie 'not fussing' if there was nothing to fuss about. Cockrill, however, gave his attention to his cigarette, standing on one foot to squash the stub out against the sole of the other shoe. He went on, as though there had been no interruption: 'Well, so the woman handed you the tray, Lady March . . . ?

'Yes, she did, she came out on the terrace with it, and I took it straight from Belle and we went down to the lodge,' said Peta. She added triumphantly that the whole thing had been weighted down with vast great covered silver dishes, let alone china and glass and stuff, and that if Cockrill thought a person could balance a tray like that in one hand while they put poison on the food with the other, that was where he was wrong.

Cockrill seized upon the only point that interested him. 'Covered silver dishes?'

'Yes, covered. So, there, Belle, darling, we couldn't have squirted poison on to Grandfather's food even if we'd wanted to.' She looked compassionately at Bella's round face, all stained and quivering with tears, trying desperately to throw a little spirit into this horrible game of question and answer, to try to make it seem a game in truth, and not the deadly quicksand that it was.

'What did you do, Peta, while your grandfather ate his supper?'

'Well I—what did I do, Bella? You sat on the sill of the un-french window delivering your oration about his coming back to sleep at the house and not staying there alone, and I . . . ' Her eyes grew wary; Cockrill knew that she was counting her words: 'I rang up the house about his fountain pen. I told you about that, Cockie.'

'Yes and then?'

'Well, actually the Turtle hadn't dusted the telephone properly and my hands were quite dirty—nobody'd *been* in the lodge for a year, you see. I went into the kitchen and put my fingers under the tap; there wasn't a cloth or anything in there, so I wished I hadn't, and I had to dry them on the seat of my bathing-dress which was horrid because it was still damp, and nasty little bits of woolly fluff came off. Then I sat on the window-sill with Belle and finally Grandfather was so cross and obviously hating us so much, that we rather tamely came away.'

'Why was he so particularly inimical?'

'Well, dash it, we were interrupting him in the middle of disinheriting us—or me, at any rate. And Belle was going on and on and *on* about his not sleeping at the lodge, in an uninterrupted monologue . . . '

'Uninterrupted?' said Cockrill.

Peta stared. 'Yes, why not? You haven't heard Belle when she's really under way!' She smiled affectionately at Belle.

'While you were in the kitchen for that minute or two, rinsing your hands, Lady March didn't stop talking to Sir Richard?'

'If you mean did she say, "Oh, just a minute, Richard, while I put a lot of poison on your food so that you won't leave Swanswater and all Peta's money to me," no, she didn't. She just rambled on and on monotonously about his sleeping alone, because I remember registering that if there was one way to make Grandfather do a thing, it was to keep badgering him not to.'

Cockrill stood looking at her with his bright little eyes, but not seeing her. Deep in thought, he wandered away to the window and stood there, turned away from them, his hands loosely clasped behind his stooping back, his fine head with its fluff of white hair outlined against the sunshine on the terrace outside. He turned back at last into the cool room with its grey and blue chintzes and tall white Adam mantelpiece, the portrait of Serafita in white dress with pink gloves, dominating the whole from her vantage point over the fireplace. Edward thought, in terror, 'He's going to ask *me*! He's going to set on *me*!'

But Cockrill attacked Ellen next; and knew again that they were resisting him, that they were all sitting taut and wary, watching him, waiting for any discrepancy in the evidence that afterwards they must support or evade. 'I thought I would have a few words with Sir Richard,' said Ellen coolly, 'and try and make him change his mind. I thought it was all exaggerated and stupid. I thought if only one of us would admit to him that we'd behaved badly and we were really sorry, he'd drop the whole show. I thought he was just—just dramatizing himself. I thought I'd just go down and tell him it was simply silly.'

'That would have been a great help!' said Claire.

'You should know,' said Ellen sweetly.

Would Ellen stand by him, by Edward, like the rest of the family? After all, she wasn't really one of them! Why should *she* lie, why should she risk trouble by sticking up for him, by saving him from the consequences of what, however unknowingly, he had done. He knew that Ellen was fond of him, that though she had laughed at his proud pretensions to psychosis, she had always had a soft spot for him in her generous heart; but to lie and cheat and try to trick the police—and perhaps be found out ... But Ellen was saying steadily: 'I watched from the balcony window of my room till I saw Bella and Peta come away from the lodge, and I crossed with them, on the lawn. I didn't want to make a family party of it; the quarrel had all originally been about my affairs and I thought I'd better talk to Sir Richard alone. But he wouldn't respond. The truth is that he didn't want to respond; he was thoroughly enjoying his Disappointed Grandfather act.'

Bella opened her mouth to protest. Just because things were true was no reason for putting them so crudely into words. But she did not know what reason Ellen might have for doing so, what subtle building up of 'atmosphere' for Edward's sake. She remained silent. Ellen, who was simply remarking upon what she believed to be the fact, continued with her story. 'Sir Richard was thoroughly cross and I saw it was all no use, so I came away. I met Edward on the—on the lawn—and walked back to the house with him.'

'Edward was going to see his grandfather, was he?' asked Cockrill, looking round at the boy as he sat huddled in his chair. (Why should they all give a little gasp, and glance at him, and turn away?) Ellen said, a little bit too quickly, that Edward had been coming down for no other reason than to walk back with her. It had been nearly dinner time. 'Wasn't it, Edward?'

'I suppose it was, as far as I remember,' said Edward, ungraciously.

'So we just walked back, talking, and then he went and joined the family,' said Ellen, rather underlining the words, 'and I ran upstairs to dress. I still had on only my bathing-dress.' She sketched its outline, a brassiere and tiny trunks.

The family relaxed. 'Why don't they tell him right out that they're protecting me?' thought Edward, bitterly watching their naive reaction to every hurdle successfully negotiated. 'Do they think they're deceiving him for a moment? They're making things worse, much worse!'

'Edward—had you been into the house before you went down to the lodge?'

'Towards the lodge,' corrected Bella, quickly. 'He never went *to* the lodge.'

The Inspector lifted an ironical eyebrow. 'Very well, Edward, when you went *towards* the lodge . . . '

'I'd been in to change,' said Edward. He added, an edge of hysteria to his voice: 'I suppose you mean had I had an opportunity of taking the poison from Philip's bag?'

'I think any of us had that much opportunity,' said Claire, smoothly, drawing Cockie's attention away from Edward, and on to herself and all of them. 'The french windows of the drawing-room were open all day, and most of us were in and out of the house during the afternoon; we spent about half the time in the hall, to our great fury, ringing up Stephen Garde, disinheriting ourselves.'

'I see. And you, Claire,' said Cockrill, 'you didn't go down to the lodge at all at this time?'

'Well, no I didn't,' said Claire, quite apologetically: for it narrowed down the circle of possible suspects to appear to exculpate herself. She added hurriedly that she *had* come into the house, away from the rest of them, that was—at about nine o'clock.

'But the paths had been sanded by then? We could have seen if you'd been up to the french window?' Cockrill had glanced at the other two paths and found them innocent of footprints or of any marks whatsoever.

'Yes, I suppose they had. Actually, I saw Brough coming away, presumably having just finished them.'

Edward had seen him go across to the lodge to begin them. 'He started at about twenty past eight.'

The silence was terrible. Outside the hot sun glared down upon the white terrace making a translucency of the thick linen of the blue and white summer curtains; but inside the drawing-room a darkness seemed to have fallen, it was as though no light had touched there for untold years, a dankness enfolded them, sick and cold upon their vitals, laying upon their spines little horrible, shuddery hands. Cockrill said quietly: 'How do you know? What were you doing at twenty past eight?' and Claire rose and went to the fireplace and stood there with her back to it, her hands clasped loosely before her, assuming, all unconsciously, the attitude of a child about to recite its party piece; and they knew that the moment had come, that she was going to tell The Lie.

They had agreed among themselves that Claire should tell it; that Claire should be the one. She raised her beautiful blonde head and looked Cockrill in the eye. 'Brough always took about half an hour to do those paths, Inspector—Teddy only means that it would be about twenty or twenty-five past eight. Don't you, Edward?' She did not wait for his mumbled acknowledgment but added, coolly: 'Of course, we were all out on the back terrace, then, overlooking the river. Edward and all of us.'

'She's afraid,' thought Edward. 'When you know a person's voice so well as we know Claire's, you can tell when she's afraid. Will Cockie recognize it, too?' She stood very straight and lovely beneath the portrait, facing Cockrill; above her, Serafita posed on pink toe-points, and seemed by contrast with the desperate sincerity of the group below her, more artificial than ever, with her gloves and her garlands, and her painted, simpering smile. Edward bit his lips, picking with his finger-nails at the arm of the chair, his leg muscles taut with the strain of keeping still, of not jumping up and ending it all by shouting out the truth—that they thought he had done it, that he was mad, that he had killed poor Grandfather, not knowing what he did . . . That they were banded together to protect him, that Claire was telling nothing but a monstrous lie. Shaking, he watched her, warily, warily, telling the story they had agreed upon. 'We all sat together on the back terrace between the time we finished dinner and the time we went to bed. Except for the ten or fifteen minutes I was in the house, doing the baby, we were all together, sitting out there.'

Cockrill gave her a long, level look. 'You're certain of this, Claire? The vital time is between twenty to eight, when Ellen left your grandfather alive at the lodge, and twenty to nine, when Brough began the sanding. You were definitely all together during that hour?'

'Yes, Cockie,' said Claire. She gave him no time for consideration but went on rapidly with her story. 'I came in at just about twenty to. As I passed the drawing-room I—I thought I would close the french windows for the night, because as we haven't got any proper servants now they always get forgotten; so I went in and did it. Of course, the—the black-out hadn't been done in there, and though it was sort of getting a bit dark by then, I didn't like to switch on the lights.' They had not rehearsed this part carefully enough; she knew she was floundering in a morass of improbabilities. 'Of course, I know it wasn't black-out time, yet, Cockie, but you know how inhibited one gets these days, you hardly dare to switch on a light in broad *day*light, do you? what with Major Lloyd George and the A.R.P. and things.'

'Besides a little matter of there being no need,' said Cockrill, watching her face and hands, quietly registering the nervously increasing volubility, the unreadiness to come to a definite point.

'Yes, that's just what I'm saying. Well, and so . . . I've forgotten where I was,' said Claire miserably.

'You were in this room, my dear, where, in spite of all these french windows and a bright, sunny evening at seven o'clock, God's time, it was so dark that—so you are going to tell me, I think—you fell over a vase of flowers.'

Claire gulped wretchedly, passing her tongue over her dry lips. 'Well, I don't say it was dark, of course not; only it *was* a bit dim when I had drawn the curtains, and I—yes, I tripped over the little table with the bowl on it, that's all.'

Cockrill was silent, flipping back the pages of his note-book. 'I see. But half an hour ago you told me that you *dropped* the bowl.'

'I can't bear it,' thought Edward. 'I can't *bear* it, I can't stand any more of this, it must end, it must come to an end, it mustn't go on.' His hands tore at the linen covers of his chair, his feet drummed on the carpet, his face was deathly white and the roots of his hair were damp with sweat. 'I'm mad, I'm mad and I can't judge for myself, and I killed poor Grandfather and now Cockie has found out, now Claire has given it all away and Cockie has found out. And they're all staring at me, they're all sitting staring with their mouths half-opened like silly fishes, not saying anything, not doing anything. Why don't they speak? Why don't they move? Why are they all looking and looking and looking and looking at *me*?' He dragged himself to his feet and stood swaying, staring back at them with burning eyes and horribly shaking hands; and opened his mouth to cry out, to scream out that he was mad—that it was he, he who had killed . . . Grandfather.

Philip got up, quietly, from his chair, and walked over to him and hit him across the face: and caught him as he fell.

CHAPTER VII

Brough, the gardener, was an exceedingly disagreeable old man. He had for many years been paid handsomely to live much about the same life as Sir Richard, the one in the big house at one end of Swanswater drive, the other in the little lodge at its gates; both ruling about equally over a large staff of undergardeners, and only occasionally themselves pottering about the grounds doing a little spraying or pruning as the spirit moved them; both quarrelling heatedly over the credit for the roses, marrows, and apples which, with monotonous regularity, were awarded the prizes for beauty, size, and profusion at all the local shows; and each heartily disliking and despising the other. The only difference between them was that Sir Richard was apparently content to continue to pay his gardener to insult and bully him, and Brough was not content with anything. He had never been beyond Heronsford, their nearest town, but, ignorant and illiterate, he yet gave his opinions upon all subjects unasked and at interminable length, and was the club bore of The Swan, the village hostelry. He had one joy in life, his small grand-daughter, Rosy-Posy; and (since the time that Philip, by a perfectly routine treatment, had seen the child through a slight attack of tonsilitis) one pride and admiration—Philip. He boasted incessantly of the complexities of the case and of the extraordinary lengths to which 'the Doctor' had gone, to save Rosy-Posy's life.

Dark days, however, had fallen upon Brough. With the increasing rigour of the call-up, all his staff had been taken from him, and he found himself obliged to turn to and do some work at Swanswater. Sir Richard had proved unexpectedly stony-hearted, saying when approached that if Brough felt too old for the job he had better retire and make room for a man strong enough to cope with such work as had to be kept going. Mrs. Brough, a gaunt woman, speechless, as must be anyone who lived with Brough, was now 'helping out' at the house, and Brough dug and delved and grumbled as never before. He was only too ready to rest, leaning upon his spade and giving of his voluble best when, on the afternoon of Sir Richard's death, the Inspector came down from the house to talk to him.

Cockie, who loved a country pub, had before now been driven from The Swan by the loquacity of Brough; but in his official capacity he stood it for just one minute. 'Well, Brough, I haven't got time to worry about your troubles with Sir Richard; they're over now anyway, and,' he could not help adding maliciously, 'I daresay you may not be at Swanswater much longer.'

He pushed the new panama hat on to the back of his head, motioning with one nicotined finger at the lodge, and said abruptly: 'Is it true that you sanded those paths last night?'

'Nine o'clock I was working till,' said Brough immediately, in a whining voice. 'Had my bit of supper at eight o'clock, all by myself, the wife being up at the 'ouse working her fingers to the bone for them as was born equal with us, *I* says, and by rights ought to be waiting on us, not us on them.'

Cockrill, not unfamiliar with Brough's ideas of an equal world, restrained himself from asking under what compulsion save that of cupidity Mrs. Brough was now working her fingers to the bone, and merely enquired as to the time she had gone up to the house the night before, and the time Brough had commenced the sanding of the paths.

'Eight o'clock, she went up,' said Brough grudgingly. 'Quarter to eight the fambly 'as their meal and she goes and helps the old woman to wash up. Eight o'clock I got in from the—the garden, and she says, "I'll put you out a bit of cheese and an onion to your bread," she says, "and you'd better 'ave a glass of beer, for I haven't got the time now to make you a cuppa tea," and off she goes to the house. I 'as me supper and a read of the paper and I'm due to go down to The Swan at nine, for me fire-watch; and suddenly I thinks to meself, "Dang it, I've still got them paths to finish, and the old beggar'll carry on if they ain't done to-night like 'e said," and I see that it isn't too late—I can just manage it; and that would be the end of the sand. Just went round, it did, and not a grain more have I got left. How the Council thinks I'm going to keep my paths nice if they don't allow me no transport, they'd better explain to Sir Richard . . .'

'Well, never mind the Council now. You started this sanding at about twenty to nine, and ended it at nine. Mr. Garde tells me that you seemed to be just finishing when he came through the gates; and a minute or two later Miss Claire saw you from a bedroom window. Now, how do you do it? Do you rake the paths over first?'

'Rake 'em over? Of course not,' said Brough, with the ineffable contempt of the ignoble mind for those not familiar with its own little speciality. 'I rolls 'em, Mr. Cockrill, rolls'em! Matter of fact, I rolled these paths earlier in the evening; then, last thing, I only had to smooth 'em out with the back of me rake and scatter a fresh lot of sand over the top of the lot.'

'So in point of fact you do rake them,' said Cockrill, with a touch of triumph.

Brough raised his eyes to heaven in mute appeal that he be preserved from those who persisted that to use a rake was necessarily to rake. 'Do you rake them (whether with the teeth or the back of the rake) *after* you've sanded the paths?'

Brough cast up his eyes again. 'I'll thank you for a civil answer, Brough,' said Cockrill irritated. 'Do you, or do you not, rake or roll or smooth the paths, after the new top-coat of sand has been scattered?'

'No,' said Brough.

'If anything—any roller or garden tool—had passed over them since you scattered the sand, could you tell?'

'Yes,' said Brough. 'And nothing has.' He added acutely: 'You mean could anyone have covered up their footsteps by tidying the path after theirselves? Well, the answer is, no, they couldn't. These paths are just as I left them last night, except for Miss Claire's footsteps here, and the mark of the tray; and her footsteps and the doctor's, running up the side of the path, there. The path to the front door and the path to the back door hasn't been touched. Those doors is kept locked and nobody uses them, even when the old man *is* at the lodge. And what's more,' said Brough, anticipating Cockrill's next question, 'if you think the paths may have been walked on and then sanded over again, I can tell you that that won't work neither, because when I'd finished last night, that was the last grain of sand in the place. If the Council thinks——'

'All right, all right, we've had all that before.' He stood looking at the rose beds, closely encircling the little house. 'Nobody could push a way through these—avoiding the paths, that is—without tearing their clothes to bits; could they?'

'They couldn't do it without tearing the rose trees to bits, that's the thing,' said Brough. He took a rake and thrust it, horizontally, between a couple of bushes; a shower of petals fluttered to the ground. 'They're all ready to fall; only that it was such a still, close night, they'd be all over the bed. But as it is . . . ' The soil beneath the trees was free of more than half a dozen petals, here and there. 'Nobody pushed no way between them trees last night,' said Brough.

'No,' said Cockrill. He dismissed the man and sent a constable up to the house for a pair of shoes belonging to each of the family. 'Try and get the ones Miss Claire March was wearing last night.'

Stephen Garde, turning in at the lodge gates, found him squatting unselfconsciously in the centre of the sanded path, poking at one of the prints with a stick. 'Hallo, Inspector? Playing at Robinson Crusoe?'

Cockrill got to his feet, bending down to rub his aching knees. He ignored Stephen's little joke. 'Mr. Garde, exactly what time did your man hand Sir Richard the draft of the will?'

'He says it was about quarter to seven. He spoke to Brough who told him that Sir Richard was sitting at his desk, at the french window, and he went round and handed the envelope to Sir Richard—he says Sir Richard put it in a drawer of the desk.'

'This man O.K.? Has he been long with your firm?'

'Thirty or forty years,' said Stephen. 'That's all. If you're suggesting, Inspector, that Briggs murdered Sir Richard because he just couldn't bear to draft out any more wills, I must remind you that several of the family saw Sir Richard alive afterwards.'

'Thank you,' said Cockrill. 'You're most helpful. However, I don't think we need trouble much about Briggs, I must say.'

Stephen asked the question that was uppermost in

his mind. 'Anything turned up about this missing strychnine?'

'No, nothing. My men are searching the place from top to bottom, the house and the grounds, but there's acres of it, indoors *and* out! Of course, nobody admits seeing the stuff after it was shown to them all and put back into the bag.' He looked Stephen straight in the eye. 'Between you and me, Garde—there's very little doubt that this is a case of murder—and by one of the family.' He dropped his eyes, fumbling with the inevitable cigarette. 'I'm sorry about it—I hate it—but there it is.'

'Somebody could have come in from outside,' suggested Stephen uncertainly. 'The old boy was a bit peppery; he must have had some ill-wishers.'

Cockrill tossed away the match. 'Don't fool yourself, my dear boy. The family and the gardener were on the front terrace practically the whole of the afternoon, or in the garden on this side of the house; who do you suppose took the risk of walking in, in broad sunny daylight, going straight to a bag he couldn't have known was in the drawing-room, and selecting from the bag two drugs which he couldn't have known were there?'

'The family didn't know that the strychnine was there, either.'

'The family had time to look for it. The family could have gone to the bag for the other stuff, and noticed the strychnine and taken that also. I must say,' admitted Cockrill, 'the disappearance of that strychnine makes me feel sick.' He stopped and then said abruptly: 'What's your opinion of Edward Treviss? All this psychological twaddle, I mean.'

Stephen was horrified by the obvious train of thought. 'You're not trying to pin anything on that poor kid?'

'I'm not trying to pin anything on to anybody. But I'm frightened.' He drew deeply on his cigarette and flung the stump on the ground and stamped on it. 'Leaving aside all question of Sir Richard's death, somebody in this house has a lethal dose of strychnine in his possession, and somebody in this house is supposed to be not responsible for his actions. Supposing that boy is really mad! Supposing there has already been one murder!' He turned away towards the lodge and seemed about to resume his work on the footsteps in the sand. '*I* can't do anything about it,' he said. '*I* can't just shove the boy somewhere to keep him from doing some mischief. I must just work and work to find out what really did happen, and be able to present a case for having him put away.'

'*If* he's unhinged, but of course he may not be.'

'Just as you like,' said Cockrill, impatiently. 'If he isn't, then Lady March, Peta, Claire, Philip, or Philip's wife—one of those five—is a cruel and calculating murderer. You pays your money and you takes your choice.' He put his small brown hand suddenly on Stephen's shoulder. 'This is no time for sentimentality, Garde; there's hideous, horrible danger in the air.'

Up at the house, Claire and Peta came across Edward, poking about among the plants in the conservatory. 'What on earth are you doing, Teddy?'

'Looking for the poison,' said Edward. He added, 'I thought, perhaps, I—if I took it, I might have hidden it somewhere here. It seems a good place.'

'If you . . . Oh, Edward *dar*ling,' said Claire, almost running to him, putting her arm about his shoulders, 'of course you didn't take it, of course you haven't got the beastly stuff. Don't get such dreadful ideas into your head.'

He looked at her rather pathetically. 'I may have taken it, and if I have and then I suddenly go and have another fugue or something—I might do something terrible with it. I might go and poison one of *you*.'

Tears filled Peta's eyes. 'Oh, sweetie, *don't*! And don't be frightened and worried, darling. I'll tell you what, just in case you have got it, we'll all be most frightfully careful, we'll all take special care that you don't go and poison us.' She tried to make light of it, to make a little joke of it, while yet reassuring his mind, but the truth was horrible and his awareness of the truth.

'Cockie's men have looked in here, anyway; if the stuff's hidden anywhere, they'll find it, don't you worry!' She glanced through the glassed wall to where Stephen was talking to Cockrill, down by the lodge. 'There's Stephen; let's all go down and talk to him and get in Cockie's way!'

Cockrill was fitting shoes into the footprints and laying them aside. Philip's and Claire's tallied with the marks leading up to the window on the left hand side of the path. 'Anyway those two alibi each other,' said Stephen, standing by, watching him.

'There's such a thing as collusion. However, I don't really suspect it in this case. Ellen March,' said Cockrill, abruptly, 'was the last to see Sir Richard alive.'

'Except Brough, of course,' said Stephen.

Cockrill had had very little time on the case as yet, and all of it amply occupied. He had not really got as far as that, but he said quickly, 'Except Brough, of course,' and called the gardener over again. 'When you were doing these paths just before nine, last night, could you see Sir Richard at his desk?'

'No, I couldn't,' said Brough, glancing at Stephen and pushing his cap slightly further back on his head, presumably by way of salute.

'He wasn't at his desk?'

'I don't know whether he was or not,' said Brough, for some reason rather aggressive. 'The curtain was drawn across the winder.'

'The curtain? The curtain of the french window was drawn?'

'Yes, it was. It was drawn across when I come out to do the paths at twenty to nine.'

'I see. Very well.' Peta and Claire, with Edward, came down from the house, and he called them over. 'Claire, good, just the person I was wanting.' He dismissed Brough. 'Now, Claire, I want you to put on these slippers—these things you were wearing last night, I understand? Now, try walking up the path here, in your own footsteps, will you?'

Claire walked delicately up the path, balancing with some difficulty, placing her feet in the first four or five prints in the sand. At each step, however, the marks of her shoes failed to coincide exactly with those made before. 'Try tip-toeing,' said Cockrill.

Claire's slippers were wedge-heeled; solid between toe and heel. It was virtually impossible to tip-toe in them, and certainly to do so steadily, keeping the toe marks within the marks made previously. 'So that's that, Cockie, isn't it?' said Peta, standing looking on.

'Yes,' said Cockrill. 'And since Claire's feet seem to be by far the smallest in the family, her footprints can't cover anybody else's, even in the event of her having wanted them to.'

'I don't see what Cockie's trying to prove,' said Edward, who appeared to have developed the notion that Cockrill could not suspect him of lunacy or murder, if in the detective's presence he invariably spoke sulkily, in a low mumble, and without much intelligence.

'He thinks I could have made the prints last night,' said Claire. 'When I left you all to go and do the baby, and then walked in them again this morning when I went up to the window. But even if I could,' she said to Cockrill, 'even if I could have covered the prints this morning, by walking very slowly and carefully up the path, which I admit I did because I was carrying the tray, and looking where I was going—I could hardly have covered the coming-back ones, because I actually ran back down the path after I saw Grandfather, as you could tell if you were a Red Indian and used to tracking.'

'I can tell without being a Red Indian and used to tracking, thank you, Miss,' said Cockrill.

It was very inconsiderate of Claire to have such little feet, that was all, because it meant that she, and only she, had been up that path, and not till this morning when her prints had been made. And the other paths were innocent of footmarks, and in any event, the doors to the lodge were closed. And nobody could possibly have pushed a way through the roses—that was more than obvious. Just by brushing her hand against them, Peta herself had brought down a shower of petals, the night before.

What it all boiled down to, thought Peta, miserably working it out, was this: that at a quarter to seven, Grandfather had been seen alive by Stephen's clerk; that after the sanding of the paths at a quarter to nine, nobody could have gone near him; that if indeed he had been murdered, he had been murdered within those two hours. At about ten past seven, she, Peta, and Bella had been with him, and after that Ellen had seen him; and then—then Edward had had that evil twenty minutes alone away from them all. Cockie was looking at Edward with that beady, bright eye of his, and Stephen was hateful and stern and thought only of what one ought to do to comply with his stupid old law, and nothing of protecting people whom he was supposed to love, or doing anything for a—a person who had *thought* she loved him. And everything was beastly and horrible, and what was most horrible of all was that Grandfather was dead—was lying, all crooked up in a sitting position, intolerably grotesque, in some cold, friendless mortuary; there to be forcibly straightened out that he might the more conveniently be slit down the middle to find out whether his nearest and dearest had murdered him. Grandfather was dead, who had been so splendid in his benevolent autocracy; and all his family could think about was who had killed him and why and by what means. The world had gone mad about them, there was no longer any room for ordinary grief and tenderness, remorse and regret. Grandfather dead, was forgotten in Sir Richard March, murdered. It was an arid and terrible thing to have no room left for sorrow.

Bella was up at the house wretchedly struggling with all the pitiful aftermath of death: the letters, the telegrams, the 'phone calls, the notice in *The Times*—how did one announce the death of a man whom the police suspected of having been murdered?—the polite insistence of the authorities in the matter of the post-mortem, the inquest, the possible postponement of tentative funeral arrangements. Tearful and helpless, she found, unexpectedly, a rock of strength in Ellen, whose brusque intolerance of sentimental muddle and delay cut like a scythe through her fluttering indecisions. 'Well, just put "died at his residence", Belle. After all, it's true, it's what's happened, he *has* died, and this *is* his residence; at least houses are always called residences when people die in them. Date? No, you can't possibly give a date because the police say that the funeral may be held up; well, but what's the *use*, Belle? You'll only have to cancel it later. Dinner? Yes, of course the old hag must get us some dinner; we hardly had any lunch, and people must eat, my dear. It's just one of those things. Well, all right, darling, *you* may not feel like food but . . . No, they're *not* heartless, it's simply that . . . Oh, lord! that telephone again!'

Philip hung about moodily, trying to help, but mostly getting in the way. Claire, returning from the lodge with the others, suggested to him, as though carelessly: 'Why not come out into the garden for a bit, and give it a rest? We'll walk down by the river.'

Philip looked doubtful. 'What about you, Nell? Would you like to come out and get some sunshine and air?'

Ellen, however, was busily addressing envelopes in her great dashing hand, and hardly looked up. 'No *thank* you! To play gooseberry to my own husband would really be a bit too much.' And she thought with deep bitterness that it was just like Claire to come in, cool and beautiful, from the garden, looking all soulful, and sweep Philip away from the horridness and drudgery which she, Ellen, had rightly kept him to; thus deliberately drawing attention to her own crumpled hot yellow linen, and the hardness of her heart. In this she did an injustice to Claire who looked only inwards and reflected very little upon the effect of her dealings on other people. She pretended now not to have heard Ellen; but Philip, following her down the back terraces and along to the little copse by the river's edge, said nervily: 'I don't know why you wanted to go and suggest this. You've upset Ellen now.'

Claire stopped, looking stricken. 'Oh, no!—do you think I have? I—I'll go back, shall I? I'll go back and say she must come, I'll tell her that we really do want her. Which is perfectly true, I mean, Philip, because of course I'd like her to come, just for a walk . . . '

Philip caught at her arm and pulled her on. 'For heaven's sake, no, don't start another scene.'

If Claire could not have a scene with Ellen, she would have one here and now with Philip; she was in the state of nervous anxiety that cried for an outlet. 'You seem very tender of Ellen's feelings, all of a sudden.'

'Just because she laughs and doesn't make fusses, it needn't necessarily mean that she doesn't feel things.'

Claire looked reproachful, drooping her exquisite lower lip. 'That's not what you said when you—when we started all this. And it's a bit late now . . . '

'Yes,' said Philip. 'It's too late now.'

They had passed into the wood, out of sight of the house. She stopped and faced him, looking up at him. 'What do you mean by that, Philip—"too late now"? Are you regretting things already? Are you sorry that we fell in love?' Her beautiful mouth worked and twisted, and for the first time he knew, for a fleeting second, what Ellen meant when she said that Claire 'made faces'. But the moment passed.

'Claire, don't be unkind, darling, don't let's be unkind to each other, for God's sake, when everything else is so awful and horrible . . . '

The corn-coloured head came just up to his heart. 'Oh, Philip, my love!' At her voice, at the weight of her clinging and the suppliance of her hands, a flame ran through him; a flame of something worthier than mere physical longing, a passion of tenderness and protectiveness because she was so deeply vulnerable with her craving for love and compassion, because she was tender and satisfying in the love and compassion she gave.

'Oh, Claire—we're two wretched people not knowing what on God's earth to do about it all.'

'When all this is over, darling, all this nightmare about Grandfather's death, we shall be able to go away and be together.'

He was troubled. He put her away a little from him. 'We ought not really to be—like this—in the middle of all this tragedy and mystery and muddle. And suppose the will never turns up.'

'Then the old will stands, Philip, and we shall both get our bit of money and Ellen will be all right. In any case that silly old draft thing couldn't count. But I must say it's extra*ordi*nary,' said Claire, moving away from him altogether and staring out over the river, 'where the thing can have got to. Who can have any motive in hiding it?'

Philip looked round as though the very trees lent listening ears. He lowered his voice. 'Of course, if— if Edward—if he had anything to do with this, I mean it wouldn't matter how irrational it was.'

Claire was silent. She said at last, 'Do you really think it was Edward, Philip? Do you really think he's—well, funny in the head?'

'What other explanation is there, Claire? And what's so terrifying is that, if he did it, he's still got this bloody strychnine—I mean, it's terrifying, because he needn't have any more reason to use that, than he had to kill Grandfather, so one can't guard against it. I don't know—I'm wondering if I ought to do something about getting him—well, certified or something.'

'*Cert*ified? *Ed*ward?' cried Claire, horror stricken.

'Well, my dear, the situation's so frightful! One can't just let things go on like this.'

'But certify him—our Edward?'

'Actually, I don't suppose he is certifiable,' said Philip. 'Unless, of course, he did kill the old boy. Oh, God, I don't know. But at least he ought to be under some supervision.'

'But, Philip, you wouldn't hand him over to the police as a murderer?'

'No, of course not,' said Philip helplessly. 'And yet . . .'

'But if you had him—certified, or—or supervised or any of those things, why, it's a plain admission that he did it. Oh, you *can't*, Philip, *prom*ise me that you won't.'

'Poor kid,' said Philip. 'The Lord knows I don't want to do him any harm.' He looked about him uneasily. 'You must be terribly careful, Claire, that's all; we must all just be frightfully careful, and watch him; you girls mustn't be alone with him. It's just in *case*——' For how could one know that he was not there, near to them, even now; poor, crazy boy, lurking behind the trees in the sunny little wood, crouching ready with death in his hands for any stray victim that might pass, or urged on by some hideous compulsion against himself or Claire. 'You must be careful, promise me you'll be careful, darling. They—they get very strong, often, and rather sort of—cunning . . .'

On the front lawn Edward sat with his long legs spread out before him, earnestly making a daisy chain, with Brough's granddaughter, Rosy-Posy, squatted beside him giving bossy advice, and Antonia staggering erratically about the grass picking the pink and white heads off the flowers. Indoors, Bella, maddened by Ellen's refusal to dither and weep, fretfully disarranged the careful heap of envelopes. 'I must say, Ellen, I think it's very unwise to let Philip go off with Claire like that—especially after what Edward said at lunch yesterday.' (Had it really only been yesterday?)

Ellen, inwardly flinching, took the envelopes irritably out of her hands. 'A fine mess you'd be in if I went off gooseberrying at this stage!' She added, half-mocking at her own lofty attitude, half-desperately sincere: 'Besides—I wouldn't condescend!'

Bella swerved over in defence of 'the family'. 'Claire is doing nothing underhand.'

'Oh, I'm saying nothing against darling Claire, Belle, don't worry! If the only way she can get a husband is to go off with mine, and if she *can* get him, well, they're both welcome to each other, that's all. Far be it from me to spoil love's not-so-young dream,' said Ellen airily, but she slapped the envelopes together and secured them with a very vicious snap of their rubber band. 'All I ask is that I and my child should eat.'

Bella looked at her curiously. She said slowly, 'It would certainly have been awkward for *you*, Ellen, if Richard had signed away Philip's legacy.'

Ellen raised her intelligent eyebrows. 'Good gracious, Belle, you've thought out a Theory, all by yourself!' But it made her angry and a little afraid. She paid back the implication and with good measure, glancing out of the window where Edward sat innocently, long legs stretched out before him, 'minding the baby' on the lawn. 'I wonder if we're wise to let Edward play with Antonia?'

Bella flamed scarlet. 'I don't know what you mean? What are you suggesting?'

'Only that with that thing of strychnine missing . . . And after all, Sir Richard *is* dead, *is*n't he?'

'Are you suggesting that Edward killed his grandfather?'

Ellen shrugged. 'I thought it was quite understood.'

'But he——You don't believe he——? Good God!' cried Bella pitifully, staring out to where the dark head was bent, intent upon the chain of daisies and buttercups, 'I'd rather you accused *me*, Ellen, of such a thing, than that—that poor harmless boy.'

Ellen rattled pens and pencils tidying up the desk. 'Well, perhaps it was you. That wouldn't surprise me either.' She added sweetly: 'After all, if Edward's mad, he must have got it from somewhere—and you're his grandmother!' and marched away down the front steps and scooped up her baby and carried it off upstairs; there to weep bitterly, lying face down on her bed, tears of self-pity and self-reproach, of anger, jealousy, and fear. Murder! The big white house sprawled lazily in the sunshine, blue skies burned cloudless down upon green lawns, the air was sweet with the scent of roses and mown grass; and through the white house and across the green grass Murder stalked in the sunshine. Up in her bedroom, Ellen wept into her pillow. Down in the woodland, Philip and Claire kissed and clung and could not keep the thought of a dead man's money from their minds. Up and down the gravelled drive Peta walked with her love and would not speak kindly to him because he had brought all this trouble upon them 'instead of just letting poor Grandfather be buried and not making any fuss'. On the marble terrace Bella sat listlessly, her pretty face swollen with tears of pity and loneliness and grief; and down on the lawn among the buttercups and daisies Edward grew weary of Rosy-Posy's artless prattle and suddenly wondered what it would be like to stick a hypodermic needle into her; and whether it was himself, the real Edward, just thinking it to frighten himself, or whether it was his other self who had put the thought into his head—and whether he was mad, whether he was dangerous, whether he was already once a murderer . . .

That night, over dinner, eyeing one another distrustfully, they kept up a brave pretence that it was all a mistake, that Grandfather had died a natural death, that there was some simple explanation about the missing strychnine which would soon explain itself. Next morning Inspector Cockrill brought the result of the post-mortem examination up to the house. An enormous overdose of coramine.

CHAPTER VIII

Bella prepared for the inquest next day in her favourite role of Grande Dame—a rather pathetic attempt to continue the part she supposed Serafita to have played in the social life of the locality. The family recognized it with groans of mortification the moment she appeared in the hall in the hat with the cock's feathers, an imposing affair of shiny black straw and a meaningless tangle of net. 'Darling, *not* your Marshall and Snelgrove!'

'It's black,' protested Bella.

'Yes, but Bella, it has the worst effect on you—it'll absolutely wreck your chances with the jury.'

Bella ignored them. The hat made her feel good, it buoyed up her self-respect, it put her before herself and the world as what she surely was—a handsome elderly lady in a secure position in the County, backed up by Sir Richard March's name and Sir Richard March's wealth and family and beautiful country home. She started off down the drive, planting her feet firmly in their rather horrid new black shoes, Peta and Claire protesting on either side of her, Philip and Ellen and Edward trailing behind. A press photographer ran backwards before them and she assumed an expression of dignified reproach, bending the cock's feather slightly forward in token of mourning. 'Noblesse obleege,' she said to Peta, who showed every sign of wishing to butt the photographer in his receding middle.

'I wish it wouldn't obleege you to wear that hat; no wonder he wants to photograph us.'

They marched wretchedly into the village hall, where a jury of seven was already wedged tightly into the makeshift jury-box, their heads and shoulders sticking out over the top like toy wooden soldiers not yet unpacked. Bella, in an undertone of fury, declared her intention to cease traffic from that day forth with Billock the grocer, Hoskins the butcher, and Matchstick, the man who sharpened the Swanswater knives. 'Not Matchstick!' implored Peta and Claire on either side of her. 'We shall never again get a knife-sharpener with such a heavenly name!' (To be sitting here at an inquest on Grandfather's body, stared at by all these people; suspected, perhaps, of murdering him!)

Billock in the jury-box stirred uneasily, seriously incommoding his all too contiguous neighbours. 'We shall lose the 'Ouse, you'll see! That Meakin and 'is police!' He glared angrily at the unfortunate sergeant held responsible for their presence in this position of trust. The public of Swansmere, jabbing its thumbs into the lumbar regions of its neighbours, shuffled slowly into a couple of inadequate benches at the back of the hall, several of the older women bobbing involuntarily at sight of the Hat. "Artnoon, m'Lady!'

'Good afternoon,' said Bella stonily, noblesse alone restraining her from throwing her parasol at them.

Little men in shiny blue or grey suits, busied themselves about the Coroner's desk, with pencils and pens. A photographer climbed upon a table, presumably to take some more shots at an original angle, of the Hat. 'The widow was imposing in black,' scribbled such youths as the popular press had been able to spare from the slightly more absorbing topic of the war— on second thoughts, however, 'imposing' seemed open to misunderstanding, and they scored it out and chewed at the tops of their already disgusting pens.

Mr. Bateman, the coroner, was a solicitor from Heronsford, and was somewhat new to the job. He looked like a sly hippopotamus, a squat, heavy man with a thick neck and narrow, cunning, pale blue eyes. His hands were small and pink and dreadfully well manicured; he polished incessantly at his little, shining nails. At his entry the Coroner's officer gave an incomprehensible shout, and they both sat down with a bump.

Cockrill had decided to let Mr. Bateman have his head. He felt that alone he was helpless against the united will of the family, trying—obviously—to protect Edward Treviss from the consequences of his innocent crime. He wondered if they realized for a moment what it was that they were doing; if they believed for a moment that this was really murder, if in their efforts to shield the boy, they were not really shielding themselves from the brutal recognition of the truth. Well, now he would have them up on the witness stand, in a public place, and see if the efforts of Mr. Bateman could wring anything out of them.

He had accordingly informed that gentleman that the
police had complete confidence in his discretion and
would not ask for any particular reticences or eva-
sions; if Mr. Bateman saw fit to lead the jury gently
to an open verdict, of course, that would suit very
well . . .

Mr. Bateman led Claire through the story of the
finding of the body. She gave it simply enough, but
it was obvious that she was intensely conscious of the
interest of the crowd. She walked back to her place,
tossing her head a little, and as Peta said, 'making
mouths'. 'She can't help it, she's just self-conscious,
that's all. She can't help showing off.' (Peta herself
showed off dreadfully, but her showing off took the
form of little breathlessnesses, hand-flutterings, and
gabblings which rather attracted than alienated sympathy). 'My dears, it's too awful,' said Claire, scraping
past them to her place. 'Everybody staring at you—
your mind goes an absolute blank . . . '

Philip having described the appearance of the body
and his first diagnosis, bore with equanimity, what
Peta would have called a Straight Talk, from Mr. Bateman on the subject of the medical bag, left open and
accessible in the drawing-room. 'It's all a question of
familiarity. You do things in your own house that you
wouldn't dream of doing outside. At home my bag's
kept on a chair just inside my surgery ready to be
snatched up at a moment's notice, on my way out. I
don't go about with it chained to me.'

'Surely you keep it locked?'

'The lock's bust,' said Philip briefly.

'There is such a thing as having the lock repaired.'

'There's such a thing as the war on and not being
able to get things done for weeks or months. I can't
spare my bag long enough—I can't do without it.'

'So you are content, Dr. March, to leave lethal doses
of deadly poison about the house, for anyone to pick
up and use as they will?'

Philip refused to be ruffled. 'Yesterday these were
healing drugs: something goes wrong and suddenly
they're deadly poisons. A car is a lethal weapon if you

knock somebody down with it and kill them, but you don't go into fifty fits if I leave my car outside the house and it's stolen.'

Argument with Dr. March appeared to be turning out an unprofitable investment. Mr. Bateman dismissed him and called Inspector Cockrill. Cockie had changed his fine white panama for a black bowler which, however, he had carried all the morning in his hand to the great sorrow of his colleagues who did not for a moment believe that it belonged to him. He placed it tenderly on the ledge of the witness-box, and automatically fished for tobacco, but controlled himself in time. He paid handsome tribute to the assistance offered to him in his investigations by the family and the fact that they had called him in from the first moment that suspicion had been aroused. Bella and the grandchildren looked down guiltily into their laps. Poor Cockie. If he only knew!

The lodge had been photographed, finger-printed, and closely examined for possible clues. 'The only things of interest were a glass on the desk bearing no finger-prints except those of Sir Richard, and containing a few diluted drops of coramine; the pen in Sir Richard's hand, which bore no prints but his own—he was clutching it when he died; and the extension telephone, up to the house, which also bore only Sir Richard's prints. I was able to confirm to a great extent the movements of the people who visited Sir Richard on the evening that he died. The pen was brought down to the house by Mrs. Ellen March; the last person known to have used the telephone was Miss Peta March; and the glass is said to have been standing on a high shelf in the kitchen. (Miss Peta March will be telling you about that in her evidence,)' suggested Cockie, insinuatingly. His mén had very thoroughly searched the house and grounds, but as yet had found no sign of the missing draft of the will, or of the stolen strychnine and syringe. It was his opinion that someone had it hidden, and was moving it about. The search continued. In his opinion the evidence of the footprints showed clearly that no one had been to the lodge after the paths had been sanded. Sir Richard had last been seen alive by Mr. Briggs, clerk to Mr. Stephen Garde, at a quarter to seven; that is to say, last seen by anyone outside the household, amended Cockie with somewhat heavy significance. The evidence of Brough, the gardener, had confirmed the visit of Mr. Briggs. Doubtless the jury would be hearing from them both.

But the jury could hardly wait to hear Miss Peta March on the subject of the glass from the high kitchen shelf. Packed tightly in their box, they turned like a hydra-headed monster to watch her fluttering progress to the stand. 'Well, yes, the glass was in the kitchen. I went in there to rinse my hands under the tap and I noticed it. I suppose it had got left over from the last time Grandfather slept at the lodge; there was nothing else in the kitchen, not even a towel to dry my hands on.'

'Why did you not wash your hands in the bathroom, where there was apparently soap and a towel?' asked Mr. Bateman, craftily, polishing away at his nails like mad.

It seemed so feeble to say one just couldn't think *why* one hadn't; one had drifted into the empty kitchen and turned on the tap and thought no more about it. 'My hands weren't dirty—only a little bit dusty. This is the sort of thing one does every day, only it isn't significant until something like this happens.' It was like Philip and the medical bag.

'And you didn't touch the glass?'

'No,' said Peta surprised. 'Why should I?'

'That will no doubt be for the jury to decide,' said Mr. Bateman, very grand. He examined the little pink nails. 'There was no towel or cloth in the kitchen?'

'No, nothing,' said Peta. 'It was absolutely bare, no curtains or anything. I had to dry my hands on the seat of my pants—well, my bathing-dress pants, you know; which was horrid because they were still damp themselves, from the swimming bath.'

Mr. Billock, Mr. Hoskins, and Mr. Matchstick looked down their noses while their minds cuddled greedily about the vision of Peta in her bathing-dress. A fine, well-developed wench for all she looked so slim. Mr. Bateman had a dear little friend in a tobacconist's at Heronsford who was often what he called 'kind to him', so he was less susceptible to disturbance of this kind. Nevertheless he did pause for a moment or two before continuing. 'Could you if you had wanted to, Miss March, have—er—interfered with this glass?'

'Interfered with it?' said Peta, startled. 'How ever can one interfere with a glass? If you mean could I have taken it down from the shelf, yes, I suppose I could, though I'd probably have had to stand on my toes to reach up to it. It's a pretty high shelf. I suppose the glass had just been put up there, some time, out of the way.'

Back among the family, Ellen and Claire were united for a moment in a paroxysm of hysterical giggling because 'interfered' always made them think of newspaper accounts of girls who were found stabbed, strangled, mutilated, and naked, but not, the paper solemnly informed its readers, 'interfered with', and as Peta said, it did really sound peculiar when applied to a glass. Bella shushed them nervously and they gulped and were silent. Hostility descended again upon them, like a shroud. Up in the witness-box, Peta glanced over at them with a tiny, understanding gleam. 'Was there any chair or other piece of furniture which you might have stepped on to reach the glass?' asked Mr. Bateman, steadily pursuing his course.

'No, there wasn't, and perhaps it'll save us all time if I add that I couldn't have climbed up on the sink or anywhere, because the shelf is at the end of the kitchen, against a blank wall. Though why it should matter, as I've already told you I could reach it by standing on my toes,' said Peta, growing impatient, 'I can't imagine.' After all it was only oily old Bateman from Heronsford, and Billock, Hoskins, and Matchstick, and all that lot. She winked largely at Ellen, crossing with her on her way back to her place.

Ellen gave her evidence with her usual air of considering everything very silly and wishing people would get on with it. Mr. Bateman, however, starting on the nails of his left hand, brought her up short. 'On your way back to the house, Mrs. March, from the lodge that evening—did you happen to see a camera—Mr. Edward Treviss's camera, I believe—on the balustrade of the front terrace?'

Damn Cockie! By what tortuous route had he learned the significance of the camera, by what cunning mathematical calculation had he juggled with two and two and arrived at four? The servants, probably, the Turtle or Mrs. Brough, had mentioned the camera lying out there with its new film in the yellow carton; had noticed it again the next morning, with the little box empty, perhaps had even watched from an upper window Philip's experiments in timing, on the morning of the murder. Ellen's little hands trembled, linked before her on the edge of the box; she knew that in the body of the court room, 'the family' were trembling too; waiting with painful eagerness to hear what she would say. She tried to make her voice casual. 'A camera? Well, I don't know . . . Yes, I believe there was one there.'

'And a film with it? A film in a yellow carton?'

'I don't know. I don't think I noticed.' She caught the Coroner's ironical glance, his significant lifting of the eyebrow for the benefit of the jury. 'Oh, well, yes, a *film*,' said Ellen, as though she now realized what they had been talking about all this time.

The pink finger-tips turned over a sheaf of neat notes. 'Recall Miss Claire March.' To Claire, very much frightened and worried now, he asked in his soft, insinuating voice: 'When you went out on to the terrace, as we have heard, at twenty minutes to nine—was the camera there then?'

Claire played for time. 'I don't think I did go out on to the terrace.' But that was unwise, for anyone could tell him that the camera and the film were plainly enough visible through the great front door, and from the drawing-room windows too. She amended. 'However, yes, I did see it. It was on the balustrade.' Anything not to seem to be making a 'thing' about the camera, anything to pass it all off as a matter of course.

'And was the film in it then?'

Did Cockrill know that Edward had put the film in the camera during that twenty minutes when he had been alone, just before Brough did the paths? Would Cockrill discover that he had been alone? If one said that the film was not in its box beside the camera, it would appear that someone—and it was Edward's camera—had put it in. If one said that it had not been put in, then there would appear the more time for Edward to have gone down to the lodge. She could not make up her mind, in the brief moment allowed to her, what to say for the best. And so hesitated and was lost. 'I—I didn't *notice* it.'

'That may have been because it wasn't there,' said Mr. Bateman, and his voice implied that quite certainly the box had not been there.

Mrs. Featherstone was the next to be called. Everyone looked up astonished to see who Mrs. Featherstone could be, but were not long left in doubt, for the voice of the Turtle commenced as she left her place and made her way, with a series of strange little bobs and curtsies, to the witness-stand. 'Can't 'elp it, Mum, if they calls me to be witness before the fac',' protested Mrs. Featherstone, apparently quite overawed by Bella's hat. "Taint my fault, Mum, can't 'elp wot I sees and 'ears, Mum, and if anyone says I was listening at any doors, then that's a lie. I got to come in and tell that the dinner's ready, and I can't 'elp wot I 'ears while I goes to the door.' She mumbled on apologetically and was only frightened into silence by the presentation of the Book and the peremptory request that she would now take the oath and wait to tell anything she knew, till she was asked. The family sat back, half-anxious, half-relieved; what on earth could the silly old Turtle tell, now that the matter of the camera had been dealt with, that anybody could care about? And yet. . . . But as long as it did not bear against Edward, they did not care what she said. What *could* she tell?

What the Turtle could tell, at enormous length and with much graphic detail, was the history of Edward's behaviour throughout the day preceding the death of his grandfather.

The Coroner recalled Philip.

By the time Philip got to the witness-box he had made up his mind. Useless any longer to resist or deny. They must plug the matter of the camera reloaded, if it came to a showdown; meanwhile, he must do all in his power to establish the fact of Edward's sanity. If Edward were not unbalanced he had no motive for killing his grandfather; he of all people could be left out of the reckoning. 'I consider that my cousin is something of a neurotic,' said Philip, in substance, leaning on his crossed arms on the edge of the witness-box, now, quite comfortable and at home, talking to the Coroner as man to man, taking him into his confidence, an expert explaining to an expert this trifling matter of an hysterical display on the part of a normal, though perhaps rather over-sensitive boy. 'But to say that he is actually mentally unbalanced is quite absurd. It's true he staged a little scene in the drawing-room before lunch on the day of my grandfather's death. My small daughter had been attracting a good deal of the limelight, and I think he subconsciously resented this. He's been rather spoilt,' said Philip, inwardly recoiling at the thought of the reckoning with Bella, afterwards, 'and has come to desire always to be the centre of attention. My opinion is, and was at the time, that he happened to notice that the wreath over the picture was awry and that it reminded him of his supposed little disability; that he dropped the glasses on the floor and deliberately waited for us to come in and make a fuss of him. I don't believe he'd just dropped them when we got there; I believe he'd been waiting for us. He then contrived to faint, which is easy enough for a neuropath. I pulled him round immediately with a little stimulant and a good time was had by all, especially by him!' He decided that he might as well be hanged for a sheep as a lamb and added: 'And by his grandmama.'

'You think he could have brought on a genuine faint?'

'Good Lord, yes,' said Philip cheerfully. 'These hysterics can bring on unconsciousness with the greatest ease. But they can't bring on fugues; they can't bring on automatism. I don't believe my cousin was in an automatic trance that evening; and if he wasn't there's no reason to suppose he might be at any other time.'

'I see,' said Mr. Bateman. His faith in the guilt of mad Edward Treviss began to waver; but it was easy enough for a doctor to get up on the stand like this and hold forth on technical matters which none of them could refute. He chawed at the corner of a nail, and polished it dry again on a bulging trouser-leg. 'If we could have . . . If you could explain. . . . If we might have some non-technical evidence for your opinion, you know: if you could give us any reason for your belief that your cousin had not just dropped the tray when you went into the room. You were all standing talking in the hall, I understand; when you entered the room your cousin was moving forward as though he had just dropped the tray and, not knowing what he had done, was continuing with his normal procedure; in other words he was in a state of—of "fugue". If you could just give us some simple explanation of your conviction that he was really acting a part . . . ?'

Something that had niggled for days at the back of Philip's mind clicked into place. He said, 'Edward had not just dropped that tray! We were standing outside the door for at least five minutes, talking in the hall; there is a parquet floor in the drawing-room and we heard not a sound of half a dozen breaking glasses and a dropped silver tray!'

Mr. Billock was puzzled and a little bothered by all this talk of hysterics and automatics and such. They had always heard in the village that Edward Treviss was a bit of a queer one, and opinion had been unanimous that he had had one of them nasty turns and done his grandpa in; but now it seemed that all that was untrue, that it had all just been a bit of play-acting. Mr. Billock didn't like it. He preferred something a

bit more straightforward. If the chap was mad, he
killed his grandpa; if he wasn't, then you wanted to
look for someone else, someone with a proper motive,
a good sound motive for doing such a thing. Money,
now, that was a motive for killing, when one was sane;
and pretty near the only motive, Mr. Billock was in-
clined to think. Well, now, who of this here lot had a
money motive for the killing of Sir Richard March?
Why, that Dr. March, that old Brough was always
ramming down their throats at The Swan: refused to
have any more children, it seemed, and had a tiff with
the old man about it; a wicked, unnatural thing, re-
fusing to have a healthy family, thought Mr. Billock,
unwilling father of seven. So the doctor was
disinherited—and rightly too. But the trouble was
that Dr. March had simply not been near the lodge
on the night of his grandfather's death, and that was
flat; much as Billock would have liked it, he could not
perceive how Philip could possibly have murdered the
old man. He mumbled as much to Mr. Matchstick,
out of the side of his mouth. 'It was the furriner,'
decided Mr. Matchstick, immediately and rather unexpectedly mumbling back.

The furriner to Matchstick and Billock and Hoskins, meant simply the one who did not belong at
Swanswater; and that, loosely applied, could only mean
Ellen, who was not of the family. There was something
in what Matchstick said; aiding and abetting her husband in his sinful refusal to propagate the March
species, and sharing naturally in his disinheritance;
and, moreover, the Last to see Deceased Alive. Her
ladyship wouldn't be sorry to see the furriner accused,
thought Mr. Billock shrewdly; rather that, than her
crazy grandson, or any of Sir Richard's own. And her
ladyship, even in peace-time, spent more money at
Mr. Billock's grocery store than the rest of the village
put together. If they could only make it out to be the
doctor's wife. . . .

'Her and her bathing-dress,' mumbled Mr. Hoskins
from the other side of him. Mr. Hoskins was obviously
following a similar train of thought.

Mr. Billock had never seen Ellen's bathing-dress or he would probably have thrown her into prison without further delay, on a charge of indecent exposure. The mention of it gave him an idea, however, and a very tremendous idea it was. He struggled to release an arm, and having with the co-operation of his immediate neighbours unpinned it from his side, he raised it, numb with inaction, in the air. Mr. Bateman turned graciously towards him, 'Yes, Mr. Foreman?'

'The jury would like to put a question to Mrs. Ellen March,' said Billock, bashfully sheltering behind anonymity.

Mr. Bateman sighed, for it was getting on for tea-time, and with the elimination of Edward he had been gathering his forces about him for the open verdict prompted by Inspector Cockrill. 'Very well. Recall Mrs. March.' As Ellen bounced up to the box again, a little astonished, but curious, he nodded slightly to Billock. 'What do you want to ask?'

Billock leaned forward, his fat fists doubled on the ledge of the jury-box; you expected him at any moment to burst into a recital of his wares, strongly recommending you to try the tinned carrots of which, it was well known, he had a large and unsaleable stock. 'Excuse me, madam; I think you told us that you walked down to the lodge, that evening before Sir Richard died, in your—pardon me!—your bathing-dress?'

Ellen was quite ready to pardon anyone for merely mentioning her bathing-dress. 'Yes, I did.' She shrugged uncertainly, looking at the Coroner for guidance.

'Her ladyship and Miss Peta met you on the lawn,' said Billock, who had known Miss Peta as a long-legged little girl in a sun-bonnet and pigtails. 'They said it would have been impossible for you to be carrying anything in your hands without their seeing it; or to have had anything—pardon me!—anywhere about your person.'

'Well, if you mean I hadn't got any pockets in my bathing-dress, I certainly hadn't,' said Ellen, still more astonished. 'There's only about half an inch of it anyway. It's a sort of kestos-and-pants thing.'

Mr. Billock shuddered. He repudiated further interest in the shameless garment. 'You couldn't, for instance, have been carrying a—er—a hipper—a hyper'—he took a deep breath—'a hipperdromic syringe?'

Laughter welled up inside Ellen like the tiny bubbles of a soda-water syphon; she pressed her lips together to prevent it from fizzing out over the top. Down in the middle of the court-room the family seethed with giggles as nervous hysteria found a new outlet. The Coroner frowned dreadfully. He said, 'Mr. Foreman, I think we have been into this matter already.'

Mr. Billock held up a ponderous hand. 'This may not seem revalent to the matter, sir, but I think you'll soon see that revalent it is.' He swooped upon Ellen as though he had found her shop-lifting a bar of soap. 'Now, madam! A—er—a syringe you was not carrying; but something else you was—I think you won't deny *that*.'

'I was carrying Grandfather's fountain pen,' said Ellen, bewildered. 'That's all.'

Mr. Billock looked triumphantly round upon his brethren in the box; they stared back blankly, like a line of fat geese, each peering beyond his leader's outstretched neck. 'A fountain pen! One of them with a plunger, I wouldn't be surprised.'

'I haven't the slightest idea,' said Ellen impatiently. 'It was just a green fountain pen. Rather a thick one; it held a lot of ink.'

'Of ink!' said Mr. Billock, on a rising note.

'Well, yes. What else would it hold—tea or coffee or something?'

She had played right into his hands. Cockrill made frantic signals to the Coroner, but Mr. Billock swept all interruptions aside. 'No, Madam! Not tea or coffee, and not ink, neither!' He paused, savouring it, looking round proudly upon the court-room, and knew that his name would go down in the annals of Swansmere as long as The Swan flourished and a man could still get a pint of beer to toast him in. 'Not tea; and not coffee; and not ink neither. Coramine, Madam, that's what!' The ranks of the jury closed up like a concertina as he sat down heavily in his place again.

Mr. Bateman hushed the chattering court and, with Cockie's indignant eye upon him, proceeded to sum up. He thought that—er—that the jury would find difficulty in ascribing this murder to any person in particular; that it *had* been murder, however, seemed almost certain. Doubtless the verdict so often given in such cases—murder by a person or persons unknown—would recommend itself to the jury? The jury looked stonily ahead of itself. Mr. Bateman sighed. Very well. He folded his pink hands upon his heavy breast and settled down to talk them out of it.

Sir Richard had definitely died of an overdose of coramine. The post-mortem examination failed to show whether this had been administered orally or by injection. Almost anyone might have obtained possession of the coramine from Dr. March's bag. Sir Richard had last been seen alive (by anyone outside the household) at a quarter to seven in the evening—after a quarter to nine in the evening, it would have been impossible for anyone to have approached the lodge. He reviewed the evidence at appalling length. The seven good men and true twiddled fat thumbs.

Mr. Bateman took the suspects one by one. Mr. Edward Treviss had no sane reason for doing his grandfather harm, as far as any of them knew; and that he had not killed him in a fit of *in*sanity seemed (to Mr. Bateman) to be now obvious. Moreover, he had not been to the lodge before dinner, and though there was some conflict of evidence, or perhaps he would say un*cer*tainty in the evidence, about the camera and the time when a new film had been inserted, he thought the jury would agree with him that there was no reason to suspect the family's assertion that they had all been together during the after-dinner hours. All, that was, except Miss Claire March. Miss

March stood to lose materially if Sir Richard signed the new will, but she also had not been to the lodge before dinner, and by the time she left the family after dinner, the sanding had already commenced.

Dr. Philip March, similarly, had had no opportunity to visit the lodge before or after dinner. There remained Lady March, the widow; Miss Peta March and—er—he scurried over the name, Mrs. Ellen March. Lady March and Miss Peta had visited the lodge for half an hour before dinner; for that time they gave each other an alibi. It would appear impossible to have introduced any poison on to Sir Richard's food (which had been prepared by Mrs. Featherstone, who, he thought the jury would agree, seemed to have no interest whatsoever in Sir Richard's life or death) before it was uncovered on Sir Richard's desk, and he began his meal. From that time on, Miss Peta attested that Lady March had sat on a window-sill some six feet from the tray, talking to Sir Richard, and that, in the brief moment that she, Miss March, was out of the room, Lady March's voice had continued steadily and with no suggestion that she had moved even for a second, from her place. As for Miss March, she was similarly proved by Lady March to have had no possible opportunity of placing coramine on Sir Richard's food. There was a suggestion, which must be looked into, that she might have introduced the drug into the glass in the kitchen, knowing that Sir Richard would later take the glass down and drink from it, not noticing, as he filled it with water, that there was already a little fluid in it. Coramine, the Coroner thought he was right in saying, was a colourless liquid like water, and the dose would have been not more than a dessertspoonful. The glass was later found on Sir Richard's desk and with traces of coramine in it. However, it did seem a physical fact that Miss Peta could not have touched that glass. Her finger-prints were not upon it; and as it was placed so high that she could only have reached it by standing on her toes, it followed that she could not have poured anything into it, except by taking it

down. Mr. Bateman thought that if the jury gave this
matter their consideration they would see that this
very simple fact did indeed rule out the chance of her
having interfered with the glass. There was nothing
in the kitchen with which she might have wiped off
her finger-prints, and she could not even have polished the glass on her—er—bathing-dress, because
there was evidence that when she wiped her fingers
on it, it was still so damp that woolly bits came off on
to her hands. All these matters were subject to inves-
tigation, but he thought Inspector Cockrill would have
commented upon it, if any of them had been untrue.
Cockie, turning the bowler hat round and round in
nervous fingers, scowled hideously at this tribute. He
was there to gather information, not to supply it, and
this was not at all the way he had intended things to
go. Old Bateman was taking matters far too much
into his own hands, the overstuffed old hippopotamus, and the lord knew what was going to happen
now that Billock had hit upon that business of Ellen
March . . .

Mr. Bateman noted the scowl and shivered; for Inspector Cockrill had an acid tongue and laid about
him right lustily when upset, and his was a name in
North Kent to conjure with. However, the jury must
be headed off any verdict but an open one. The Coroner took a deep breath and came to Ellen.

He thought the jury would not be unduly swayed
by the fact that Mrs. March had been the last to see
deceased alive. If he understood it aright, said Mr.
Bateman, kindly making matters clear for those of the
jury who had not yet arrived at a conclusion, their
foreman had propounded a theory that the coramine
might have been carried down to the lodge in the
green fountain pen, and—Mr. Billock would correct
him if he overstated the case—used as a syringe to
inject the poison. Well, now, that was a very ingenious
notion, a very ingenious notion indeed, but he felt
sure the jury would ask themselves if in fact such a
thing would be possible; if it would be possible to
introduce the nib into the skin—by a sharp jab, per-

haps, he could not help elaborating, warming a little to the theory himself; and pressing the plunger which would—er—squirt the liquid possibly into a vein. It sounded very unlikely and silly when he put it into words, and he apologized for his own momentary enthusiasm, by repeating that he supposed that the jury would consider it unlikely in the extreme that such a thing could have been done. And yet, medically speaking, he supposed it was just possible. He dithered and havered, and Cockrill's brow grew steadily more black. Mr. Bateman noted it and became all at once perfectly convinced that the thing would have been impossible—im*poss*ible! He felt sure the jury would perfectly agree with him; and suddenly grew tired of the whole thing and closed his speech with a rather peremptory instruction that they should bring in a verdict of murder by person or persons unknown . . .

The jury, without retiring, brought in a verdict of murder, against Mrs. Ellen March.

CHAPTER IX

If Cockrill's bowler were really not his own, the owner was in for a shock. He stood twisting it ruthlessly between his nicotined fingers, facing the stricken family in the fast-emptying court room, the Coroner having apologetically scribbled out a warrant for Ellen's arrest and bound over the witnesses. 'She'll have to appear before the magistrate's court to-morrow or the next day,' said Cockrill. 'I'll arrange it as soon as I can. Meanwhile, I'm afraid . . . '

Ellen stood helplessly, staring at him. 'You're not going to take me to *prison*?'

'It isn't like prison exactly,' said Cockie gruffly,

looking down into the hat. 'Just the police station at Heronsford. You'll be quite comfortable. It won't be too bad.'

They all stood looking at Ellen, speechless, dumb-founded by the suddenness of the blow. Bella said at last: 'Inspector, can't you do something? Can't you stop this—this awful mistake? You can't really let her be taken away. She—it's all too horrible, it's impossible. I can't believe it's *hap*pening.' She ran to Ellen and put her arms round her neck. 'Ellen, my dear, my poor child, it's too dreadful, it's the most ghastly mistake!'

Ellen seemed hardly to hear. She looked over Bella's shoulder to Philip and for a moment all her brave jauntiness was gone.

Claire said into the silence, 'Oh, *God*, this is too awful!'

Peta went to Ellen, gently disengaging Bella's cling-ing arms. 'Don't worry Nell just now, Belle, darling. She'd rather be left alone.' To Ellen, she said: 'Don't think that we believe one word of this, not for a mo-ment: it's all just a stupid and fantastic mistake. But if they insist on taking you to this frightful place for a little while, look, darling, I'll cope with Antonia for you, I'll look after her every *min*ute of the day, I promise you she shall be all right . . . '

Ellen thought of those long, fluttering, incompetent hands doing their loving best for her baby; but she summoned all her courage to smile and say: 'Thank you, Peta, I know you will, and I'll try not to worry. Stick to her diet and don't—don't drop her in the bath, darling! She's so slippery, it's like trying to wash a poached egg.'

Philip had pulled himself together and was rushing between Cockrill and the departing Mr. Bateman, im-ploring them to see some sense, to realize the utter absurdity of this decision, to take his word for it as a doctor that such an injection could not possibly have been given, to *do* something, to *un*do something—well, for God's sake only to *say* something then. Mr. Bateman was frightened and being frightened became pompous and non-committal; he could do nothing to reverse the verdict of a jury, and he regretted that important affairs, urgent affairs, impelled him to hurry away. Cockrill merely stood staring at Ellen, twisting his hat. 'I'm sorry, Dr. March, there's nothing to be done about it. Except for—for being alone, she'll be all right.'

Except for being alone; shut up alone in a cage, put there by the stupidity of men, with the cold fear in her heart that all men might be as stupid, that a net was closing about her which all reason, all truth, all innocence could not destroy. Philip shivered. He started forward to go to her, as she stood pathetically a little apart, as though cut off from them already, by invisible bars; to go to her with comfort with promises that he would look after things, that all would be well; with reassurance, with love. She saw the movement. She glanced from him to Claire, standing by, watching his face, watching with agony the return, in pain, of his tenderness: and she lifted one eyebrow in her cynical way, and once more was the Ellen he had come to believe in—indomitable, self-sufficient, unresponsive, cool. Claire lowered her lovely head into her hands and wept; Philip turned away with a hurt and angry frown; and Ellen nodded cheerfully to Cockrill and the two policemen who waited behind her: and turned and went with them.

Claire slept in Ellen's room that night, with the baby, Philip having moved temporarily into hers. Peta had protested violently against this arrangement. 'I promised Ellen that I would look after Antonia, I promised her, I promised her. Bella, do tell Claire that I can have the baby to-night, do tell her not to butt in!' To Claire she said viciously that anyway it was jolly indecent, considering about her and Philip, and the last thing Ellen would have wanted. 'Philip, I think you ought to put a stop to this. You know Ellen wouldn't want Claire to be the one to sleep in her room with the baby, considering everything . . . '

Philip sat wearily at the dinner table, his head in his hands. 'Oh, do shut up, Peta; what does it matter who sleeps with the kid as long as it's someone responsible? Ellen wouldn't care two hoots.'

Bella could see that Claire was working up for a scene; it had been a terrible day and she felt she could bear no more. 'Peta, dear, let it be as we've arranged it. Claire's a very light sleeper, and you know, darling, that nothing will wake you once you've gone off.'

'I'd wake if the baby cried.'

'You wouldn't,' said Claire.

'I would.'

'The thing is, really,' said Edward, speaking in his slow, half-pitiful, half-humorous way, 'that Claire's room is nearer mine than yours, Peta, and Philip has to be near me in case I go barmy in the night and come and try and kill any of you. I mean, it's quite true what Philip said to the Coroner about me to-day, but we're not sure yet that I'm *always* acting. I may really be quite batty for all we know.'

Bella gave Peta a miserable half-nod. 'Well, all right,' said Peta ungraciously. To Stephen, as they stood together on the front terrace after his evening visit, she repeated: 'All the same, I think Ellen'll be furious when she comes back. Fortunately, I don't think that can be long, Stephen, do *you*?'

'Well, I can't promise that,' said Stephen. 'She's been committed on a coroner's warrant, you see.'

'Yes, but Stephen, surely you——? I mean, surely it's just a question of the magistrates or whoever it is next, saying that it's all too silly and letting her go.'

'Not quite,' said Stephen.

'But, good Lord, *you* think it's silly, don't you? *You* don't think anyone could give an injection with a fountain pen? Though I must admit that Philip says it could just *poss*ibly be possible.'

'And there was some ink on your grandfather's desk, Peta; the pen could have been brought down there with anything in it, and refilled with ink afterwards.'

'Yes, but——'

'You see, there's no witness to what Ellen did, is there? You had Bella there with you, but Ellen didn't. No, I don't say for a minute that she did kill your grandfather, but it isn't all so utterly fantastic as you want to think, and I'm looking ahead to what the magistrates may say—and beyond that. You see, it is true that Ellen *could* have got the glass down for your grandfather, from the shelf; she *could* have polished off her finger-marks in the sitting-room behind his back, or even gone into the bathroom and done it there; she could have polished the telephone for some reason—which would account for your finger-prints not being on it, though you were the last to use it. I don't say that Ellen did it, but I have to face the fact that she could have done it. She was admittedly the last to see Sir Richard alive.'

Peta looked at him, biting her lip. 'I just want not to believe it. I just want Ellen to be free!' She took his arm, walking down the broad, shallow front steps with him and along the curving drive, leaning her weight a little against him, confidingly, more nearly loving and friendly than she had been since that ugly moment when he had insisted upon sending for Cockrill—a hundred aeons of hell ago. The lodge lay before them, small and pretty and white in the gentle evening sun. And suddenly she stopped, clutching at his arm. 'She couldn't! Ellen couldn't have killed Grandfather! Someone was in the lodge after her; when Ellen left the lodge the curtain was pulled across the window—but when Claire saw it in the morning it had been pulled back! Who pulled that curtain back?'

Stephen looked at her, miserable at having to prick the bubble of her naive triumph. 'Well, I suppose your grandfather pulled it back.'

'But then he couldn't have been injected with coramine from the green fountain pen; because he pulled it back after Ellen left the lodge.'

'Nobody supposes for a moment that he was injected with poison from the pen,' said Stephen, 'except that old fool, Billock, I suppose, and his chums. But Ellen could have put the poison in the glass, Peta; she could have left the glass beside your grandfather— possibly he asked her to get it for him; we don't know. And after she left the lodge, hours afterwards, if you like, he may have drunk from the glass and died. Death from over-stimulation of the heart isn't a violent affair, it seems. He would have a little spasm or two perhaps, but it would be largely a matter of coma, gradually coming on. He might easily have just sat on at his desk, simply falling against it as he lost consciousness. He may have been all by himself when he died.'

'But *Ste*phen,' said Peta, 'that's right back where we started from. How could Ellen have put the poison in the glass? She went down to the lodge in her bathing-dress, she wasn't carrying anything except the pen, and we surely agree that it's impossible that she could have used the pen to inject the stuff. Well, that being so—how did she take down the poison?'

'Well, she may easily have *carried* it there in the pen,' said Stephen apologetically.

Claire, having won her point, tucked up the baby after its ten o'clock potting, and herself went to bed. At eleven a siren screamed and a flying-bomb droned its relentless flight between the balloon cables and made for London, there to disappear in a mushroom of mauvey-grey smoke licked through with flame—with flame and destruction and sorrow and pain and death. She put on her light and looked over at the baby, sleeping, tight-curled as a rose-bud in its cot; and settled down to rest again. Through the open windows the summer moonlight shone pale and glimmering into the room; and outside in the corridor a board creaked.

A board creaked. And was still. And creaked again. Someone was creeping stealthily past her door.

She sat bolt upright in her bed, holding her breath, listening. Only the soft breathing of the baby, only the terrible thudding of her own heart. But now on the painted woodwork of the door came a little fluttering sound, a little scratching sound of fingers moving there. They felt their way down the panel, softly moving in the darkness of the corridor, to the handle of the door. She knew that soon they must find the handle; that the handle would turn, the door would slowly open; and in a moment she saw the brass knob move and the almost imperceptible widening of the crack between the door and the jamb. Into her numbed brain came one thought: 'Edward!' And almost as the thought was born there was a tiny whisper: 'Claire!' And she knew it was his voice. It whispered again: 'Claire!' With a violent effort of will she fought down her terror and, fumbling for the bedside light, clicked on the switch. Edward stood in the doorway, blinking. He said, quite naturally: 'Hoi—mind the black-out!' and padded across and drew the curtains to. He padded back.

And suddenly it was only little Edward after all, standing blinking apologetically in the sudden lamplight, smiling at her, saying that he had a simply *brilliant* idea and he had to talk to *some*one but he'd listened at Peta's and Philip's doors and they were both snortling away like hell, and though he'd knocked and whispered, nothing woke those two up. He perched himself on the edge of her bed, curled in his gay silk dressing-gown. 'What I thought was this, Claire; you know about Peta's finger-prints?'

'Not being on the telephone, you mean?'

'Yes. Because that definitely means that the telephone must have been wiped. And surely to goodness it could only have been wiped by the murderer.'

'Stephen seems to have said to Peta this evening that Ellen could have wiped it, before she went away, leaving the stuff in the glass for Grandfather to drink later.' She added hastily, 'Not that *I* think Ellen's guilty; and I'm sure Stephen doesn't either. He only says she could have.'

'Well, *I* don't see how she could; what on earth excuse would she make to Grandfather. I don't believe Ellen wiped the telephone at all; and I don't believe she put the poison in the glass, and I don't believe she took it down to the lodge in that fantastic idea of the pen. I believe something quite different —something *mar*vellous!'

'I don't see what you're getting at,' said Claire.

'I'm getting at Brough,' said Edward, and kicked up his feet with triumph so that his scarlet slippers flew into the air.

There was a long silence while Claire thought it all out. She said at last, slowly, 'Of course, Brough never did like Grandfather. On the other hand, Teddy, you don't kill people just because you don't like them—not even if you're Brough.'

'Yes, but the will,' said Edward.

'Brough didn't lose or gain by the change of the will. Of course, there was the Serafita-brooch for Rosy-Posy; and he is fond of Rosy. In fact, I believe she's the only person in the world he really cares for.'

'Except Philip,' said Edward.

'Except Philip! My God, Edward—the will! Brough does care for Philip and he didn't care two hoots for Grandfather. If Grandfather was cutting Philip out of the will. . . .'

'I know,' said Edward, hugging the bed-post, grinning all over with delight. 'That's what I thought. That was my idea. I mean, it would be so lovely if it could have been Brough all the time, Claire, because it would show I wasn't a murderer and barmy after all. The only thing is, how could Brough have known about the will?'

'Oh, I don't know, but he could easily have found out. At any rate, he knew all about giving Grandfather injections of coramine, because Dr. Brown showed him and Mrs. Brough in case Grandfather was taken ill in the grounds; and when you passed out that day and Philip gave you the injection and afterwards showed us the syringe and the coramine, Brough was just outside on the terrace, doing the geraniums. I remember Philip saying "sorry", because he nearly squirted water on Brough.' She added: 'I daresay the Turtle was listening at the door afterwards at lunch, and heard Grandfather shouting at the top of his voice that he was going to disinherit us all; and she's sure to have told Mrs. Brough.'

But Edward was still nursing the heart of his great discovery. 'I think it's more likely that Grandfather told Brough himself!'

'Grandfather told Brough he was changing his will? Why on earth should he? And anyway, when?'

'When he called Brough in to witness the signature,' said Edward, and sat up expectantly regarding her with shining eyes.

The sirens wailed on and off all night, but nobody cared. They all got up and crowded into the kitchen and made cups of cocoa, rejoicing at Edward's discovery, and afterwards went back to bed, excited and relieved. Just before dawn another siren howled, and the All Clear did not go till half-past six. This time Philip got out of bed and dressed and went to the telephone. 'I say, I'm frightfully sorry to be so early, Inspector. I hope I didn't wake you up?'

'I'm up and dressed long ago,' said Cockie austerely, standing in his pyjamas still warm from his bed.

'Only my cousin has had the most brilliant idea during the night, he's absolutely discovered how the whole thing was done, and I was terribly anxious to let you know so that you could tell my wife and put her out of her misery. Of course, it wasn't her at *all*. It was Brough!'

'Oh, was it?' said Cockrill sourly.

'It's extraordinary how it's never been thought of yet. After all, one of the oddest things has been—where was the draft of the will? It'd been hidden or destroyed; but, as Edward says, why, if it hadn't been signed? So it must have been signed.—Are you there, Inspector? Are you listening?'

'Intently,' said Cockrill, holding the receiver against his hunched shoulder with his chin and groping in his pockets for the first cigarette of the morning.

'Well then, the thing was, if it had been signed, who witnessed it? No one in the house, because we were all involved; but Brough and his wife were just across the drive from the lodge, and just before eight o'clock Brough was rolling that path outside the lodge. So what do you think of this, Inspector? Grandfather

called him in and told him to fetch Mrs. Brough before she came up to the house for her work at eight
o'clock, and made them both witness his signature.
Because Brough thought it was wrong and unfair, and
because, for some idiotic reason, he happens to be
particularly devoted to me, we think that when she'd
gone he killed our Grandfather, drew back the curtain
and all that, and then backed away from the lodge,
scattering sand over his own footsteps as he went.' He
waited breathless to hear what Cockie had to say to
that.

Cockrill had contrived to roll and light the cigarette;
he took the first deep puff of the morning and suddenly was galvanized into action. 'Well, all right, all
right, all right, Dr. March. Now, look here—you get
your family up and dressed and I'll be along in twenty
minutes. I daresay Lady March will give me some
breakfast when you all have yours. Meanwhile I don't
want a word of this, not one word, to anyone outside
the house.' He had long ago taken the precaution of
putting one of his own men at that centre of rumour,
the telephone exchange. 'Above all, of course, not a
hint to that old servant woman, or the Broughs. Nobody is to leave the house, and above all, nobody is
to go near the lodges. Got that? Goodbye.'

Philip rattled wildly at the telephone hook. 'Here,
Inspector—Inspector, don't go! What about my wife?
Can you get a message to her? Can somebody let her
know? You won't leave her in suspense a minute longer
than you must? You will tell her right away, won't
you? Tell her it was Brough all the time . . . '

'I told her last night,' said Cockrill, and rang off
with a click.

Sergeant Troot came round for him in the police-
car. 'They've tumbled to it up at the house,' said Cockie,
settling himself next to the driving seat, holding the
white panama hat in his lap. 'I shall have to move
now. However, it doesn't matter, I was more or less
ready. As long as it didn't all come whooshing out at
the inquest, that was all I cared, and if only that fat
fool Bateman hadn't lost his head and let them bring

in that absurd verdict against poor Ellen March, all would have been well. It's rough luck on the girl, but I shall be able to get her out now, I think; once I've brought Brough in—and anyway, the Assizes are next week. I gave her a pretty broad hint last night that there was nothing to worry about, but I didn't dare tell the family in case they gave it away before I was ready for him.'

'I never did like that beggar Brough,' said Troot who, also, had often been driven from a favourite pub corner by the loquaciousness of Brough.

'This may not be a bad thing after all,' mused Inspector Cockrill, nursing the hat as they sped along the dusty country road. 'It might be just possible to force an admission out of him, if he thinks Ellen March is suffering for his crime. After all, she is Philip's wife, and that's where Brough's devotion appears to lie—not that I think for a moment there was much philanthropy behind all this. Anyway, I'll have a shot at it—let him see that his own chance is hopeless and then get him to own up to the whole thing and set the girl free. There's nothing like a nice, neat written confession to plonk before a jury!'

It was a nice, neat written confession; but it would never be plonked before a jury for it was written in dust. Brough lay beside it on the floor of the sitting-room in the little lodge, the room where Sir Richard, also, had died. His body had fallen from the dreadful, convulsive arch, but his face was cyanosed, his eyes wide-open and protuberant, his hands and feet like claws; and in his left arm the needle of a hypodermic syringe had broken off. On the dusty tiles of the little hall, close to his right hand, was written in printed characters: I KILLED SIR R. And underneath, like a signature, his initials, J.B.

The police seal had been carefully prised from the doorpost and the front door opened with Brough's own key—his bunch still hung in the lock. Inside the lodge, nothing appeared to have been disturbed. The windows were securely fastened from inside as was

the back door, with the outside police seals intact.
Brough lay across the doorway leading from the little
hall to the sitting-room—his footprints made a straight
line between the two doors, a distance of perhaps six
or seven feet. He wore pyjamas and a dressing-gown;
his heel-less slippers had apparently been kicked off
during his paroxysms and were tumbled at his feet.
One hand lay just through the doorway, on the tiled
floor of the hall; and near it were the printed letters,
firm, small characters, evidently made with a broken
matchstick which lay beside them: I KILLED SIR R.
and the initials, J.B. For the rest the dust was undisturbed as it had been on the day on which Sir Richard
had died, when Bella had bundled the vacuum cleaner
into the hall, out of the way. It still stood, propped in
its corner, just inside the door, and but for it, the hall
was entirely bare. At Brough's left hand was a phial
of crushed glass that had once held strychnine—he
had been dead since dawn.

CHAPTER X

Mrs. Brough stood gaunt and tearless beside the sofa
in her stuffy little parlour. Ugly lace curtains kept out
the brave morning sunshine, and everywhere were
fringes and bobbles and hideous china plates. From
beneath the merciful covering protruded a stiffened
hand. She took it and held it in her own warm live
one, and so holding it, faced her questioners.

'When did you last see Brough alive?'

'I haven't seen him since last night,' said Mrs. Brough
sullenly. 'He went off to bed same as usual. I don't
have him in my room no more; I've done with all that.
He usually got up and made hisself a cuppa tea and
went out to his work and came in again for his break-

fast at half-past seven or eight; he slept badly, and he liked to get the work done while it was cool. I'd be up and have breakfast ready for him when he come in. I didn't hear him go out this morning, but I often don't. I sleep 'eavy,' said Mrs. Brough, eyeing Inspector Cockrill as though about to add that he could put that in his pipe and smoke it.

Cockrill considered. 'He looks to me as if he'd been dead some time—an hour at least, perhaps two.' He stood watching her, his short legs apart, a cigarette, as always, pinched between thumb and forefinger; and suddenly changed his tack. 'Mrs. Brough—when I asked your husband for an account of his movements on the night of Sir Richard's death, he told me you had gone up to the house at eight o'clock; he said: "I came in from the——" and he hesitated a minute before he said "the garden". He had been going to say "from the lodge". Hadn't he?'

'I daresay,' said Mrs. Brough.

'Sir Richard called you in—*did*n't he? And you witnessed the new will before you went up to the house; you and Brough witnessed it. Brough told me about his supper that evening; he said that you had told him you "would get him an onion and some cheese to his bread", and that you hadn't time to make him tea— he'd better have a glass of beer. The reason your meal wasn't ready, Mrs. Brough, was that he had taken you over to the lodge to witness the will. Wasn't it?'

'He told me to say nothing,' said Mrs. Brough, glancing down at the covered body on the couch. 'But I suppose I'd better, now. Yes, the old man called us in and he showed us a couple of great long sheets of paper and he says, "I want you to watch me sign," he says, "and then put your names here." "I'm signing nothing I don't understand," said Brough—he was always a fly one, was Brough. "I'm changing my will," says Sir Richard, impatient. "That's all it is, it's nothing to do with you. I'm leaving all to her ladyship," he says, "and after her to Mister Edward. I'm leaving all away from my grandchildren," he says, and he starts in leading off something dreadful about them and their wicked ways, ungrateful and immoral and such. "Oh, get on with it," I thought, "I got to get up to me work at the 'ouse," and at last he's finished his rig-marole and signs his name and I signs mine, and Brough signs his as I've taught him to do, me being the one that had the schooling, for all he talked so grand; and then I went over to the lodge to get his supper. After about ten minutes or so he came in and a little after eight I went on up to the house. The old woman gets the dinner, but I helps with the clearing away and washing up.'

'Did Brough say anything to you about the will when he came over for his supper?'

'He said it was a shame to do the doctor out of his birthright. He was fond of Dr. Philip, along of what he had done for our Rosy, once. He thought the doc-tor ought to be master here, not a pack o' women, and he said he would've been, only for that Mr. Garde interfering. When Mr. Philip came home first, Sir Richard would've changed his will then, but Mr. Garde went round asking a lot of questions and in the end he persuaded the old man to leave the whole lot to Miss Peta—meaning to marry her himself some day, I suppose; these lawyers are that sly!'

'When did Brough tell you that Sir Richard was dead?'

'He told me next morning,' said Mrs. Brough. 'He came up from 'is fire-watching, so called—sitting up drinking with his pals at The Swan, more like—and told me he'd heard it straight from Mrs. Hoggin, her whose daughter runs the telephone exchange. I'd been out at the back of our lodge, and I hadn't heard the commotion over the way. "They've found the old man dead," he says. "Florrie Hoggin heard Mr. Garde ring-ing up for Inspector Cockrill. He said there was some poison missing; and that they couldn't find the will. This is our chance to do something with—something for the doctor," he said; meaning that now the doctor would keep his own,' elaborated Mrs. Brough; but she was walking warily among her words.

Cockrill considered for a long time, scattering the

spotless linoleum with a layer of cigarette ash. 'I see. And he didn't—didn't tell you before you went up to the house that evening, that Sir Richard was dead?'

'How could he? The old man was alive and kicking ten minutes before.'

'He's dead now,' said Cockrill; 'so perhaps we could have a little more respect in speaking of him. Now, Mrs. Brough—is there any reason why, between the time you left the lodge and went up to the house, and the time Brough went off to his fire-watch in the village, he shouldn't have slipped into the drawing-room at the big house while the family were safely at dinner, taken the coramine, and gone back and given it to Sir Richard, or placed it in the glass on the desk beside him; and then have left the lodge, covering up his footsteps with the sand as he went? Can you see any objection to that theory?'

'No,' said Mrs. Brough. 'I don't think there's any reason why he couldn't have done that—no reason at all.' She added calmly, 'And no reason why I shouldn't have been in on it with him.'

Cockrill lifted an eyebrow. 'Well, I don't know what you're trying to provoke me into, Mrs. Brough, but, of course, we both know that that would have been impossible. Mrs. Ellen March left Sir Richard at a quarter to eight, and you were up at the house a few minutes after eight. There wouldn't have been time for you to be called in, witness the will, obtain the poison and murder Sir Richard, let alone discussing the whole thing and working it out. As to whether you knew about it, that's different; but Brough had gone off to his fire-watching before you left the house. The Turt—er, Mrs. Featherstone, testifies that you and she were in the kitchen at the back of the house all that time.'

'*So* we were!' said Mrs. Brough, rather sneeringly, as though she were humouring an objectionable child.

Cockrill ignored the sneer. 'He could have managed it all sometime between eight, and twenty to nine; and hidden or destroyed the will, and concealed the strychnine and the hypodermic—in case of accidents.

He didn't think there'd be any accidents, but there was one. Mrs. March was accused of the murder that he had committed. He had thrown the blame on to just the person he had done it for. He couldn't save her without confessing to the murder; so he killed himself.'

Mrs. Brough ejected a sort of horrible, snorting laugh; she still held the dead hand in hers, and she gave it a rough little jerk, looking down at the covered body with a curling lip. 'Well, well, Brough,' she said sneeringly again. 'Fancy you!'

Bella, entering the narrow doorway, stood appalled; but she came forward immediately and, ignoring Cockrill, went up with a little gesture of pity and kindliness to Mrs. Brough. 'I came down to tell you. . . . We're all so sorry, Mrs. Brough. It's dreadful for you; if there's anything in the world any of us can do—though I don't know what there could be . . . '

'Thank you, m'lady,' said Mrs. Brough stonily. She lifted the cover of the couch and pushed the cold hand under it. 'Such sights are not for the like of you,' she said.

For answer Bella went up deliberately to the sofa and pulled back the rug and looked down pitifully on Brough's terrible dead face. The grey hair had become disarranged by the covering and she put out her hand and gently brushed it back. 'Poor Brough,' she said; and covered him up again. Cockrill, watching her from the hearthrug, could scarce forbear from giving a little cheer.

'It's very good of your ladyship, I'm sure,' said Mrs. Brough coldly.

Bella took her unresponsive hand. 'Oh, Mrs. Brough, I do feel for you, I do understand. After all, I've just lost my husband, too, and though perhaps it isn't as bad as this—well, it *is* dreadful, you know, to have to bear the loss and to know as well that the person you loved has been—murdered.'

'If you care so much—it's funny you don't seem to hold it against Brough and me,' said Mrs. Brough, but without humility.

'Well, this isn't quite the time or the place to hold it against you or him; I try to remember that whatever he did—however terrible it has been for me, and for all of us—at least when he found someone else was to be punished for it he—he prevented that.'

Mrs. Brough laughed again.

Bella had driven herself to come, meaning only to be kind. She said now, growing indignant: 'Considering everything, Mrs. Brough, I think you are—well, not very polite. All I have done is to tell you that I and my family are sorry that so much of this tragedy has fallen on you, the innocent one.'

'Innocent's right,' said Mrs. Brough. 'And well you know it.'

It was more than a gibe; it was an accusation. 'What do you mean?' said Cockrill quickly, coming forward, tossing his cigarette-butt in among the pleated crepe fans in the fireplace.

'I mean that she's right when she says I'm innocent; and she knows it well enough; and she knows he's innocent, too.' She jerked her head in the direction of the sofa. 'Her and her sympathy! Do you think I don't know that you're all rejoicing up at the house because your precious Mrs. March can come out of prison now? Much you care, the whole pack of you, as long as you can go free, that he lies dead, to pay for your sins for you. Let the servants suffer! Don't dream of punishing the rich or suspecting the rich, or saying a word that might hurt the precious feelings of the rich—not if you can find a servant to suffer in their place! You know as well as I do that he never killed Sir Richard! Brough! Brough kill a man to prevent an injustice! *Him* get himself into trouble to help somebody else! I can just see him! And then kill hisself to prevent another injustice.' She laughed again, the same short, ugly, mirthless laugh. 'He kept back the business of the will and that's all he did. *He* never killed the old man—not he!'

'But then—but Mrs. Brough, then who killed *him*? And why? Why should anyone kill poor old Brough?'

'Because poor old Brough could use his wits, my

lady! Oh, yes, he saw you sitting there all right: sitting in the window-sill with your back to the garden, talking to Sir Richard while he ate his dinner, while Miss Peta was in the kitchen. Brough was outside the lodge, rolling the paths. "They asked me if she moved," he said. "Well, she didn't move, and I told them so. It wasn't for me to put ideas into their heads—what do I care who killed the old beggar!" says Brough. "But didn't I see Dr. Philip squirt out the water from that there syringe, the afternoon before?—squirted it out across the terrace, and it went in a big curve a couple of yards across and landed up in a little pool right near where I was standing. And haven't I seen her, time after time," he says, "chucking lumps of sugar and bits of biscuit to that dog of hers? Is it the dog that's clever, sitting still with its mouth open? No, it isn't, of course. It's her. If she didn't aim straight—but she does; she's got a damn good eye, that's all," he says. "Sir Richard looks round for a minute, perhaps to call to Miss Peta in the kitchen," says Brough, "and her ladyship presses the plunger of that there syringe and the poison stuff squirts in a curve across the desk and lands on his plate of food!" That's what Brough knew, my lady, my fine lady!—and that's what you knew he'd tell if you let Dr. Philip's wife be accused of your dirty work. So you killed him, too. You and your "innocent"!' She bent over with a swift movement and stripped the cover right off Brough's misshapen corpse. 'There—look at him! *Look* at him! Look how he suffered, look at his poor face and his eyes sticking out of his head, look at his mouth and his hands . . . ' And suddenly she threw herself down on her knees beside the couch and burst into hysterical tears.

Bella stood, stricken, staring down at her. 'You don't really think . . . ? You can't believe . . . ? Inspector!' she cried, turning round upon Cockrill, holding out her hand to him, '*you* don't believe this, *you* don't think it's true, you don't, you *can't* . . . ?

'No,' said Cockrill. 'Nobody killed Brough but himself. He was lying in the sitting-room near the door leading into the hall; everything was locked and sealed from the inside and there was no possible way of getting there except across the hall. It's the old story of the sand again; the dust in the hall has not been crossed by anybody but Brough. Nobody could have followed him and killed him—they couldn't have got in and they couldn't have got away. He killed himself and he wrote a confession in the dust of the hall to say why he had done so. Nobody else could have written those words. Brough wrote them himself.'

Mrs. Brough knelt by her husband's body, with uplifted head, staying her tears to listen. When he had done, she got to her feet again, brushing away her tears with her big, bony knuckles, straightening her ugly black dress, pushing back her disordered hair; and facing them, upright and calm, she returned to her former hostility, cold and sneering, and blackly menacing.

'He wrote it himself,' said Cockrill steadily; steadily meeting her eyes.

'But he couldn't write,' said Mrs. Brough; and broke once more into her dreadful laughter.

The funeral was a terrible experience to them all. It seemed so incredible to be walking there behind Sir Richard's great, handsome coffin, in a tiny group of which, almost certainly now, one was a murderer; to be walking there slowly and solemnly, black-clad on this sunny day, beneath the avid stares of great crowds of unknown people sprung suddenly from nowhere to see a murdered man laid at last to rest; to be looked at askance by a huddle of relatives and 'friends of the family', anxious, curious, angry at all this publicity, and afraid; to be importuned by and photographed by The Press—impudent young men and brazen young women—and yet, young men and women who only had their job to do; to be crowded and jostled and pushed past; to have the lovely flowers all broken and bruised, the sheaves torn apart by the ugly hands of souvenir-hunters, the cards made dirty by numberless fingers, turning them over to read the brief sad messages of sorrow and farewell. They stood at the graveside, eyeing each other tearfully, grimly, distrustfully, trying to believe that one among them was wicked and cruel, a murderer for greed; trying to believe that after all it must have been Edward who was mad, poor child, and not responsible for what he did; trying to think only of the dear departed and not all the time so selfishly of the effects of his death upon themselves . . . But now there was Brough. Brough had been killed too. Murder and all its terrors were among them, and God knew where it was all going to end and when. You could not be truly sorry for an old man who was dead; you could only think of him resting and at peace from all this.

They went down to the churchyard again in the evening, when the sensation-seekers were dispersed; and at the trampled graveside, tidied and regrouped the scattered flowers and placed at their head a new wreath which Bella had brought. 'I've made so many,' she said. 'Richard had me taught when I first came to Swanswater.' It was a narrow circlet of Ophelias from the rose-beds round the lodge, such as she had hung many a time at his command above the portrait there, and in the great rooms up at the house. On a card she had written, 'From Serafita.' 'I didn't bring it before,' she said. 'I knew there might be people, and they wouldn't understand.'

Peta took her trembling hand. She voiced the thought in all their minds when she said, 'Darling Bella! With all her charms and all her marvels, Serafita would never have thought of a thing like that!'

Stephen had gone with them, to ward off possible intervention from the police—who, however, had no right to prevent them from going anywhere they would. They all walked slowly back to the house. 'Well, thank God the aunts and uncles and cousins and things have gone. Stephen, dear, you'll come in and have some supper?'

'Thank you, Lady March, if it isn't a strain on the rationing?'

'It's only cauliflower cheese anyway, and hardly any

cheese at that,' said Bella, the sorrowing widow swallowed up for a moment in the distracted housewife. 'The relations have eaten up everything I had in the house. I don't know if they imagine special ration cards are issued for what I believe one should call funeral baked meats, though there was no meat baked or otherwise, except my one precious tin of American sausage.'

'You managed jolly well, darling,' said Peta. 'The relations were terribly impressed, actually, I expect, and went away muttering among themselves what a wonderful woman you must be.'

'They went away muttering that I was not a lady and never would be,' said Bella, with shrewd irony. 'That aunt Ethel of yours with her lah-di-dah ways! And after all, it was very embarrassing not even being able to have the will read!'

'Well, honestly, Bella, it isn't your place to provide a will for your deceased husband's relatives, like the bridegroom doing the bouquets!'

'If *I* killed Grandfather,' said Edward, walking along at Bella's side, peering round her at the others, straggled out to her left, 'I suppose I know what's happened to the will; only I don't. Isn't it peculiar?'

'What do you think happens about the will now, Stephen?' said Peta.

'Well, I don't know. It's really frightfully difficult. We know a will was signed, but we've only got Mrs. Brough's word for it and she says she doesn't know what was in it. Of course, *I* know what was in it, because I made out the draft, but that's not to say he didn't make any alterations. Unless the new will turns up, the whole thing will have to be decided in court; if they take Mrs. Brough's evidence to be true, then I should think the first will would be cancelled and Sir Richard would be deemed to have died intestate.'

Claire looked alarmed. 'Good lord—does that mean the Government would get all the money?'

'Well, hardly,' said Stephen, laughing. 'If he was declared to have died intestate, there would be a life interest for the widow, that is, you, Lady March, and after her death, an equal division between the direct heirs, that's to say, Peta, Claire, Philip and Edward.'

'What about our mothers and fathers and things?'

'Well, actually you haven't got a father between you, have you?' said Stephen with a slight air of apology. 'I mean, Peta's parents are both—both dead . . . '

'You needn't put on a Voice, darling,' said Peta. 'They have been dead for twenty-four years, so I really am getting over it!'

'And mine, in that accident,' said Edward, kindly refraining from throwing a fugue at the bare memory of what he had not seen happen.

'And my mother abandoned me at the age of two to the tender mercies of Grandfather,' said Claire, trying to keep up Peta's genuinely serene acceptance of affairs, but failing dismally; for this was a bitter thorn in her memory. She added, 'I wonder if she'll turn up, all smiles, when I become a part-heiress!'

'She isn't entitled to anything by the will, of course,' said Stephen hurriedly. 'Nor is Philip's mother. It goes entirely by blood-relationship; so the children of Sir Richard's children are the only interested parties, in this case.'

'Well, I think that's the best thing that can happen,' said Peta, cheerfully. 'I don't want to be a beastly old heiress, but I *would* like us all to have some money eventually, and not have to be buried in paupers' graves; and meanwhile Bella would have Swanswater and the income from the capital, I suppose, so she would be frightfully rich and could be very kind to us and always giving us enormous cheques.'

'Grandfather said that he would put it in his new will that she wasn't to,' said Philip.

'Yes, but the new will has disappeared and the law will assume that he may have altered some of its terms, so I don't see why Bella shouldn't do some assuming too, and say that that was one of them—you will, Belle, won't you, pet?'

Bella was warm with assurances of assistance, though protesting that she should hate to have Swanswater and all that horrid money to manage; and on this more cheerful note they sat down to the cauliflower cheese. Philip had visited Ellen during the day at the police-station and she had sent buoyant messages to them all. It was quite fun, declared Ellen, *much* more to eat than at home and a heavenly sergeant sat with her throughout every meal and told her about his wife's operations which were sure to interest her, she being a doctor's wife! As long as Antonia was all right, they were not to worry about her, Ellen, at all.

Cockrill was moving heaven and earth to set her free. Of course, now that the second murder had been committed while she was tucked away in prison— thus, surely, freeing her of suspicion of having committed the first, some sort of arrangement must be arrived at, even if it was only bail. Stephen struggled manfully to explain the intricacies of English law. 'Once people are charged, they're charged; you can't just set them free because the local detective makes up his mind that they weren't guilty after all . . . Yes, but it's nothing to *do* with Cockrill . . . But the Coroner hasn't the *power* . . . Well, I know, but after all the fact of Brough's death doesn't necessarily mean, not necessarily, that he was killed by the same person as killed Sir Richard; not to remote people at King's Bench, anyway, and that's where application will have to be made.'

But that brought them back to Brough's death. 'Fancy all our fine conclusions going bonk like that! And Cockie's too, because, though he now says he suspected murder from the minute he saw how carefully the seal on the door had been prised off, as though Brough meant to stick it back afterwards, I'm sure he thought all along that it was suicide. And Bella,' said Peta, 'have you told Stephen about this fantastic accusation of Mrs. Brough's?'

'I'm not worrying about it any more,' said Bella firmly. 'Cockie's been trying experiments and he says it couldn't have been done.'

'Of course it could be done,' said Philip. 'I did it myself on the terrace that day, only I didn't happen to be aiming at anything.'

'Oh, Philip, *no*!' said Claire. 'It dripped water everywhere.'

'But the main lot did go in one little pool . . . '

And so once again ill-feeling and distrust were at work. 'Of course, Philip, if you think I did kill your poor Grandfather, if you think I killed my own husband, well, you'd better say so and be done with it! As long as Ellen comes out of gaol, I suppose you don't care who's accused!'

'Now, now, Mrs. Brough!' said Peta, teasing. Philip said, half-laughing, half-apologetic: 'I'm not accusing you, Bella, old girl—only if Ellen's out of it because she couldn't have killed Brough, and Claire and I are out of it because neither of us went near the lodge, and you're out of it because I'm not allowed to say you're not, well, that only leaves Peta and Edward.' He skated hastily over the question of Edward. 'I must say, Peta, *most* peculiar about your fingerprints, my dear!' Out on the terrace, over the coffee cups he produced a syringe which he had fetched from his room. 'We'll try it here and see whether Cockie's right or not!'

Peta was fed up and cross. 'I wish you'd stop going on and *on*, Philip, and let us think of something else for a change.'

'How can we possibly think of anything else, anyway? Look, there you are! At least half the syringeful concentrated in one spot.'

'Yes, but a whole trail of drips,' said Edward. 'It's only when it's at full squirt that it hits the same spot. While it's revving up, and while it's petering down, it drips across all the intervening space.'

'But a lot could still have gone on the plate of food; the drips wouldn't have shown on the carpet, and they'd have dried up overnight, especially with all that sun on the window.'

'Surely,' said Stephen, 'the post-mortem would have told them whether he'd taken the coramine with food or not?'

'No, it wouldn't. I'm sick of explaining that with coramine you couldn't tell whether it was injected or

taken orally; and how much more could you not tell
if it was taken with water or food or by itself.'

Claire saw that Bella was hurt and upset. She said:
'If this is tending to show that Bella could have killed
Grandfather, I *must* point out that she was the very
last person to want to do so. After all, the new will
gave her possession of Swanswater and all its wealth.
Why should she do anything to prevent him from
signing it?'

Philip ignored Bella's protestations that she didn't
want Swanswater, she didn't *want* all that money, if
she could just have a nice little house and garden like
she'd had in—well, yes, in Yarmouth in those old days.
He said, 'She might have killed Grandfather to prevent him from *un*signing the will!'

Stephen thought it over carefully. 'If Lady March
killed Sir Richard as soon as the new will was signed
—which was so much in her favour—then why did
she conceal the will? It's to her advantage that it should
be found.'

'I daresay it will be,' said Philip calmly. 'When the
hue and cry has died down and everybody has got it
firmly into their heads that Bella is the one person
who wouldn't have wanted to kill the old boy.'

Peta, sitting on a footstool on the dry terrace, shifted
her position so as to lean against Bella's knee. 'Don't
take any notice of him, angel; he's only doing it to
annoy because he knows it teases. Look, Philip, my
dear idiot—Grandfather signed the thing some time
after a quarter to eight. If Bella put poison on his
food at—well, it would have had to be at a little before
half-past seven—surely he'd have been dead before
he could call Brough and Mrs. Brough in?'

Philip was slightly taken aback. He said, however:
'Well, not necessarily. He could only have had about
half the dose if it was put on his food from the syringe,
because of losing the drips; and, besides, coramine is
a stimulant—he might even have benefited a bit at
first; then, after the Broughs left him, he fell into a
coma and died. And, as for Bella hiding the will,' said
Philip triumphantly, having only just thought of it,

'who says she did? That interfering old bustard Brough took a fancy to protect me from an injustice and made away with it. So poor Bella's work was all in vain.' He got up lazily and went over to Bella and said, taking her hand and giving it a little peck with that sort of careless grace which all the Marches could so readily assume: 'Darling Bella—I don't believe a word of it, not for a moment! I'm only being difficult.'

Bella, innately generous, responded as always to generosity. She gave his hand a little affectionate shake. 'I know you wouldn't really think I would do such a thing, Philip—and for money! Edward and I will have all we need anyhow; and as for Swanswater . . . !' She looked across the lovely lawns and to the river, and over her shoulder at the house, its essential beauty spoilt by its sprawling over-building, but touched to charm by the soft light of the evening. 'As for Swanswater—well, it's never been home to me, you know. I—I don't like it very much. It may have seemed a great thing to others that I should come here and be mistress here, that I should own a part in all this; but it hasn't been all honey, by any means. You children make a joke of my past, and I don't mind that, not from you—I know you only do it in affection. But other people haven't always been so friendly; and—well, then there was always Serafita!'

Peta sat stiffened into immobility at Bella's feet. All that was deep and delicate in her soul went out in compassion to this soul, seeking, perhaps for the only time, ever, to put into words a host of feelings too deep and fragile for adequate expression. As Bella was silent, she protested, gently: 'Serafita's been dead for ten years, darling—fifteen years!'

'No,' said Bella. 'She hasn't been dead. As long as Swanswater stands, Serafita won't die. That's what your Grandfather intended, and as it was in his life, so it will go on being now that he's gone. To you she's a sort of charming shadow—she smiles down at you from oils and water-colours all over the house; her little shoes and her coloured gloves and her roses and her fans and her programmes. She's a legend, a ghost, a—a fragrance to all of you and nothing more. But she's a reality to me. I was your grandfather's mistress, so you think of me as having been just a laughing creature, sweet and cosy in my little bijou house with the frilly curtains and the geraniums in pots at the windows; and that's how Richard thought of me, too. But even mistresses have hearts, poor dears; I don't think I ever was one to sell myself or my affection for money and possessions any more than I would have killed your grandfather for them. I was in love with him, even if I was only the Yarmouth Bella, as Serafita used to call me. Oh, she wasn't just an adorable ghost to *me*! There she was, always in his background, cool and secure and mocking, the wife; giving him his fine sons to be proud of, while I must hide my little girl away in shame, a child conceived and born unwanted, and always an irritation to him. Poor Bella—with her pathetic little aspirations to gentility, and her pathetic little aspirations to "intellectuality"—buying long books and reading them up, trying to educate myself to be good enough for Richard. Serafita's jokes, proudly repeated to me, soon cured me of all that! Once, you know, I was with him in London, and Serafita passed us in the street. She didn't make a scene or cut me dead, or anything like that—not she! I shall never forget the sweet, condescending smile she gave me and her little ironical bow. He was in ecstasies at her handling of the situation; and the worst of it was,' acknowledged Bella, ruefully smiling, 'that I couldn't help admiring it myself. When she died, then I married him, and I thought I should be happy beyond anything I had ever known; and so I was—but she was still in his background, more securely than ever. When she was alive, she used to weary him often, and annoy him, and he turned to me for tenderness and, well, he used to say for generosity; he said she was mean of emotion—I don't quite know what he meant, but that's what he used to say. But when she was dead, he forgot that; more and more the memory of her came to dominate his life—and my life.' She paused, as though afraid of saying too much; but, as they remained silent and sympathetic, she went on, bursting out now with old wounds and grievances. 'Swanswater became my home. I wasn't young any more, but I came to it as eagerly and tremblingly as a young girl, anxious to live up to it, to make it all that he would wish: and found that what he wished was that I should make it a memorial to Serafita. I left my little house with all its bits and bobs of nonsense and its lovely yellow-painted front door, where I'd been happy living my own life in my own way; and came to this great mansion as a servant to the memory of Serafita. There was no dusting to be done any more, no shopping, no little chores; here I was to sit back like a lady and my only task was to "do the flowers", to keep the vases filled—under Serafita's portraits! To study Serafita's recipes! To keep Serafita's feast days and festivals. To see that nothing was moved from the place where Serafita had—probably quite carelessly —arranged it.' She pointed suddenly down to the long beds of roses, hanging their heavy heads, a-swoon with their own scent after the heat of the day. 'Shall I tell you something?—I hate roses! My mother died about this time of year, and all the flowers at her funeral were roses. I was a little girl then, and I've hated them ever since. But Serafita liked roses, and so there were roses, roses, in every inch of the garden, under and over and round every picture of her in the house. For fifteen years now, it's been part of my— my stewardship—to fill with flowers I detested a home I was supposed to call mine!'

There was another silence. Philip said, smiling at her: 'Now that Grandfather's gone, darling, we'll have an orgy digging them up.'

'No, that's just it, Philip—we can't have any orgies where Swanswater's concerned. I owe everything I've ever had in my life to your grandfather, and he brought me here to keep Swanswater a mausoleum to Serafita—and so it must be. I couldn't not do it now, just because he isn't here any longer to keep me to it. He was leaving it to Peta and Peta could have kept it as he wanted it, of course, and done no harm to her feelings; but I can't. And yet, if it's mine, I shall have to.' She said, suddenly, viciously, tearing at her foolish little lace-edged handkerchief, '*I* kill for possession of this place! I hate every stone of it! And if I inherit it I'm chained to it for ever . . .'

Inspector Cockrill stood in the doorway of the house behind them, listening spell-bound while the passionate voice went on and on; and thought that if Bella had rehearsed this speech over—was it four days?—she could hardly have done it better.

Bella became immediately the considerate hostess; it was extraordinary to see the intensity die from her face leaving it merely round and pretty again, a face without fire or character, without more than a rather gentle, foolish charm. 'Oh, Inspector Cockrill, come and sit down. Would you like some coffee? I'm afraid this is rather cold, but one of the children will run in and get you some fresh.'

Cockrill was very weary. 'Do you know, Lady March, it *would* be rather nice. Is it a lot of trouble?'

'No, indeed, Inspector. Peta, darling, you'll go?'

'I'll come in with you,' said Claire, 'and we can go and pot the baby at the same time.'

Peta was offended by Claire's determined preoccupation with Ellen's baby, but mercifully forebore to start a wrangle. Edward, sitting on the balustrade, idly teasing Bobbin, said, 'Poor Nell—will she hear the nine o'clock news? Life will be insupportable to her if she doesn't.'

To Philip the idea was intolerable that Ellen should be locked up; even in comfort, even with the nine o'clock news, even with instalments of the surgical case-history of the police sergeant's wife. He said, turning away from it: 'How are you getting on with the case, Inspector? We saw you fussing about down at the lodge.'

'I was trying to see if one could get into the lodge from the front door, without leaving footprints,' said Cockrill briefly. 'And one couldn't.'

'Not by jumping?'

'Well, it's seven foot wide, and no take-off.'

'Bella, could you jump seven foot?' said Philip.

'Well, I could try, I suppose,' said Bella. 'And, of course, I'm suspect number thingummy. But the thing is this—I can just manage to picture myself doing it *out* of the lodge, after I'd killed Brough; but how surprised he'd have been to see me come leaping *in*, like a middle-aged kangaroo!'

'Let's all go down and try,' said Edward. 'It would be fun. I bet *I* could jump in from the front door to the sitting-room, Cockie! I bet *I* could!' His voice trailed off as he reflected that it might be better not to claim this particular accomplishment.

Cockrill was quite pleased with the suggestion. He liked to get his suspects talking; if they all discussed the case the murderer was obliged to join in or remain conspicuously silent—and sooner or later, among the innumerable intricacies of time and place, of lies told, of reservations made, of apparently careless suggestions deliberately put forward, was liable somewhere to take a false step. Despite his weariness, therefore, he agreed that it would be a good idea if, in the cool of the evening, they all went down to the lodge. 'I've just had the p.m. report on Brough,' he said, as they trailed down the drive. 'He definitely died of strychnine; nothing to show whether or not self-administered; the syringe was near his right hand. He'd been dead not more than two hours when I found him.'

He had that morning taken their evidence as to their movements during the early hours of the morning; but none of them could pretend to any alibi but that of their own beds which must, of necessity, be unsupported. Philip had been up suspiciously early, but declared that the All Clear had woken him, though he had slept through the Alerts. 'You all sleep like the dead,' said Claire. 'The wretched things went on and off all night.' Like many other light-sleepers, she could not prevent a slight suggestion of hoggishness in those more fortunate than herself.

There had been coming-and-going and finger-

printing and photographing and measuring down at
the lodge, but now the police had left it and only a
solitary constable stood sentry inside the big iron
Swanswater gates. Cockrill led the way up the path to
the french window, only a day or two before so jealously guarded, but now giving pride of place to the
dusty hall. It was horrible to see the smooth expanse
of the tiles with only the printed message—written
there by a murderer—by one of themselves! But they
did not, in their hearts, believe that—not really! They
subconsciously revolted against propositions put forward by the reasoning mind. There must be some
other answer, and that was all there was to it.

As soon as you looked again at the hall, you saw
that by no possible means could anyone have jumped
across it, into or out of the sitting-room. The hall was
seven feet across, the steps up to the front door prevented any take-off, and the inner door was set at
an angle. And as for leaping out . . . ! 'Among other
things,' said Cockrill, indicating the floor just within
the sitting-room door, with his toe, 'a body, heaving
in convulsions probably, was lying there. There's no
mat in the hall, and you'd have had to land on that
narrow step outside; there was nothing in the path to
suggest that anyone had scuffed it up, running up it
and taking-off; or tumbling on to it out of the door.
We've tried it; my men reproduced the conditions,
more or less, inside the french window, marking off
a square to represent the hall. You can have a shot if
you like, but you'll only prove the same thing.'

Philip and Edward had several shots; Peta also leaped,
long legs flying, landing two feet short of the objective.
'Quite right, Cockie, pet. It couldn't be done.'

'Yet here are Brough's footsteps walking inwards
across the hall, and that's all. How did the murderer
get in, and how did he get out?'

'I suppose somebody could have stepped in his footprints,' suggested Claire, tentatively.

'Not Edward or me,' said Philip. 'Our feet are just
as big.'

'Claire's only showing off because her own feet are smaller than ours,' said Peta.

'You ought to be jolly thankful they are,' said Claire, crossly. 'Otherwise Cockie might suggest that you'd walked in my footprints up to the french window and killed Grandfather.'

'How could I, you fool, considering that they were made just before you found him dead, when he'd already been killed hours ago?'

'Children, children!' said Bella.

'Well, Claire's such a show-box!'

'You're just jealous, that's all,' said Claire, trying to laugh it off; but, honestly, Peta behaved like a spoilt *child* sometimes, and just because *she* wanted to look after Antonia all the time. 'After all, if Philip hadn't met Ellen soon after he came home, and before he really had time to get to know me,' thought Claire, 'Antonia might have been mine.' The bitter grievance flowed like poison through her veins, bursting out in a hundred ugly little sores.

The rest of the party ignored a mere feminine outburst of cattery. 'I'll tell you what, Cockie,' said Edward: 'suppose the murderer never did come in! Suppose he just gave Brough a jab with the hypodermic and pushed him in, and these are Brough's footsteps staggering through the hall?'

'Then how did the murderer write the "confession" in the dust?' said Philip.

'Oh, well, that's a bit of a stinker, isn't it? Perhaps he—perhaps he had a long stick,' cried Edward, triumphantly, 'and wrote it terribly carefully, upside down! Leaning in from the front door, I mean!'

'Hardly,' said Cockrill. 'The letters were small and thin and neat, just as though they'd been made with a matchstick, which, in fact, I think they were. There was no jiggling about, no little marks that the stick would have made—it would have had to be at least eight feet long! Think how much control you'd have over a thin stick of that length. And don't forget that all this took place in the dark, or at least the semi-

dark. Oh, I know it was bright moonlight, and anyway
round about dawn; but there wouldn't be much light
in the hall. And they wouldn't dare to use a torch,
not with police about on the watch.'

'A lot of good your police did us, Cockie! What a
rotten outfit!'

'I had a man on, patrolling,' said Cockrill, mildly.
'But this is a big place, and we're very short of chaps,
with everyone away at the war. I'll pass on your com-
ments to the constable concerned, Peta; but I'm afraid
they'll be rather lost in the rush. I bet he hopes he'll
never be on a murder case again. And he needn't
worry—he won't!' he added grimly.

Peta's kind heart melted. 'Oh, Cockie, the poor *pet*,
don't be so fierce! Is it that nice one with the funny
nose? Poor lamb, he couldn't really help it, I don't
expect—not having a funny nose, I don't mean, but
not seeing Brough being murdered—I mean, if he
was at the back of the house, it would take him ages
to go round and he could easily miss what was going
on at the lodge. Do let him off, Cockie! Do tell him I
pled with you for him, and that for my sake you'll
forgive him!'

Claire was worn out. The drama of the morning's
discovery had been hideous to her, her grandfather's
funeral a terrible strain, and she knew all too well that
in his anxiety over Ellen's imprisonment, Philip's love
for his wife was returning; that her own hopes of
keeping him, were slipping away. She felt she could
not endure another minute of Peta being sentimental
and silly about the police constable, flapping her hands
and treating Cockie (and the attendant Stephen), to
a display of pretty blandishment, the sweet, the ten-
der-hearted, the considerate, the all-forgiving one.
She said irritably, 'Oh, Peta, don't put on the pot, not
at this stage, for heaven's sake; we've got enough to
bear! The man was here to guard us and he failed in
his duty. If Cockie thinks he should be punished,
surely that's good enough for us.'

Inspector Cockrill was a past-master at the art of
prodding into flame the damped-down fires of ner-

vous irritability, of fanning to a blaze the embers of
shock and restraint. He said, shrugging, 'You talk as
though I were a sort of nursery governess to the con-
stabulary of Heronsford. What do you want me to do,
Peta?—give him back his toffee apple?'

'Well, but the poor sweet . . . '

'Don't take any notice of her, Cockie! Who's showing off now, I should like to know?'

'What on earth's the matter with *you*, Claire? Can't
I just say I'm sorry for the poor man?'

'For God's sake,' thought Claire, 'why should I suddenly crack on this idiotic little point?' But she was
beyond control, and she leapt to her feet with a gesture of final exasperation. 'Oh, Peta, don't be so sickeningly affected!'

'Claire, Claire!' cried Bella, flapping.

The fire began to burn—everywhere the dry, frayed
sticks caught and kindled, as chafed nerves sought
comfort in speech, as muscles too long tautened, relaxed into gesture, as hands deliberately steadied,
trembled unregarded. '*Hon*estly, Claire . . . ' 'Well,
damn it all, Peta . . . !' 'Anyone would think . . ,' 'Why
don't you say straight *out* . . . ?' Cockrill darted to and
fro like an evil spirit, throwing fresh fuel to the flames.
'You don't suggest, Claire, that Peta isn't dis*tress*ed
about these murders?' 'But do you mean, Peta, that
you think Claire was con*cern*ed in your grandfather's
death?' 'But, Doctor, Claire has just said . . . ' 'But
Lady March, Peta insists . . . ' 'But Edward, my dear
boy, your cousins are accusing each *other*.'

'Just because of this idiotic business about my finger-
prints, Claire, you think you can say these terrible
things to me. I tell you, I don't know why my finger-
prints weren't on the telephone. I picked it up with
my bare hands, just in the ordinary way. Didn't I
Belle? *You* were there, Belle, *you* can say what I did.
Could I possibly have worn gloves or any nonsense
like that?'

'Peta dear, Claire hasn't suggested . . . '

'Yes, she has. Just because she couldn't have done
it herself, she thinks she can lightly accuse other peo-

ple of it. Well, if you ask me, Claire, you're the one
and only person in this family who *might* have done
it! I wouldn't believe it of Bella, or Edward, or Philip,
not if I'd seen them doing it with my own eyes—but
as for you . . . '

'For heaven's sake, you fool, do you think I would
kill Grandfather for the sake of three or four thousand miserable pounds?'

'Yes, I do, if you wanted it badly enough. You never
think of anyone but yourself.'

'Well, will you explain why I should want it at all?
I've got a job and I don't owe a penny in the world,
and strange though it may seem to your evil mind,
I'm not even being blackmailed!'

'You've got a job for the moment; but only because
all the decent journalists are in the forces. Good Lord,
after all these years in Fleet Street, you hadn't even
enough pull to get us a little peace and quiet in all
this filthy publicity! As soon as the men get home
from the war, you'll be out on your ear—and then
what?'

This was too shrewd a blow for Claire to essay to
contradict it; but the very truth stung her to further fury. 'Just because I don't choose to lower my
standards, to write vile grammar and snappy para-
graphs . . . And anyway, the same goes for you. Being
a V.A.D. now, doesn't mean you'll be able to earn a
living after the war, it counts for nothing, absolutely
nothing, in proper nursing—so what will *you* do if you
find you're cut out of Grandfather's will? God knows
you never earned a penny until you had to join the
Red Cross, to dodge the Services or munitions.'

'Of course, there's the likelihood of your both mar-
rying,' suggested Cockie sweetly, scattering powdered
dynamite.

Peta just lifted one eyebrow.

It was not prettily done, but both of them were far
beyond consideration of good manners or good feeling. In both, the deeply running blood of their grandmother welled up to the surface; that little hot-blooded

hybrid, whose much advertised poise and control had arisen always and only from indifference.

In vain Bella wept and interceded; Edward, rue-fully grinning, tried to inject placatory facetiae, Philip and Stephen sat white and ashamed, each on the arm of a chair in the little sitting-room.

'. . . and at least I'm not frittering my youth away hanging round the neck of a man who doesn't want me,' finished Claire, passionately at the end of a two-minute tirade.

'You—you insufferable little beast!'

'You sneering little show-off!'

'You murderess!'

'If either of us is a murderess, Peta, it's you, for the simple reason that it *can't* be me!'

'Oh, can't it?'

'No, it can't.'

The family burst into deprecatory beseeching. Cock-rill said: 'How do you suggest, my dear Peta, that Claire could have killed your grandfather?'

'I couldn't have—she can't!'

Peta stood looking about her wildly. 'You *could* have! You were the one who'd have liked to, and you did —you could have! I don't know how, but—my God, Cockie, I do see now, I can see now how she could have done it! Claire, you did, you did kill him, poor Grandfather! You little beast, you little murderess, you did, you killed him!' She burst into tears.

Claire faced her, white and shaking dreadfully. '*How* could I? You know perfectly well I never went near the lodge that night; you saw for yourself my one line of footsteps up to the window and my one line of footsteps running back, as I made them that morning.'

'As you made them the night before,' said Peta.

There was an utter silence. Claire spoke at last, and now her voice was much quieter, and only her hands hung twitching at her sides. 'What do you mean, Peta?'

'I mean that you made the footprints the night be-fore,' said Peta, stifling her tears, speaking almost in a whisper. 'Just after nine o'clock, after you'd seen to the baby. There'd have been time then; you were away for twenty minutes or more while we were all listening to the news out on the back terrace; the Turtle and Mrs. Brough would be safely in the kitchen, and Brough had gone off to his fire-watching. The paths had been sanded. You—you took the poisons out of Philip's bag—Stephen interrupted you when you were in the drawing-room doing it, and you were startled and knocked over the vase. It all fits together like a piece of machinery. You ran across the lawn and then walked carefully up the path to the window; of course, Grandfather let you in, and you told him some story and he let you give him an injection; you probably said that Philip thought he ought to have something to do his heart a little good, as he was staying alone down there; then you—yes, you got the glass from the kitchen, or if Grandfather had already got it, you only noticed it, but anyway, you put a drop of coramine in there to muddle things up; just like you to be so cool and uncaring, Claire—you never really loved poor old Grandfather! Perhaps you knocked against the telephone; anyway, you had to wipe it. And then, finally, you drew back the curtain. That's always been a mystery—who drew back that curtain, and why it was done. It was done for a jolly good reason—you wanted to see in, the next morning. You ran away down the path, leaving your footsteps going up the path and coming down again; it was you who carefully drew Philip's attention to them the next morning! You said they were the footprints you'd just made; but they weren't—you'd made them the night before. You stood on the drive, twenty feet away, and looked in at the window, to where Grandfather was sitting, dead. You never went near the lodge that morning, at all.'

Claire stood absolutely silent, not moving; and Peta threw herself into Bella's arms and burst again into a storm of tears.

CHAPTER XI

Ellen was released from her incarceration on the morning after the funeral. She took a tender farewell of her gaolers, adding with much laughter that she would probably soon be back, accepted her bail from the magistrates with an ironical smile and, a jaunty little ship with her paint unscratched and her flag still flying, was convoyed safely home. Bella chugged down from the terrace to meet her as, with her escort of battleship and two destroyers ('And me the dirty little dinghy with one small boy madly cheering,' said Edward), she sailed across the green lawns. The baby was wearing its best white smock in her honour, with a chain of forget-me-nots which Bella had made while she waited; and nothing could have been more satisfactory than the way in which, for the very first time, it actually did say 'Blut-blut-blut' which everybody perfectly recognized as meaning 'Mum-mum-mum.'

Bella had a tray of drinks ready and they all got mildly tight before lunch. 'It's the first time we've felt sort of relaxed and reasonable since Philip came up that morning and told us that Grandfather was dead. It's got worse since you've been away, Ellen,' said Peta, holding the gin bottle up to the light, and deciding that it would do just one more round. 'We've all been on edge and hateful and suspicious and cross. Last night Claire and I let our back hair down and had the most frightful slanging-match, didn't we, Claire?'

'Sheer Serafita,' agreed Claire, in Ellen's own phrase.

'*I* taunted Claire with her spinsterhood . . .'

'And *I* said Peta was throwing herself at Stephen's head . . .'

'Well, so she is,' said Ellen, laughing and holding out an apologetic hand to Peta.

'I know, but she needn't have gone and said it bonk out in front of Stephen; only, fortunately, it never entered his head that she meant him, and now I suppose he thinks I have a secret passion for some doctor at the hospital, only I haven't, because they're all married and about a hundred, anyway.'

'The being married part wouldn't occur to Claire as a deterrent,' said Ellen.

Edward crashed gaily in on the ugly little pause. 'And also, Nell, we had a great scene out here. Bella broke down and made a dramatic speech about how she really hated Swanswater . . . '

'Because of the hang-over from Serafita.'

'And we all got most terribly emotional and Peta wanted to come out at night and dig up all the roses just to show our devotion.'

Ellen looked mildly astonished at this original way of displaying devotion. She said: 'Well, of course, it's obvious that Bella, of all people, couldn't have had any motive for murdering Sir Richard. She lost nothing if the first will stood, and if the second will was signed it only gave her something she didn't want.'

'The question now remains,' said Philip, 'whether Bella didn't want Swanswater so much that she would commit murder to prevent herself from getting it.'

'We forgot to tell you, Ellen, that Brough had a theory about Bella having squirted the poison on to Grandfather's food from the window-sill . . . '

'And my dear Peta's worked it out most brilliantly that Claire could have made the footprints the night before . . . '

'And then it's most peculiar about Peta's fingerprints . . . '

'You seem to have been having a wonderful time while I've been away,' said Ellen dryly. 'Before the inquest the great idea was that nobody could have murdered Sir Richard; now nearly everybody could have; and you've added Brough to the——' She had

been going to say, 'to the bag', but, for once, considered Bella's feelings and trailed off into a mumble.

They broke into a flurry of repudiation. 'Whoever
could have killed Grandfather, *none* of us could have
killed Brough. Cockie can't make out how the murderer can have got in and out of the lodge. There
were simply acres of dust untrodden between him and
the door.'

And the old irritation was at work again. All very
well for Ellen to start dragging in Brough, when, after
all, this was something *she could*n't have done; all very
well for her to be so snooty about them all getting
horrid and accusing each other. After all, she had
been away from it; it might have been awful in prison,
but not more awful than having to go to poor Grandfather's funeral, being stared at and talked about, staring at each other and talking about each other, going
over and over this thing like a cageful of squirrels.
Who *was* Ellen, anyway? Not one of themselves—not
really, just an outsider, that was all—sitting there,
calmly receiving their welcoming attentions, taking it
all so much for granted, treating them like so many
eager children jumping through their little hoops for
her entertainment; mildly reproving them for quarrelling with each other while she had been away. 'She
makes me mad,' said Peta to Edward, punting up the
river that afternoon in the lazy sunshine, escaped for
a moment from it all. 'It's utterly irrational, Teddy,
but last night I felt as if nothing really mattered as
long as the beastly old magistrates let Ellen out of
prison to-day, because it was so awful for her; and
now she's out and—well, honestly, I begin to wish all
over again that it was her that had done the murders,
and then at least we, the real family, you and me and
Philip and Claire and Belle, could be clear of all this
horrible suspicion.'

A kingfisher held for a moment all the world's blue
in its darting flash through the branches at the river's
edge. The willows dipped green fingers into the running stream, shaking them with a scatter of brilliants

in the breeze to dry. On either side the quiet cows browsed in the flower-starred fields and behind them Swanswater lay, white and rambling, in its ordered pattern of dark oak and pale larch and burning copper beech. Edward forgot for a moment the ugly puzzle that obsessed their minds. 'When I hear the word "England", Peta—this is what I think of. Don't you?'

'Yes, only there ought to be cricket.'

'The boys who would be playing cricket are up there in bombers, I suppose, or under the sea in submarines, or just marching about on land—but all killing people.'

'And here we are in all this fuss and excitement and horror because one man is dead; two men, with Brough—but both old and at the end of their lives anyway.'

'It does seem strange,' said Edward. His young muscles rippled in his thin arms as he stretched with unconscious grace, hand over hand, up the punt pole. 'If only I could know for certain that I didn't do it, I could go to a real proper psychologist and get him to say that there was nothing wrong with me and—and go and be a pilot or something, Peta. Don't you think I could?'

'I should think you could, darling, if you were absolutely unphoney about it; only I think, if you don't mind my saying so, that you ought to go in for something not so spectacular as being a pilot, because that's always been a part of your sort of mixed-up neuroses and things. I mean you do dramatize yourself a bit.'

Edward immediately had a vision of himself splendidly sinking his identity in some humble job in the most appallingly dangerous part of the army; doggedly enduring the deadly monotony of carting high explosives from continually burning buildings. ('Corporal Edward Treviss—there can be no fuss, no public recognition, you understand? but the C.-in-C. has asked me to say a quiet word to you. We're proud of you in the regiment, my boy!') But after a moment he said, miserably, 'Well, anyway, Peta, what's the use?

Even if it's not proved that I did it, I shall always be afraid that I did.'

'Unless someone *else* is proved to have.'

'Well, but that would only mean one of us, and in a way it would be worse. In a way I'd rather believe it was me; at least I wouldn't have been cruel and wicked; I'd only have been barmy.'

'Oh, Edward, you are sweet,' said Peta.

They moored the punt and scrambled ashore at a tiny island where they had played and picnicked as children. 'I don't know whether I would rather it was me than Ellen,' corrected Edward thoughtfully, as they threw themselves down in the long cool grass and sucked through straws at the lemonade bottles with which Bella had provided them. 'I can't go as far as that. But you and Bella and Claire, of course, and—well, I *think* I'd rather it was me, dotty, than Philip sane.'

'I don't see how he could possibly have done it, so you needn't worry either way, but concentrate on us four.'

'After all, we haven't known Philip for very long, even if he is our cousin—only since he came back from America. I don't see why I should feel awful if *he* turned out wicked and horrible.'

'Nobody's asking you to, pet. Don't start a Thing about it.'

Edward made satisfying noises by blowing into the bottle. 'Do you like Philip, Peta?'

'Yes, I do, frightfully; I'm terribly fond of him. I didn't like him much when he first came home though.'

'I was only twelve or something.'

'Well, he was rather off-hand and peculiar. I suppose it was awkward for him,' admitted Peta, 'because, of course, Grandfather went all haywire in his usual fashion, and made a terrific fuss of him, and wanted to make over the house and estate and all that to him as being the only male heir and carrying on the name and so forth.'

'Good Lord, how grim for you!'

'Oh, I didn't mind much. How did you make that sort of moaning noise, Edward?'

Edward explained the mechanics of the moaning noise and for a little while the woodlands echoed dismally. 'I must say, I didn't think Grandpop would ever really disinherit me for Philip,' acknowledged Peta, afraid of having appeared to put on the pot by her claim to indifference as to the disposal of her fortune. 'But I daresay he raised poor Philip's hopes. After all, I mean, Philip's human.'

Edward sat up and began to throw small stones into the river, just for the sound of the lovely little plop! At the third throw he paused suddenly, arm uplifted, struck by an idea. 'I say, Peta—good Lord!—you don't think by any chance Philip *is*n't Philip?'

'What on earth do you mean?'

'Well—good heavens, Peta, this is terrific—suppose Philip is somebody else who knew Philip in America, well the real Philip I mean, and he died or something, and the other Philip, our one, pinched his diary and read up all about his childhood and us and Grandfather and everything, and came home and impersonated him. *You* know, intimate stories about this island that only you and he would know, and things like that. How long is it since Aunt Ann went to America?'

'They went when Philip was a little boy, about five or six or something.'

'Well, there you are; people change like anything between six and thirty-whatever-Philip-is. And he wouldn't have to pretend to remember very much; he could have been a very bad-memoried little boy!'

'And we were just *say*ing how odd Philip was when he first came home,' agreed Peta, slowly.

'I know. Of course, he was sort of feeling his way. I expect he worked on Grandfather like anything, really, to make him change his will from you to him, and only pretended to be thankful when he didn't.'

'Good *Lord*, Edward!'

'Yes, isn't it terrific? Come on, let's go back and tell them.'

'No, no don't be silly, we mustn't tell a soul; we must just watch like mad and try to prove it.' Nevertheless she got up with great despatch and scrambled back into the punt.

It was harder work going back upstream; with the exertion, Edward began to lose some of his effervescent confidence. 'Of course, I don't see exactly what difference it makes, really. Philip had no more reason to kill Grandfather if he was the real Philip, than if he was a pretence one.'

'Grandfather might suddenly have found him out!'

'Oh, gosh, so he might,' said Edward.

'On the other hand, it still remains impossible for Philip to have done the murder, whoever he is. He just was not near the lodge that evening before the paths were done, and the next morning he was dressing in his room when Claire came and said she'd found Grandfather dead.'

'Well, she said she *thought* he was dead.'

They stared at each other across the length of the punt. 'But he—he'd been dead all night,' said Peta. 'He was sitting at his desk. He'd been sitting there all night.'

'Unless he'd just got up and was sitting there waiting for his breakfast. Perhaps he was only—only keeping very still, and Claire thought there was something wrong, and there wasn't really.'

'Or perhaps he'd just had a little weeny heart attack.'

'And Philip rushed in and—and when Claire wasn't looking quickly gave him a terrific thing of coramine, so that he'd never come round. After all, if anyone had access to the stuff, it was Philip. And so carefully drawing our attention to it and all that, so as not to be the only one to be suspected! And, Peta, Philip knew all about the sand having been put down, because he'd walked to the gate with Stephen the night before.'

The punt pole, used most energetically to prod home Edward's excited reasonings, finally embedded itself deeply into the mud. He gave it a jerk, wobbled perilously, and only just regained his balance. Peta started forward in a purely impulsive attempt at rescue. 'But, Edward—Edward, look *out*, darling!—Edward, Philip can't have murdered Grandfather then. Grandfather had been dead for hours. I mean, Philip said so to Claire; he said, "He's been dead for hours . . ." '

'Yes, *Phili*p said so,' yelled Edward, just in time; and overbalanced completely and fell with a splash into the river.

And while, miserably, the family eased their tortured nerves in accusation and argument, wrangling unceasingly among themselves, siding now with one and now with another, irritable, dejected, over-excited, ashamed, Inspector Cockrill prowled, ever watchful, through the house and grounds. Now and again he put a sharp question; now and again he stood unblushingly outside a door to listen; now and again he appeared among a group of them, stirring up with a sort of mischievous joy those easily-ignited fires; but all through the day and half through the night, he harried his men in his ceaseless search for the will. 'It hasn't gone outside this place. Whole or in pieces, it's somewhere inside the walls of these grounds. Burnt? Well, it may have been burnt, but I doubt it. It's in human nature to hang on to the thing, just in case it might some day be necessary to produce it—as proof of this or that—don't ask me why. Signed or unsigned, I say that that will exists, and if you dig the whole place into allotments in the search for it, I don't care—it's got to be found.'

'Somebody's moving it about,' confided Sergeant Troot to the minions beneath his immediate command. 'That thing's not buried nowhere, nor yet hidden in any one place. Somebody's moving it about, if only he'd be got to see it.'

Mrs. Brough watched the search with a smile of tolerant contempt. 'They don't even know what they're looking for,' she said to Bella, who came across her standing in the grounds outside her lodge.

'They're looking for the will,' said Bella curtly, for she was now by no means enamoured of Mrs. Brough,

and only wondering how soon, under the circumstances, one might decently give her notice.

'The will—what will? There's two wills, m'lady, isn't
there? Never mind where the new will is—where's the
old one, that's what I want to know!'

'It's in Mr. Garde's office, of course,' said Bella,
suppressing a desire to add that what it could have to
do with Mrs. Brough she did not know.

'It's along of our Rosy's brooch,' said Mrs. Brough,
as though in reply.

'Well, I've no doubt the brooch is down in both wills.
In any event, Mrs. Brough, I should think you would
know me well enough after all these years, to be certain that Rosy would have her brooch if that's what
Sir Richard intended.'

'Yes, m'lady,' said Mrs. Brough submissively. She
added as though merely politely enquiring, 'If the new
will isn't found, m'lady, I suppose the old one stands.'

'It would probably have to be settled in court,' said
Bella, recollecting that on Mrs. Brough's word only,
would their future depend.

'I see,' said Mrs. Brough. After a moment, she asked:
'I take it you'll be there at Brough's inquest to-morrow, m'lady—you and the family?'

Belle was not familiar with the etiquette involved;
but since it was evidently expected of her, she said
with a sort of idiotic heartiness that of *course* they
would.

'Gabble and talk, gabble and talk,' said Mrs. Brough,
suddenly and viciously. 'I wonder who they'll find to
pin it on to this time. That Turtle, I wouldn't be surprised.'

'Serve her right for saying all that awful stuff about
Mr. Edward the other day,' said Bella, half smiling.
Edward's eccentricities could be no secret from such
old servants as the Broughs.

'Well, they can't pin nothing on Mr. Edward this
time,' said Mrs. Brough triumphantly, for though she
did not care two pins for daft Edward Treviss, it was
good to have any theory in opposition to 'them'. 'This

was a woman's murder, my lady, and they can't help but see that. No man killed Brough—no man would have thought of that trick.'

'What trick?' said Bella, surprised.

'The trick with the dust,' said Mrs. Brough.

Bella stood staring over at the opposite lodge; a little, pretty, dumpy woman in her 'good' grey summer mourning, beside the big gaunt woman in her uncompromising black. Had Mrs. Brough got another of her terrifying theories? She said nervously, 'Do you mean that you know about—about how they got away across the hall?'

'I daresay,' said Mrs. Brough. She folded her big hands in front of her waist. 'The police have been experimenting with carrying somebody in—I suppose they think Brough might have lifted the murderer in—which at least fits in with my idea of its being a woman.'

Bella had a wild vision of Brough, playfully carrying a mock bride across the threshold of the little house of death, his thin legs tottering under the weight of lanky Peta or muscular, plump Ellen, or even Claire who was slim and not very tall. 'I can't think of any earthly *reason* for such an action, Mrs. Brough.'

'No more can I,' said Mrs. Brough coolly. 'No, no, m'lady, Brough just walked in there alone, by hisself, of course he did. There was a sireen just before dawn, they say, though I didn't hear it; but I daresay it woke him up, and for some reason he got up and put on his dressing-gown and slippers and went over to the lodge; why I don't know, though maybe I could guess. He unstuck the police seal, meaning to put it back again so as not to show—he was clever with his fingers, was Brough—and in he went, not thinking how his footprints would show in the dusty hall. And in went the murderer after him. I can't say what happened there, my lady, nor what they said, but she killed Brough then and there with her dirty syringe—killed him in agony, poor old devil.' She turned her hard face aside, staring into the rhododendron bushes that bordered that part of the drive.

'It's dreadful for you, Mrs. Brough,' said Bella, once more daring to be kind.

'I don't set up to have been a loving wife,' said Mrs. Brough abruptly. 'He was a hard man to live with, was Brough—an ignorant know-all and bad-tempered and dishonest to boot; but I'd lived with him for thirty years and he was my husband; and I wouldn't let a dog die the way he died.'

Bella was silent. 'Well, she killed him,' said Mrs. Brough at last. 'And there were her footsteps clear across the hall, giving her away to all the world.'

'You keep saying "her".'

Mrs. Brough looked her full in the face. 'I told you I knew that this was a woman's job—too.'

Bella walked away from her without waiting to reply, up the sanded path now free of barriers, and in at the french window. Inspector Cockrill was in the sitting-room of the lodge, standing looking down as though he had been for a long time standing looking down, at the floor of the hall; seven square feet of dust, evenly laid and undisturbed, but for the three footprints and the neat row of letters. No other mark. He did not seem to resent her presence and she stood beside him first looking casually, then staring at the floor. And after a minute she said, 'But where is my squiggle?'

'Your squiggle?' said Cockrill.

'That day—the day Richard died—I came down here with him, Inspector. The hall hadn't been cleaned. I said to him that it wouldn't be used anyway, and I just shut the door on it. But before I did so, I—I put out my foot and made a little squirl in the dust and said something about how thick it was, after a whole year; or even more, because possibly the hall wasn't dusted *last* time either. Well—where's the little squirl?'

Cockrill clapped his hand to his mouth and stood gazing at her with wide open eyes, pinching the end of his nose between finger and thumb. 'Ye Gods! I believe you've got it!' He took his hand away and said—more clearly: 'That dust has been removed— and put back again!'

'*Non*sense, Cockie!' said Bella. 'How could it?'

'God knows,' he said. 'But that's what's happened. The floor's been polished free of dust and the dust put back again.'

'But why? Why put it back? Even if such a thing was possible? Why not just leave it polished and come away with no footprints showing?'

'Oh, well, that's easy,' said Cockrill. 'Because of the confession, of course. The murderer suddenly saw that the whole thing could be turned to advantage— stage a suicide to account for Brough being dead— forge a confession to account for Sir Richard being dead. If he could only make it clear that no one but Brough had been in the lodge, he freed himself and everybody else of suspicion and everything would be all right again.'

'Well, I'm glad you say "he",' said Bella, fresh from Mrs. Brough's rough handling.

Cockrill did not seem to hear her. 'He polished this floor free from dust—that would have been simple enough with this vacuum cleaner standing there so handily.'

'Vacuum cleaners don't like tiles,' said Bella, the housewife. 'They're for carpets.'

'Well, it would pick the dust up sufficiently. Here,' said Cockrill, taking the curtain-cleaning attachment, 'this would have sucked up most of it, if you just put the nozzle down near the floor. Then—but heaven knows how he did *that*—he covered it with an even layer of dust again; and in it he wrote the "confession" with the matchstick and threw the matchstick down. And then he took off Brough's slippers, which, if you remember, weren't on his feet, and walked backwards in them to the front door, and standing on the step, threw them across to lie by the body. All that was always obvious enough if you tumbled to the fact that it wasn't the original film of dust.'

Bella in her turn was not listening. A dusty floor, a vacuum cleaner with its bag half-full after the annual cleaning of the lodge. She moved forward suddenly and, unhitching the bag from its hook, shook out some of its contents on to the floor, uncoiled and connected the long tube used for sucking or blowing the dust from crevices, and adjusted the switch. The little pile of dust stirred and was gently blown about the floor; the letters and the footprints on the tiles were delicately filmed over, then more thickly coated, and finally completely covered with a thick coat of the dust. She straightened her back and stood looking down at it. A shadow came between her and the sunshine pouring in at the french window behind her; a voice said, 'I *thought* your ladyship would know how the trick was done.'

Stephen Garde was sitting on the steps leading down to the river when Peta and Edward got back. 'Hey— don't shake yourself all over me, Edward, there's a good dog!'

'Teddy, rush in and change, darling, Bella will have fifty thousand *fits* if she sees you so wet!'

'No, but we must tell Stephen, Peta! Well, all right; but look, if I go in and change you're not to say a word to him about what we've found out, till I come back.'

'All right, cross my heart, only hurry up!'

Edward loped off, shivering, into the house. 'What's all the mystery?' said Stephen, tying up the punt and sitting down beside Peta on the grassy bank.

'Well, it's awful, Stephen, actually. I mean, Edward and I have found out that Philip—well, we think we know who killed Grandfather, only I can't tell you till Edward comes back, so if you've guessed, don't say so. And, of course, I'm glad, really—at least I am if what we think about him is true and he isn't really Philip; but if he *is* Philip, then it's awful. Though, of course, if he is Philip, there's no need for him to have done it, is there?' said Peta, bewildered.

'No, my love,' said Stephen helplessly.

'Do you mean my love or my *love*, Stephen?'

'Just my love,' said Stephen.

'Oh,' said Peta. 'Well, anyway, I mustn't tell you, having promised Edward, but honestly Stephen you'll be absolutely staggered when you know what the answer is.'

'Oh, Peta, you are a little funny,' said Stephen, and picked up her hand and kissed the palm of it very lightly and folded her pretty fingers over the kiss.

Edward's head appeared at the bedroom window as he struggled, flapping like a scarecrow, into his shirt. 'Hoi, Peta, you're not telling him anything?'

'No, only do hurry up!' shouted Peta, her hand still curled on the kiss.

He vanished and reappeared at the window jiggling himself into his trousers. 'I say, Peta, I've just thought—I suppose the same thing couldn't have been done to the other one? The real one, I mean.'

'Good Lord,' said Peta to Stephen, clapping her fist to her mouth and regarding him over it with startled eyes. 'How *fright*ful! Do you think it could?'

'Not the slightest chance, I shouldn't think.'

Edward dashed out of the house, vigorously towelling his head as he ran, in great lolloping hops, over the lawn. 'She hasn't told you, Stephen, has she?'

'Not a word,' said Stephen gravely.

They poured out the story, one on each side of him, half-appalled, half-excited, only partly believing in it themselves. 'You mean that Philip killed your grandfather then and there under Claire's very eyes? But the police surgeon confirmed afterwards that Sir Richard had been dead for several hours.'

'Well, so he had by the time Dr. Newsome saw him; he didn't come till about one o'clock, and those things about how long people have been dead are frightfully vague really, it's only in detective stories that you can tell to the minute.'

'Yes, but there's a slight difference between eleven or twelve hours, and two or three hours.'

'On the other hand it was old Dr. Newsome, young Dr. Newsome's father, and he's frightfully ancient and probably quite past his job, and, Philip being a doctor, the old boy will have accepted all his evidence about the finding of Grandfather's body and everything and gone by what Philip told him—he's sure to.'

Stephen looked unconvinced. 'Anyway, Philip had really awfully little to gain by killing Sir Richard, you know. After all, he only stood to get five thousand pounds or so, and though, of course, that ain't hay,' said Stephen, who would never have five thousand pounds in the world, 'Philip had a flourishing practice; he didn't *need* the money.'

'He might have if he was going to hop off with Claire, which we've rather forgotten about in all this drama, but after all, he *was*! And anyway, we don't think it was for the money; we think Grandfather had found out that he wasn't really Philip.'

'Of course he's really Philip,' said Stephen, laughing.

'Well, *we* don't think he is.'

'Then I'd better be looking out for another job. Do you seriously think that, as your grandfather's solicitor, I'd let any odd stranger walk in and claim to be his long-lost grandson, without suggesting a few discreet enquiries—especially when Sir Richard was so keen on making him the heir! And anyway, look at the fellow—he's exactly *like* Sir Richard, only all on a less magnificent scale.'

'That's probably what first gave him the idea. So he murdered the real Philip.'

'Why are you so keen for it to be Philip, anyway?'

'Well, if it wasn't, then it has to be Teddy or me or Bella or Claire, and Teddy says he'd rather it was him just doing it when he was dotty, than one of us being so awful when we were sane. But he wouldn't rather it was him than Philip; especially as it would mean that Philip wasn't Philip, if you see what I mean.'

'To listen to the way you gaggle on, Peta, anyone would think it was you who was the dotty one,' said Stephen.

'She can be jolly glad she's not. After all, it's jolly grim not only knowing that you've killed your own grandfather, even though not exactly meaning to; but that, if I did, it means that I *am* slightly barmy after all, and I shan't be able to go into the Air Force or the Army or anything and—and kill other people,' finished Edward, with a gleam of irony.

'Though you'd imagine that Edward would be just the person they'd choose, when you come to think of it,' said Peta, interested.

Stephen considered, his hands linked under his knees, watching the river water gently swirling by. 'Edward—I've known you for ages now, ever since you were a small boy. I'm fifteen years older than you, enough to have been able to judge you fairly sensibly all along. I've never thought for a single moment that there was anything wrong with you that hadn't been put into your head by all this cackle of phoney psychiatrists and people; and I don't now.'

'Well, Stephen, that's all very well, but we don't know what sort of a state I can have got myself into, without there having been anything wrong to begin with. I mean, I can faint and make scenes and things, and I really don't know I'm doing it; and after all, the fact remains that after I had staged that thing about the glasses and the crooked wreath, the same thing did happen again next night. I don't remember doing it; but then I wouldn't anyway. If I did it and I've forgotten it, then perhaps I did the murder too and I've forgotten about that. If I didn't drop the vase— who did? You can say that the murderer did—but why? How could it help *him*, to do such a thing?'

'By throwing suspicion on you, Edward—just as it has done.'

Edward said nothing for a moment; he picked up a stone and threw it aimlessly into the river. 'Well, I —I don't like to think that. I mean, if—if one of the family killed poor old Grandfather, that's pretty ghastly; you don't honestly think that on top of that, any of them would deliberately try and put the blame on *me*?'

Bella, Claire, Peta, Philip, Ellen—you could not imagine any of them stooping so low. 'Though I suppose it's irrational to think of it as being worse than actual murder,' acknowledged Peta.

Philip strolled towards them across the lawn; he looked very charming in his white flannels, tied carelessly round his waist with a twisted coloured tie. 'Bella's clamouring about tea. It's on the front terrace.'

Peta put out her hand to be hauled up. 'Hallo, Philip, we've just been having the most terrific discussion about how you could have been the murderer.'

'Shut up, you fool,' said Edward.

'Well, of course, you might *not* have been; but anyway, Philip, if you're really not Philip March but an impostor from America, you may as well say so straight out, because we've realized it now and we shall soon go into it and make certain. Not that I really think you are, for a minute,' added Peta, bewildered by her own inconsistency.

Philip went off into roars of laughter. 'Well, what a mouldy lot! Sitting and tearing your poor cousin to shreds!'

'But you *were* rather peculiar when you first came, Philip, and then all that early business about Grandfather changing his will in your favour——'

Philip stopped laughing. 'Are you suggesting that I tried to influence him to change it?'

'Well, no, of course not, Philip, not exactly.'

'When I think of all the trouble I had to talk the old boy out of it! Damn it all, this *is* a bit too much! Of course I was awkward, crashing in on an unknown family and having Grandfather immediately wanting to make me his heir; what do you think I felt like, doing Peta out of her estate? Naturally, I didn't know him as well then as I did afterwards, and that he'd only change it back, or change it another way, in about five minutes. I do think this is a bit thick, Peta,' grumbled Philip, working up a grievance. 'It's you who's talked Edward into all this. I'm sick of being harried and heckled about who did this bloody murder; first it's Ellen, and then it's Claire, and now it seems it's to be me! The truth of the matter is that *you're* the only one who stood to lose anything substantial by it, and just because you're all gaga and girlish, nobody thinks of its being you. You could easily have left coramine in that glass in the kitchen, and if it weren't that your finger-prints weren't on it, that would be the obvious explanation; yet we know you touched the telephone and your prints aren't on that either.'

'Well, what do you suggest I did?' said Peta, taunting him. 'Wore a large pair of gloves, I suppose.'

'There *are* some gloves of Serafita's in the casket down at the lodge.'

'My dear, good Philip—a pair of long black gloves! What was Bella supposed to think when she saw them?'

'Bella isn't a chicken; her eyesight probably isn't marvellous; she may not have noticed.'

'Considering that Bella can throw sugar-lumps into Bobbin's mouth at a distance of several feet, I think she might notice at the same distance if I suddenly went black to the elbows!'

'Oh, lor', come on you two and don't argue,' said Edward. As they started across the lawn, he asked, leaning across Stephen to look at her: 'Have you hurt your hand, Peta? Why are you holding it all scrunched up?'

Peta went scarlet and immediately unclenched the hand. 'She's practising a bit of Yogi,' said Stephen, easily, ambling along beside her, his heart in song, because she was still so foolishly nursing his little kiss. 'She's trying to see if she can keep her fist closed till the nails grow right through to the other side.' He added regretfully, 'I see that you have returned to the ox's blood!'

'Yes, I kept on the colourless varnish till after the funeral in deference to Grandfather's "known wishes", but he can't be caring now, poor pet, so I may as well do as I like, and it keeps up my morale.'

'Colourless varnish!' said Philip.

'Philip, what a peculiar face, darling. You look quite dotty.'

'Colourless *var*nish!' cried Philip.

'Well, Edward, you'll have company in not being able to go into the Army or the R.A.F. Philip's gone completely off his head.'

'Oh, have I!' said Philip. He seized her wrist, bending her hand back to look at her nails. 'Look at them! *Look* at them! Hard, shiny enamel. Look at them, Edward, and you too, Stephen—if that was what she calls colourless varnish, you couldn't see it, could you? Just a plain, hard shininess it would be, just a film of pale, hard shininess over her nails. But that wasn't where it was on the evening that Grandfather died, Peta, was it? Why, good God, only five minutes before you went down to the lodge, you were sitting there on the terrace doing your nails, in front of all our eyes—doing your nails with colourless varnish! Putting a thin, hard coat of colourless varnish over your finger-tips!'

Claire sat on a fallen tree in the little wood down by the river, waiting for Philip. Through a gap in the branches above her head, the sun gleamed in a circular patch, very gay and comforting in the cool green shade of the evening. A squirrel scuttered down the bole of a tall tree and paused to look at her with his side-ways glance, sitting up alert and bright-eyed, clasping his little hands; and somewhere above the meadow across the river, a lark was singing out its heart with joy of life. Philip came through the trees to meet her, still in his white flannels tied round with the shabby tie. 'You look very woodland and romantic, Claire, all bosky undergrowth and the wee wild creatures grouped about your little feet!'

'Which you've frightened away with your own clumping great ones,' said Claire, as the squirrel scampered off up his tree again.

'Ellen's putting the baby to bed,' said Philip, sitting down beside her and beginning rather aimlessly to chuck bits of bark at an opposite tree. 'Antonia is still saying, "Blut-blut-blut," and I feel that the day will come when we shall find it in our hearts to wish that she had thought up some different phrase.'

Claire knew that a scene was coming; all that was honest and real in her rebelled at it; all that was over-romantic, over-dramatic, egotistical and 'exhibitionist' gloried in it. 'Why are you playing for time, Philip?'

Philip stopped throwing bark about. 'Claire—Ellen has just asked me once and for all, finally and for the rest of our lives, which it was to be: herself or you.'

It seemed as though the lark had stopped singing, as though even the wood and the river hushed for a moment their multitudinous whisperings to listen to the beating of her heart. At last she said, 'Well—what did you tell her, Philip? Is it Ellen or me?'

'It's Ellen,' said Philip.

There was silence again. She did not reply directly to him, but said, as though to herself, and with an infinite pathos, 'So I'm alone again!'

'She—she was bathing the baby,' said Philip blundering on with it. 'And I said that Peta had done it last night, and how fiercely she'd been fighting for her ascendancy in the matter of looking after Antonia, because of her promise. I—I was sort of making a joke of it, not thinking about you in relation to it all. But I suppose it made her think of you, and she suddenly stood up straight, right in the middle of a sentence, as if she couldn't bear it all a moment longer; and asked me if it was to be her or you. I've been terribly weak and—and wrong, Claire; you and Ellen have meant different things to me, and I wanted them both, and you've both suffered and it's been my fault. I suppose I'm a rotter, I suppose I'm just weak and mean. But anyway, when Ellen said that to me, I knew that she was the one. There's only one thing to do, Claire, and that is to tell you straight out. I know it doesn't do *you* any good if I—I loathe myself for all this, but I feel despicable . . . '

'What did Ellen say?' said Claire.

'She didn't say anything. She—she just stood there looking at me, pushing a little strand of hair off her forehead with the back of her hand; and then she bent over and went on bathing the baby.'

Out of the aching silence, Claire said: 'You don't often see Ellen with her hair untidy.'

'I—her sleeve was rolled up, Claire; and I stooped down beside her and kissed her bare arm; and came away.'

The lark's song screeched through her mind, the green of the woods seemed to close in about her, suffocating her; her very soul shuddered with the shuddering of her physical revulsion at the thought of his kiss on Ellen's round white arm. She said, loudly and crudely, deliberately wounding: 'At least you can spare me the recital of your amorous attentions to your wife.'

'That's just it,' said Philip, 'she *is* my wife.'

'Yes,' said Claire. 'I'm sorry.' The reality of her pain robbed her for a little while of all emotionalism and affectation. Her beautiful face, staring out over the river, was quiet and still. 'I'll tell you something, Philip; it's—it's an extraordinary thing to say, but perhaps, at least, it'll make you feel less bad about the whole thing. I think all this time it's been because I needed *some*body—not necessarily you. I wanted a man to love and to lean on and to be friends with and to—to share my troubles.' She gave a little half-laugh, and a little half-shrug. 'I wanted a husband in fact!' And suddenly, she interrupted herself, putting out a hand to clutch his arm. 'Who's that?'

It was Mrs. Brough, coming quietly down the little path towards them. She said with her ugly smile: 'I thought I might find you in the wood. You often come here, don't you?'

'Did you want something, Mrs. Brough?' said Claire.

'Not exactly,' said Mrs. Brough. 'I thought that I might just have a word with you.'

'What about?' said Philip curtly.

'Well, it was about the will, Doctor; the will we witnessed, you know; it was the one disinheriting you and Miss Claire here.'

'Well, yes, thank you, I think we know the general trend of it. What about it?'

She stood before them, a tall, gaunt woman in her black dress, like a blot against the gay green of the trees, with her big hands folded in front of her in an attitude of nicely blended mockery and respect. 'Brough felt for you about that will, Doctor, indeed he did. "I don't think it's fair," he said to me, coming away from the lodge with it in his pocket.'

'With the will in his pocket?'

'Sir Richard signed it while we stood there, Doctor, and he folded it up and put it in an envelope and he said to Brough, "Take this round to Mr. Garde's office

in the morning. Take it yourself, Brough. By hand.
You can do it on your way home from your fire-
watching, at nine o'clock".'

'Good God!' said Philip.

'So Brough took it along, Doctor, and I daresay
thought no more about it; but before he left the village
after his fire-watching, he got the news that Sir Richard had been found dead. Mrs. Hoggins on the exchange, and that daughter of hers—they spread
everything,' said Mrs. Brough, sniffing virtuously.

'Yes, yes, we know; they always have.'

'So then Brough thinks to himself, "How can I do
the Doctor a good turn? Why, now, who knows about
this here will the old man signed last night? Nobody
but him and the missis and me; and his mouth's shut,
and the old woman isn't one to open hers about what
doesn't concern her," meaning me, Miss Claire and
Doctor, you understand? So he kept the will in his
pocket and came home and said nothing about it,
meaning to wait for events.'

'Good Lord!' said Philip again.

'But it was absolutely illegal, Mrs. Brough,' protested Claire. 'He could have got into terrible trouble
for doing such a thing.'

'I don't see why Miss, really,' said Mrs. Brough com-
fortably. 'If things got awkward he had only to hide
it somewhere in the grounds, and pretend to dig it
up—him being the gardener—all innocent like. He
wasn't one to take risks for nothing, wasn't Brough.'

'Well, it was very—it was very kind of him to take
all this trouble for me,' said Philip uneasily. 'Especially
as I don't see how he could expect to gain anything
by it.'

There was a short silence. 'Well, as to that,' said
Mrs. Brough, sweetly, after a moment; 'as I've just
said, Brough wasn't one to take risks for nothing.'

Philip gave a long, low whistle. 'Oh, I *see*. That was
it, was it? As a matter of interest, Mrs. Brough—how
much was it going to be?'

'I think Brough reckoned, sir, that twenty per cent.

wasn't a great deal to a man who wanted a few thousand pounds as badly as you wanted them. You and
Miss Claire.'

'I don't know what you mean by that,' said Claire.
'Why include *me*?'

Mrs. Brough just lifted an eyebrow. 'Why, I told
you, Miss, that I knew you'd been here before.'

Philip got to his feet with an angry jerk. 'This is just
a try-on, Mrs. Brough. Miss Claire and I have often
walked here and often sat here and talked; we happen
to be cousins. There's nothing in the least wrong or
odd about it.'

'Well, that's not what Brough thought, Doctor,' said
Mrs. Brough calmly. 'And it was he that used to see
you here—him being head gardener and in charge
of all the grounds. As far back as last autumn, he's
seen you here when you've all been down for week-
ends. "Mrs. Philip wouldn't like it," he said to me,
referring to your wife, Doctor, of course. "But I shan't
say a word," he said. "On the other hand, they need
some money very badly these two young people and
I'm the man that can see that the Doctor isn't done
out of his lawful rights. I shall bide my time," said
Brough to me, "and then put a little proposition to
the Doctor. 'Two thousand, five hundred to me,' I
shall say, 'and you and Miss Claire gets twelve thousand between you.' Then I'll produce the will and
hand it over to him and he can tear it up or do what
he likes with it. I won't hold it over him," Brough said.
"I'll give it to him outright and he can destroy it and
after a while the old will will be taken to stand; you
and me, old woman," Brough said to me, "being the
only ones as knows t'other was signed." Blackmail, sir,
all the same, *was*n't it?' finished Mrs. Brough, piously
looking down her nose.

'Yes, it was,' said Philip furiously. 'And Brough would
jolly soon have known it, because I'd have taken him
and his will and the whole boiling and handed them
over to the police.'

'Ah, but then the trouble would have been that it

would all have come out about you and Miss Claire,' said Mrs. Brough, shaking her head as though that were something that did not quite bear thinking about.

It brought Philip up short. 'The devil!' said Claire, standing beside him trembling. 'He was going to blackmail you into buying the new will from him, for this outrageous sum of two thousand five hundred pounds!'

'Why, what would *you* think a proper sum, Miss?' asked Mrs. Brough smoothly. '*I* was thinking of asking two thousand. Would that be more reasonable?'

The lark sang, the leaves rustled in the gentle evening breeze, and the river drifted, whispering caressingly to its flowery banks; but in the woods the three faced each other and spoke not a word—a girl in a gay frock, a man in white flannels and a big, ugly woman in an ugly rough black dress. Philip said at last: 'Have you got the will here?'

'No,' said Mrs. Brough. 'I'm not a fool. But I know where it is.'

'Well, that's good enough,' said Philip. 'All right, Mrs. Brough; I've decided. I haven't got any choice, anyway. You'd better go ahead now—it wouldn't do for us to be seen coming out of the wood together; besides, I want to talk to Miss Claire. I'll see you again after dinner to-night.'

'Two thousand pounds,' said Mrs. Brough warily.

'Very well; two thousand pounds.'

She turned to go. 'And don't play any tricks, now; for I have a vivid imagination and Brough used to say that I had an ugly mind—and if you start any trouble now, why, the things I shall tell them I saw going on in this wood between you two—you'll hardly believe your ears! But other people will believe theirs all right. Poor old Brough—scum that he was, I wish he'd been alive to see this day.' She turned and walked away.

Down by the river the old landing-stage and boat-house had been reconstructed by Serafita, with much marble terracing, and yet another of her innumerable little summer-houses. Inspector Cockrill was sitting there with Stephen and the rest of the family, when Claire and Philip emerged from the wood. It was intensely hot and Bella had brought down a tray of glasses and an enormous jug of ersatz lemonade. Philip poured some out for himself and Claire. He appeared to have forgotten all about his recent accusation of Peta, and said to her, perching himself on the balustrade and swinging his white-flannelled legs: 'Peta—how much do you want Swanswater and a hundred thousand pounds?'

That afternoon Stephen had kissed her hand. He had done it lightly, half-teasing her, and yet. . . . If she were not an heiress, would Stephen be in love with her? She said, avoiding his eyes: 'Not very much.'

'Well, that's a good thing,' said Philip. 'Because you're not going to get it, my love.'

'What do you mean, Philip?'

'I mean that you're a pauper, my pretty one; and so is Claire and so am I. And Bella—like it or not—you are mistress of Swanswater!'

Cockrill jumped out of his cane chair, putting down his glass hastily on the little table. 'Do you mean that the will's been found? Do you know where it is?'

'No, but Mrs. Brough does,' said Philip calmly. 'She's just been talking to us down in the wood. She says that Claire and I have been carrying on something dreadful in the undergrowth and threatens that if I don't buy the will off her and destroy it, she'll tell Ellen of my goings on and wreck my married happiness for ever. Fortunately Ellen knows that, despite rumours to the contrary, she has my entire fidelity.' He looked across the terrace at her and said deliberately, and perhaps a little pleadingly: 'Don't you, Ellen?'

Ellen never would play up to that sort of thing. She said: 'Yes, *now* I do,' and appeared to think it necessary to explain to the assembled multitude. 'Claire and Philip seem to have decided that they have been suffering from a slight midsummer madness; and Philip and I have had a dramatic reconciliation over the baby's bath.' She was deeply happy, nevertheless.

Bella was staring open-mouthed at Philip. 'Do you mean to say that, after all, this place, this—this memorial museum, will belong to me?'

'Well, it looks that way, Bella, old girl; and surely the extra hundred thousand quid will go some way to consoling you for your gain? You needn't live here, after all; with all that money you can splash around like anything, and, as Peta and Claire and I will be homeless and penniless, we'll keep the place aired for you and the relics dusted, during your dashing absences in the south of France and Miami and places like that.'

'That isn't what Richard would have wanted,' said Bella sadly, but doggedly; and she glanced over her shoulder and up at the house and said: 'I'm a prisoner here for ever now,' and fell silent.

Peta lay back in her deck-chair, just a tiny bit white under her always lavish make-up. It is not every day that a young lady loses a fortune and likes it; and supposing that Stephen hated her after all! 'Cockie, pet, aren't you going to *rush* down to the lodge and brow-beat Mrs. Brough into telling you where the will's hidden?'

'Yes, perhaps I'd better,' said Cockrill. He went indoors in search of his men but, having given his orders, returned immediately to the terrace, where the family had now started on a new tack. Wouldn't it be *too* heavenly if it could turn out to have been Mrs. Brough all the time! Or Mrs. Brough in collusion with Brough could have murdered Grandfather, and then she could have murdered Brough. Couldn't it possibly have been that?

'No,' said Cockrill.

'But, Cockie, why *not*?'

'Mrs. Brough was up at the house at eight o'clock on the evening Sir Richard was killed; she had nothing to do with his murder—there wasn't time.'

'Well, she could have killed Brough, afterwards; there could be two murderers.'

'Why should she?' said Cockrill.

'Well, she hated him.'

'Not in that way; not in the murdering way. In any event, why not have waited until he'd collected the money off Philip which they thought he was going to get? Why not let him do the dirty work and get the blame if Philip wouldn't allow himself to be blackmailed? Brough was going to ask for more money, anyway.'

'But that means—it literally means, Cockie, that you think it was one of us?'

'Work it out for yourselves,' said Cockrill.

Bella was looking very pretty that evening; her hair was charmingly done in nonsensical curls on the top of her head, her grey frock was becoming, and two modest diamonds glittered in the lobes of her ears. Beside her, Peta was tall and lanky, but she lounged in her chair with her usual extraordinary grace, the wild rose in its hot-house setting, all aflutter with her elegant little absurdities. Claire sat in the background, very lovely, her face pale under the crown of her corn-coloured hair, but in its resignation, more serene than it had been for many months; next to her Ellen was dark and vivid, restless, intelligent, alert. Philip sat on the balustrade, his tall, cool glass beside him, and, in his white flannels, had much of his grandfather's grace and charm, though nothing of Sir Richard's rather unreasonable splendour; and on the steps running down to the river, Edward perched, his thin brown hands dangling between his knees. A good-looking— on the whole a very good-looking—family; pleasant, ordinary, English people in a more than usually pleasant, ordinary, English setting. Bella, Peta, Claire, Ellen, Philip, Edward. And one of them, reflected Cockrill, was a murderer. One of these six. He wished it were not true, but he knew it was. He had wasted a great deal of time in the past five days, trying to prove anything to the contrary.

Edward bounced a rubber ball down the steps, for Bobbin. 'Definitely one of us, Cockie?'

'Don't ask the Inspector things like that, darling,' said Peta. 'It isn't etiquette. But doesn't Bella's good lemonade choke you under the circumstances, Cockie?'

It was very hot; and yet, suddenly, there was a chill in the air—a chill of cold fear. It came to them, to each of them as they idled there, that this was no ordinary evening; that the shadow of terror had crept very close upon one of their company, that there was not much longer to go now before this horrible game of hide-and-seek was to come to an end. As though to give point to the unspoken thought a siren wailed and was taken up by a second and a third, until all the air was filled with their dismal cries. The sound shattered the icy silence; and as it died away Edward got slowly to his feet and faced them and Cockrill saw that the boy's face was white, that his hands were trembling, that there was a beading of sweat along the lines of his hair. He said, speaking slowly and wearily at first, but rising to a pitch of something very much like hysteria: 'Cockie, I'm—I'm sick of this, I can't stick any more of it. On and on and on, discussing and arguing and accusing—I'm —I'm sick of it, I can't bear it any more. Why don't you make up your mind and arrest me and take me away and—whatever it is they do? Surely you can see, surely we can all see plainly enough that it was me—it must have been me. They all know it was me; they've been trying to pretend to you that it wasn't, but they know it was. I don't remember it. I don't think, not really in my heart, that I did it; but—but I do do things that I don't remember, and there you are, the vase was found broken in the drawing-room where the wreath was hanging crooked; and I don't remember dropping the vase, so I suppose I don't remember what happened afterwards. I do do these things; I've done them before.' He swung round upon them all suddenly and his young face stared piteously at them, his thin young hands were half-held out in unconscious pleading. 'You won't. . . . They won't. . . . I won't be put in a loonie-bin, will I? I couldn't bear that.'

Stephen sat on the balustrade beside Philip, very silent, his cigarette smoking itself out between his fingers. When the family flutter had died away he got to his feet and pushed forward and took Edward by the arm, forcing him into a chair. 'Look, old boy—I told you down by the river, a little while ago, that I knew you weren't mentally unbalanced. Now I know something very much more to the point. You aren't a murderer, either. I don't just think. I know.'

Edward stared up at him, exhausted, half-sullen, half-eager. It was pitiful to see the gradual dawn of hope on the immature young face. 'All that business about the crooked wreath,' said Stephen, speaking more to Cockrill now, than to Edward, 'that was a plant to shift the blame on to him, poor kid. If a thing hung crooked, it might catch his attention and cause him to glance up quickly at it; and it's a perfectly good medical fact that in people subject to fugues and automatism and what-not, glancing up quickly may bring on an attack. Whether it was Edward who dropped the vase, or not, I don't know; Claire found it broken on the floor when she came into the house just before nine—didn't you, Claire? But do you remember what I said to you when I came into the hall and you were picking the bits up?'

'You just said was it Edward again? didn't you, Stephen?'

'Not quite,' said Stephen. 'I said—I must have said something more like, "*Not* Edward this time?". Can't you remember?'

Claire looked half-hopeful, half-incredulous. 'Well, I can't exactly remember the words. I know I said that it must have been him, because he'd just been in, and Peta had been teasing him and he was a bit upset and so forth; I'm afraid I just took it for granted that he'd dropped the vase. I've always thought so, all along.'

'We all thought so,' said Bella. 'We know the vase was dropped and broken and the water and roses spilt; we saw it next morning, all of us. And the wreath over Serafita's picture was hanging askew.'

'So Edward said just now,' said Stephen. 'The wreath was hanging askew.'

'Well, but Stephen, so it *was*,' said Peta.

'Not when I saw it,' said Stephen.

CHAPTER XII

Edward got up slowly from his chair. He was absolutely white now, his hands shaking, the sweat rolling down his forehead; he faced them again, pathetically young and coltish in his adolescent weediness, but with a dignity about him, a passion of pain and disillusion and bitterly contemptuous reproach that had nothing in it of childishness. '*You* did this to me! One of *you* did this to me! You let me go through this hell. You let me think that I was mad and a murderer, a dangerous lunatic not fit to be loose on the world. Not fit to play with the baby, not fit to sleep alone in a room without the man of the family near, to protect the others, not—not fit to . . . ' He broke down for a moment, then said: 'This has been torture, the most horrible kind of torture. None of you can know what it's been like; you can't know what it's like not even to be certain that you're thinking sensible thoughts. You suddenly wake up and think, "Perhaps this is all just drooling idiocy; perhaps I don't really know what's going on about me; perhaps I'm living in a sort of dream, not recognizing what people are actually saying to me." You—you make jokes and pretend you don't care, but all the time you're driving yourself mad, thinking that perhaps people are only humouring you by smiling and pretending to respond: perhaps you're not even talking sense: perhaps you think you're a poached egg or—or Queen Victoria, or something, like the funny stories about lunatics. You—you wake up in the night and think and wonder, and—and dread being taken away to some terrible place, and then say to yourself that perhaps *that's* part of a 'persecution mania'; and you make a terrific effort all over again to seem as if you're normal and don't care. And one of you did this to me! One of you broke the vase and spilled the water and arranged the wreath, so that all this hell should fall on me. Not to speak of the fact that I had to believe myself a murderer.'

Bella rose, putting out her hands to him. 'Oh, Edward, darling, for God's sake . . . '

'Don't touch me, Belle,' he said. 'I don't want anyone to touch me or come near me. One of you, one of my own family, *one of my own family*, let me think I was mad. One of my own family . . . '

Peta said, 'Darling, don't go on and *on* saying, "one of my own family" . . . '

He whirled round with a face of cold fury. 'God help me, Peta, I believe you would walk through a battlefield, looking at the wounded men lying there in the mud—and make a joke of it!'

'Summer time, darling,' said Peta. 'No mud.'

He was dreadfully white. 'No one should know better than you, Edward,' said Ellen in her matter of fact voice, 'that the Marches are never more flippant than when they're minding about something very much. As for your family, well, most of us aren't exactly your family, my dear, are we? That's what you seem to mind most, that one of your own flesh and blood should do this to you; so perhaps it'll make you feel just a little better if you remember that, after all, you're not a March. If *I* did this thing—but I didn't actually—well, I'm not your family at all: and Peta, and Claire, and Philip—they're only half-cousins, or whatever it is; you've only got a grandfather in common, haven't you? You and I, Teddy, we're outside this lot really, aren't we? I only belong to it through Philip. Your grandmother was Bella; theirs was Serafita. You and I and Bella, we haven't really any part, darling, in the ancestor worship and ballet-dancing and rose-wreaths and coloured gloves . . . '

Her level voice went on and on, trying to calm and soothe him; she knew that it did not matter very much what she said. While she spoke, Cockrill got up quietly and, almost unobserved, went into the house. He went into the drawing-room and stood for a little while underneath Serafita's portrait, looking up at her. 'You have a lot to be responsible for, my dear,' he said to the smiling face, and so returned to the terrace again and sat down quietly in his chair. Ellen had stopped speaking and they all sat silent while Edward still stood, towering above them, given over to his ashen rage. 'One of you, one of *you*! Letting me bear the blame! I'll tell Cockie, I'll tell him everything we've worked out; he thinks it couldn't have been any of you and so it must have been me. But it could have been *any* of you, I'll tell Cockie, I'll make him see . . .'

'Oh, Edward, *dar*ling!' pleaded Bella.

He turned on her furiously. 'Keep quiet! Keep *quiet*! If—if it hadn't been for you, filling me up with stupid nonsense, taking me to see the wrong kind of doctors, phoney ones, sensational ones, who told me I might do things and made me experiment and want to see if it would really happen: making me think I was queer and different . . .' He broke off, but shouted, standing over her, both of them white and shaking, both almost in tears: 'If I'm mad, *you're* mad! If I'm mad, where did I get it from? perhaps *you* killed Grandfather; perhaps you did squirt poison over his food—you could have! Perhaps *you're* mad, Bella; if I am, why shouldn't *you* be?'

'But the whole point is that you're not, Edward,' said Stephen in his quiet way. 'And if you're not, there's no reason to suppose that Bella is. And unless she was mad and did it without a motive, she surely wouldn't have killed Sir Richard—why should she?'

He turned away with a sort of half-movement, like a hurt animal. 'Well, I don't know. Anyway, it was one of you. Wasn't it, Cockie? Her or Peta, or Claire, or Philip, or—who's left?—Ellen.'

'It was one of six people here,' said Cockrill steadily.

'Well, all right, counting me.' He looked round him almost as though he were the centre of some game at a children's party. 'It couldn't be Ellen, because of Brough. And it couldn't be Philip because we don't really believe, not seriously, that he isn't Philip, and of course Dr. Newsome wouldn't make such a mess of the time-of-death business. We were silly to think of that.'

'Thank you,' said Philip, sarcastically; but one couldn't really resent what he said, poor desperate boy.

'So that leaves—it leaves Peta and Claire. And Claire—well, Peta showed, that day, how Claire could have gone up the path the night before and killed Grandfather and come away, and only pretended to go up it the next morning and see him sitting in the window.' He looked rather frightened; and shame-faced. 'You heard Peta say it, Cockie; *I'm* not telling you. It—it could have happened.'

There was a silence. Claire said at last, 'Well—Ellen!'

'Yes?' said Ellen.

'Aren't you going to tell Edward about that morning? You were standing on the balcony outside your bedroom; you could see right over the bushes at the edge of the drive—you could see down to the lodge. You must have seen me walking up the path to the french window, and running down again. *You* know that I really did go up the path.'

Ellen said nothing. She thought: 'This bitch tried to steal my husband: she nearly succeeded in stealing him (which is what hurts!). She wanted him because she wanted somebody—not because she really loved *him*. She's self-centred and—and not real; she'd have made him miserable and unhappy, she'd have driven him mad with her emotionalism and scenes and play-acting. Why should I help her out? Let her suffer a bit!' She tipped back her garden chair and looked at Claire coolly. 'Did you? I don't think I noticed.'

Cockrill, with sardonic amusement, watched her face. 'It doesn't matter anyway, Ellen. If Claire hadn't gone up the path as she says she did, how could she have left the breakfast tray in the middle of it?'

'Oh. So that leaves me,' said Peta. 'What fun.' She did not look as though she found it fun at all.

Cockrill sat rocking pleasantly back and forth on the hind legs of his chair, nursing his white panama

hat. 'The case against Peta is an interesting one. She
had a great deal to lose if the new will was signed.
She went with Lady March down to the lodge clad
only in her bathing-suit, of which there isn't much,
because I've seen it. She couldn't have concealed a
hypodermic syringe about her person, but I suppose
there's no reason why she shouldn't have carried two
or three tiny glass ampoules tucked up the leg of her
slip; it was so closely fitting that it would have kept
them there; that would have been enough if she could
have got down the tumbler from the shelf and introduced the coramine into it, so that your grandfather,
when he went for a glass of water, would fill up the
glass and drink the whole lot off. But the point about
the glass is that Peta couldn't have got the stuff into
it without touching it; and that if she had touched it,
she must have left finger-prints on it. That glass hadn't
been polished—it was still a little dusty on the outside.
So Peta couldn't have murdered Sir Richard either;
her prints were not on the glass—only his.'

Now was the time to tell Cockie! Now, if he really
was going to put his threats into action, was the time
for Edward to tell Cockie that Peta *could* have touched
the glass, and left no marks, to tell Cockie how it was
that though she had touched the telephone she had
left no marks on that either, to tell Cockie how Philip
had suggested that Peta might have covered her finger-tips with colourless varnish; that she could be—
must be—the murderer! Now was the time. They had
deceived him, terrified him, they had let him suffer
to take responsibility for this horrible crime; now was
the moment to pay them all back, to speak out and
tell Cockie all he knew. He opened his mouth to speak,
to tell about Peta, to send Peta to—to God knew what
horror of prison and trial and condemnation and death.
Peta, so pretty and sweet and gay and laughing—so
vulnerable, in her foolishnesses and her tendernesses.
Yet if Peta was a murderess—if Peta had let him suffer. . . . He turned away and went to the edge of the
terrace and stared down at the river. Let someone else
speak. Not he.

It was Peta who spoke. She said, 'Oh, Teddy darling—thank you!' and to Cockrill added, quite gaily: 'The family have a theory about my finger-prints, Cockie; we're so full of theories and this is the one about me. They think I put colourless enamel over my finger-tips to stop them making prints. They think I could have done it that way; but the important thing is—do you?'

'No,' said Cockrill. And he put his hand in his pocket and fished out something and laid it on the table before him, not taking his eyes off her face. Peta said, 'Good God!—what's that?'

It was a pair of flesh-coloured, elbow-length gloves.

They all stood staring at them. Bella said, 'Gracious, Cockie: where on earth did you get those?'

'From the little casket under the portrait in the drawing-room,' said Cockrill. He picked them up and bundled them back into his pocket. 'I thought it was my handkerchief; I'd forgotten I had them there.'

'I thought you were going to tell us that Peta had worn a pair of Serafita's gloves,' said Bella, laughing a little nervously. 'There *is* a pair in the casket in the lodge, only, of course, they're black, and Peta couldn't possibly have worn them without my seeing them; and Richard too.'

'You frightened me, Cockie,' said Peta.

'You were right to be frightened,' said Cockrill. 'You ought to be frightened; you *all* ought to be frightened, because something very bad and horrible and cruel has taken place and I think it's time you all faced up to the fact—really faced it; didn't play with theories and suspicions and silly accusations that you don't really believe in, but looked the fact square in the face, that one of six people here on this terrace is twice a murderer.'

Not Peta. And not Claire. And not Belle and not Philip and not Ellen and not Edward. Cockrill waited. And suddenly Edward said, in a whisper, 'You can't mean—Stephen?'

Even Cockrill look startled. 'I'm sorry, Stephen,'

said Edward. 'I didn't mean *I* thought that! I only thought Cockie did. And, of course, after all, you being keen on Peta and wishing she wasn't an heiress and all that.' To Cockrill he said, 'You did it on purpose, Cockie. You're playing with us all; you're going on and on at us, hoping that someone will break down and give themselves away. You're—you're like a cat with us poor little mice, scared to death all round you; you're doing it deliberately to make the murderer confess!'

'Yes,' said Cockie. 'I could put my hand out and take the murderer now, this minute—the murderer of Brough and of your grandfather. But I think it would be—well, less terrible all round, if he'd confess; if he or she would confess. I have known you all for a long time. I knew your grandmother, Serafita; I knew Lady March when she first came here—I remember very well how naïve and charming she was in her eagerness and inexperience. I remember Peta and Claire and Edward when they were little children; I remember Philip when he first came home to Swanswater and Sir Richard killed the fatted calf for him; I remember Ellen as a bride. That's why I am giving the murderer this one chance. That's why I say to the murderer, "This is the end. These are the last minutes; for God's sake, get this thing off your soul! Isn't there a little gleam of reparation to be made for the irreparable harm you've done? By putting out your hand now and saying 'Take me,' instead of just letting yourself be ignominiously taken." '

Bella, Peta, Claire, Ellen, Philip—one of these five. Edward looked round at them imploringly. 'One of these five, Cockie; one of *these five*? There isn't anyone else. There's nobody else.'

'Well, only one other person,' said Cockrill.

'One person? One other person?'

Cockrill took out his little tin of tobacco and his papers and with great deliberation, concentrating deeply after so uncharacteristic an outburst, he made himself a cigarette. When it was rolled and lighted he tossed the match off the balustrade into the river.

'Edward, my boy—this is as clever a frame-up as ever I have known. Somebody such as yourself is the perfect scapegoat. You are, or you are not, mentally unsound—nobody knows. If anything inexplicable occurs the responsibility may easily enough be fixed on to you and even you yourself need not know for certain whether or not you are the real culprit. The family will fight tooth and nail to protect you from discovery, but if you are finally accused and convicted, nothing very dreadful can happen to you after all. You will be detained "at His Majesty's pleasure", which, in your case, would largely be a matter of seeing that you could never again do any harm, to yourself or anyone else. Ye gods, yes!' said Cockie, ruminating over it, 'this was a cleverly thought-out plan. At the worst you would be an object of interest and pity, living a life of comfort, subjected only to proper supervision. The chances were that by the united efforts of the family you could be protected from discovery and the thing would simply resolve itself into an unsolved mystery; but if somebody had to take the responsibility, why you were the one person who could take it and not be held responsible.'

Bella, Peta, Claire, Ellen, Philip. 'But Cockie,' cried Edward, 'who is this? Who did this? Who thought this all out? Who do you mean?'

Almost in a whisper, Cockrill said: 'I mean you!'

Far above their heads, what had been a low, grumbling drone grew to a roar; a steel wire whanged and split asunder with a stinging crack; and, one-winged after its impact with the balloon cable, a flying bomb came hurtling through the summer sky.

CHAPTER XIII

The noise of the bomb-burst fanned hotly against their recoiling nerves. It was as though with a great, thick stick, an invisible giant struck at the very softness of the brain behind the frontal bone; all the flesh shuddered from the impact of the sound, from the thrusting suck and eddy of the blasted air. The spirit screamed to the mind to fight its way to the surface of the engulfing dark; the mind struggling against more merciful nothingness feebly implored obedience of limbs held captive by horror; wide eyes, open upon the uprush of devastation, sent no message to the unasking brain. Like a ship destroyed at sea the great house seemed to rise piecemeal into the air, settling down slowly, low in the water, a huddle of tangled wreckage afloat on the wide green lawns. And as the dust cleared and the wave of the blast that had tumbled them backwards, withdrew, leaving them spent and gasping, Ellen cried out: 'My baby!' and staggered a few steps forward and fell fainting to the ground.

Edward did not know that he was running towards the house; that they were all running towards the crumbling house, that he was outstripping them, was rushing, two steps at a time, up the rise of terraces, into the hall and up the crumbling stairs. As he gained the first-floor landing the structure of the staircase gave way; a beam, crashing past him, glanced off his shoulder; he caught at his arm, unconsciously, with his other hand, and, holding it, looked down into the hall below. Philip and Stephen stood, warding off the falling masonry with their arms, staring up at him helplessly; on either side of them the new parts of the house were already a mere mass of lath and plaster and slowly-settling dust; but the sturdy Georgian brick stood proudly, defying till the last possible moment an enemy of which its builders had never dreamed. He leaned against the carved wooden banisters and screamed out over the din, 'I'll get her! Go outside! Go out under the balcony window. I'll try and get her down to you.'

It was terrible to leave the comforting support of the strong oak to which he clung; but he dragged himself away and, still holding his arm, began to stagger through the falling bricks and beams, towards the baby's room. In a world where everything else was giving way, the door had jammed; he beat against it wildly with his uninjured arm—and behind him a little red tongue of flame savoured the wooden banister of the fallen staircase and, caught by a gust of draught, licked up suddenly into a leaping flame.

With the door the inner wall collapsed and fell about his head. Stunned and blinded he stumbled across the overturned bedroom furniture to the cot. Antonia was not there, but his heart turned sick with relief as, somewhere in the corner, he heard her lusty howling. He groped his way through the dust-filled air towards the sound. He tried to call out, to reassure, to comfort her, but no words would come; he put his hand to his throat and found blood there. Blood was trickling down from a small wound in the side of his head; but he felt no pain.

The baby was heavy on his single useful arm, and turned and twisted in an abandonment of terror, but she did not seem to be injured. It was terrible to be able to find no words, no sound, to sooth her. He dragged himself towards the balcony window. Through the gaping roof and tottering outside wall, fantastically, unimaginably, sunshine was pouring in through the veils of thickly falling dust. The roar of the fire behind him lent a panicky strength to his failing legs.

Philip and Stephen had torn down the heavy linen curtains from the drawing-room, and were trying to fashion a cradle from them, for him to drop the baby into from the balcony; but the blast had slashed them

to shreds and they were useless. He stood swaying on
the edge of the little balcony, clinging to the stone
balustrade. Philip screamed out at him, 'Stand back!
Don't lean against it! It's giving way. Drop the baby,
try to throw her to us; but be careful, the balcony's
giving way.'

He leaned over perilously, letting the child slither
through the grasp of his one hand, dropping a few
feet into the safety of their outstretched arms; and,
thrusting himself backwards and away from the balustrade, fell back into the room as the stonework broke
and crumbled and toppled with a crash to the terrace
below. With it went the outside wall; and he was alone
in a prison of falling stone, with the red fire raging
outside the open door.

For a moment it was almost peaceful, shut in alone
there with his task accomplished. The baby was safe
—the baby who had danced for Grandfather on the
terrace, a thousand aeons ago, the baby who had sat,
crowned with buttercups and daisies, on the green
grass of the lawn, the baby who only yesterday had
greeted its mother in its white silk smock with forget-
me-nots round its neck; the baby was safe and he,
poor mad Edward, had given his life to save it. There
was nothing more now to do—for a moment he, who
of late had known so much evil and terror and pain,
who surely could never know happiness again—for a
moment, he was happy.

But the time for surrender had not come; surrender to death might be preferable to struggling on,
since life held so little of joy; but not to this death,
not to a death creeping upon one in a cloak of curling,
suffocating smoke slashed with bright flame, not to a
death in choking and agony. He staggered once more
to his leaden feet and, with heavy reluctance, drove
his dragging legs towards the door.

The heat of the flames beat him back, but in the
moment that he stood there, he had glimpsed a small
opening in the conflagration; if he could get through,
could creep out on to the landing, he might perhaps
manage to drop down into the hall; might even find

masonry so broken and heaped that he could clamber down over it. He did not think that his aching head could stand the jar of another fall. 'I must keep my mind clear,' he thought. 'Whatever happens I must try to keep my mind clear.' Catching up a tatter of linen from one of the beds, he mopped at his bleeding wounds; and, holding the bloody cloth across his mouth and nose, fought his way out through the heat and smoke, brushing himself against the walls of the corridor to crush the small sparks that caught at his tattered clothes. The smoke caught at his aching throat, the hot breath of the fire smote at his eyeballs; breathless and sobbing, he thrust his way through hell, and was out once more into a tiny haven of calm and peace, sheltered by a corner of roofing from falling stone, safe for a moment from immediate threat of the flames.

Outside in the incongruous, unbelievable sunshine, Bella and Ellen wept over Antonia's safety, watching, faint and dizzy the slow destruction of the burning house; and, cut off from him by the mountainous toppling of the outside walls, Claire, Peta, and the three men tore with frenzied hands at the piled brick and concrete of Edward's tomb. Inside, crouched in his corner, he fought against the desperate longing for surrender, surrender to oncoming death, even to the agony that must precede the peace. Peace! Peace and rest! No more struggling, no more fighting, no more fear. Surrender, unconsciousness, death. Surrender . . .

Only the spirit now had courage to go on. His head ached, his eyes were blinded by the pain and the heat and the smoke and the dust-clotted blood; from his temple to his shoulder, pain tore at him now, with terrible hands; blood poured down his arm and across his breast, and through the torn flesh a bone gleamed whitely for a moment and was engulfed again in a fresh clot of blood. 'I can't go on,' he thought. 'I'm dying. Nobody can live with wounds like this.' His knees gave way beneath him and for a moment blackness poured in upon him like fluid velvet, softly lapping him into eternal rest. 'I can't go on. I needn't struggle any more. I'm dying. Let me die in peace.' But the failing spirit drove on the rebellious flesh to one effort more, and he stumbled to his feet and started perilously down the shifting masonry into the hall; and there in the shattered cavern whose marbled beauty had been Serafita's pride, he crept as near as was possible to the great front door, and like a dog locked out, lay panting and sobbing, and could try no more. 'Let me die, what do I care? Why should I want to go on? Only to be caught and imprisoned and at last done to death because I killed my grandfather, because I'm mad, or not mad—God knows!—and a murderer. Why should I change one imprisonment, and one death, for another imprisonment and another death?' He crouched up against the plaster-strewn rubble, shielding his eyes with his one good arm from the sight of the oncoming flames. 'I'll die. I'll just give myself up to death, poor mad Edward, dead and done with it all . . .'

Over the doorway, the delicate woodwork and glass were shattered to a thousand splinters; but in a sea of fallen stones, the arch stood firm. Philip and Stephen and Cockrill struggled frantically to clear a way through. 'But we don't even know what we shall find on the other side. We don't even know that he's been able to get downstairs . . .'

Claire, the lightest and smallest, climbed up the slope of the stones to the height of the transom. 'I believe if I could get some of this stuff away, I might see in . . .' Her little hands clawed at the stones and plaster. 'Yes! Yes, I can make a hole right through. I can see into the hall . . .' She paused for a moment, peering in, with a face of horror. 'My God, the fire! It's awful, inside. It's all up the stairs and on the top landing—not down in the hall . . .' Scraping fever-ishly like a terrier at the small aperture, she thrust through her head and called, 'Edward! Edward!' and wriggled her shoulders after her head and called again. After a moment she pulled herself back. 'I can see him. He's down in the hall. He's hurt. I'm going through,' and she plunged back into the aperture again, gave a thrust and a wriggle and, headforemost, disappeared. The transom reshifted, resettled; and the gap was gone. But almost as she dropped down beside him, they saw a gleam of sunlight as Philip's hands tore a way through. 'Quick, Edward, be ready; as soon as the hole's big enough, I'll help you up.'

He crouched on the rubble looking up at her, his hand to his throat. 'Oh, Claire—why did you come? The fire will get here before they can get you out. You'll be killed. Oh, why did you *come*?'

'I'll help you up, Edward. I'll get you out.'

At least the speech had come back to his lacerated throat. 'Claire, of course I can't get out and leave you here.' He gasped and choked, swaying against a boulder. 'When they get through again—I'll lift you with my arm—my right arm's hurt—and they must haul you out. After that . . . ' He looked up at the ill-balanced heap of masonry above their heads. 'One more move, Claire, and the whole thing will come down. One person scrambling through . . .'

Above them the hands scraped and tunnelled. They faced each other in the stifling, flame-licked dark. 'Edward—for God's sake, there isn't time to argue. When Philip gets through to haul you up—you're to go! For heaven's sake don't waste time with this fantastic argument. You're hurt. I'll help you out; and you're to go!'

The gap above them imperceptibly increased. It was true that there would be no time to argue. 'Look, Claire—I don't think more than one of us can get out. I think it'll collapse. If only one of us can be saved—it mustn't be me. Why should I live? I'll be sent to prison, or a lunatic asylum, or hanged. Why should I be saved just for that? I don't want to be saved, I don't want to, I only want you to get out and be saved, and leave me here to die.' He looked round desperately. 'Oh, why can't I die now and put an end to this? What can I do, just to die and be finished with, so that you won't have to save me?' To their right the roofless ruin that once had been the drawing-room, gaped dimly through the flames; Serafita's portrait, spared by some freak of incalculable blast to hang, though crookedly, on the in-bulging wall, simpered down at them in the light of the fires, with its painted, artificial smile. 'I must do something. I must make an effort, I must drive Claire into saving herself.' He staggered to his feet and before she could stop him, had stumbled forward at a little blundering run down the sloping heap of the rubble, and, through the smoke and flames and out of her sight. In a brief flare up of flame, she saw him lying on the floor beneath the portrait, arms outstretched.

Philip with Stephen and Cockrill, scraped and battered at the place where the transom had been. 'It won't hold much longer. The whole thing's giving way. But there's nothing else to do, it's the only hope of getting to them now.' Cockrill, small and agile as a monkey, worked at the top of the heap, delicately balancing on the rubble, peering into the hole. 'The whole place is filled with the smoke and flame . . . I can't see . . . Yes, she's—she's just below me here.' His small brown hands worked frantically, digging a widening gap, trying to steady the tottering wall above. Stephen was the first to put the terrible truth into words. 'It's no use. We might get one of them out, but then the whole thing will collapse. One person pushing through will bring the lot down.' He did not pause in his work, but his voice was sick with horror of the thought. 'We can only get one of them out.'

'Yes,' said Philip. 'It's true.' He did not hesitate. He called up to Cockrill, 'Can you call through to Claire? Never mind if she doesn't answer, she may hear you anyway. Tell her to be ready. Tell her she must leave Edward. Tell her only one of them can get out.'

Peta stood weeping below them on the broken terrace. 'Oh, Philip, you can't—you *can't*! She mustn't just leave him to die!'

'It's Claire or Edward,' said Philip. 'If the wall doesn't fall, I'll go down and get him. Go on, Cockrill, call down to her!'

Cockrill spared a word for the sobbing Peta. 'He's right, my child. If only one can be saved, and one's a murderer, then the murderer must be abandoned.' He leaned through the gap and called down into the smoky blackness below. Claire's voice, faint and high-pitched, answered him, and, as the gap suddenly widened beneath the strain of the infalling masonry, he leaned forward, groping, clutching wildly at the upraised hands below. Stephen and Philip, taken unawares, could only grasp at his legs and his body, dragging him backwards as the wall toppled in. From the house there came one terrible scream, piercing through the rumble of stones; and then silence. Bruised and battered, Cockrill was hurled to the terrace below, and picking himself up, staggered away from the falling rubble and down the broken steps and laid his unconscious burden on the lawn. They stumbled after him, wiping the blinding sweat and grime from their eyes, and stood in a silent circle, staring down. At last, in a whisper, Philip said: 'You said—you told us—we should leave the murderer!'

'So we have,' said Cockrill; and kneeling beside Edward began tenderly to examine his wounds.

CHAPTER XIV

And so Swanswater burned. There was the clang of a fire-engine bell in the distance, and soon skidding wheels churned up the gravel of the drive; there were curt orders, the hiss of river-water driven high from heaving hoses, and in the late afternoon light the flames glowed red on the helmets of toiling men. A rescue squad began methodical preparations for the removal of Claire's body from the ruins of the hall; and down on the lawn, Philip pushed Cockrill aside and took over into his expert hands, the tending of Edward's wounds. He said briefly, 'He's not very bad. They're ugly, but they're all superficial; he can be stitched up, and the arm set, and he'll be all right. Don't cry, Bella, he'll be quite all right.' An ambulance drove into the iron gates and a little way along the drive. Philip glanced at it. 'Tell them to wait a few minutes; there's no urgency about Edward, and we shall want it just in case Claire ... In case ...'

The baby slept, exhausted, wrapped in a rug on the grass. Cockrill, Stephen, Bella, Peta, and Ellen, were silent, looking down at the unconscious boy on the stretcher. Cockrill said, almost grimly: 'My dear Philip—there's no "in case".'

Philip, his task completed, stood up. He turned away his head. He said, 'Well, never mind: let him wait.'

Ellen went over to him. 'Philip—don't mind so terribly. You think it was your fault, but it wasn't. If it hadn't been you—it would have been someone else.' She looked at the others. 'Tell Philip—put him out of this awful agony. It's true, isn't it?'

'Yes,' said Bella. 'It *is* true, Philip. Claire—well, she dramatized herself so much. And she was unhappy; she wanted to be loved—she knew that she was beautiful, and clever, and yet people didn't love her, and she couldn't understand why. I think myself, it was because she never *had* been loved. From her childhood she'd lived here with your grandfather, and Peta had always been the darling, the petted one. It wasn't your fault, Peta, dear, don't reproach yourself; but you were the heiress, you were the child of the favourite, and Richard didn't really need Claire or want her; he didn't really love her. When she was old enough to be conscious of the need to be loved, well she—she tried too hard. And it was more than that. She was a failure at her job. Just as she was beautiful and it didn't make her any more loved, so she was clever, but it didn't make her a success. I think there again, she tried too hard. She couldn't be content with doing an inferior job well, she wanted to be "literary". Anyway, she knew that when the war ended, her "career" would be over; she'd be a failure, a failure as a journalist, because she hadn't got a job, and a failure as a woman, because she hadn't—hadn't got a man. Nothing in her life was satisfying and secure. And then, when this need was most urgently upon her, suddenly something flared up between her and Philip; he was unhappy and restless and she felt that he needed her; for the first time in her life, I believe, she felt that she was "needed"—it's what all women want, I think, underneath: to be necessary to somebody or something . . . ' Bella broke off and looked about her. 'I'm not putting this very well. I'm not very clever.'

Peta stood in the shelter of Stephen's arm. 'You are, darling, you're very clever. Go on!' It eased that terrible tension of waiting, to talk; and if they were to talk of anything it could only be Claire.

'Peta said it all that day down at the lodge,' said Bella. 'If your grandfather signed the new will and died—as he might easily do—before he changed it back, then she lost Philip and everything that Philip stood for.'

'She may have thought,' said Ellen, 'that he was old; that he'd had his life; that she was only anticipating things a little. It may not have seemed so very terrible to her after all . . . '

Beneath God knew what weight of fallen masonry, Claire lay dead. Cockrill, looking up at the ruins, said almost sternly: 'Because she has paid for her crime, Ellen, there's no need to try to make less of the crime itself. It isn't good or healthy that you should. She was a murderess—twice a murderess—and she let this poor boy here suffer—well, he told you this evening what it had meant to him. I tried to make her own up to it; I tried to make her be the one who told Edward that all his nightmare was at an end; that he wasn't mad; at last I tried to shock her into doing it; I thought if I accused him point blank she would break down. I knew that it would mean a lot to him, if she confessed; it would restore something of his faith. But she wouldn't speak. And then the bomb fell.'

Peta said, 'It's true. She let him suffer; she let him think that he was mad; she let us all think that he was mad; she let us behave towards him and be frightened of him, as though he were some mad, dangerous dog, that we ought to have had destroyed, only we had once been fond of him. She did that deliberately.' She turned her head aside, to conceal her tears.

Stephen answered. 'Not deliberately. I don't think she planned it. I think it all grew up and she couldn't stop it; she always tried to disprove and deny that Edward was mad, as all of you did. Looking back on it all, in this new light, I think that Claire knocked over that vase in the drawing-room by mistake; she'd gone there to get the poisons, I suppose, from Philip's bag, and she knocked the vase over. And then I came into the hall and found her there, and she had to say something, she had to account for her being there. She took it for granted that I thought Edward had had another of his "turns"—when I'd gone, she put the wreath crooked to bear the theory out. But only to account for the broken vase. I don't suppose for a moment she foresaw its implications.' He looked down at the pale face lying on the flat stretcher pillow. 'Don't you think, Philip, he ought to be got off?'

Up at the house, men toiled with ladders and shovels and picks. 'In a moment,' said Philip. 'In a moment.'

'You're building up a bitter disappointment for yourself, Philip,' said Cockrill, 'if you hope that Claire will be found alive.'

'I don't hope she's alive. I pray to God that she'll be found dead. But just in case there's a chance . . . Edward's all right, heaven knows it's warm enough here with this bonfire raging, and there's no great loss of blood. There's no other ambulance in this one-horse place; I can't take the risk of letting it go.' Philip brushed the dust and grime from the glass of his watch. 'I'll keep it ten minutes more.'

'While we wait, Cockie,' said Ellen, 'tell us about Claire. We shall have to know.'

Cockrill responded at once. He thought it unwise

and unhealthy that, because she had died for her sins, Claire should be allowed to grow into a martyr in the family's eyes. He thought they should face the facts. 'She made up her mind to do this thing and she worked it all out thoroughly and acted quickly and cleverly. She chose her time when you would all be listening to the news, the servants in the kitchen, and Brough gone to his fire-watch. She took the coramine and told your grandfather some story and, of course, he trustingly let him give him an injection—"instructions from Philip", no doubt. She put a little coramine into the glass to confuse the issue—she was cool and calculating. She must have accidentally touched the telephone, because it was necessary to wipe it and press his hand to it, hoping that it wouldn't be noticed if there were no other marks. Then, I suppose, she couldn't find the will; but she had no idea that it had been signed and she thought it was only the draft, so it wouldn't have worried her much. And she hadn't much time, she had to get back to the family soon. She'd seen Brough sanding the paths, and she had her plan all worked out. She pulled back the curtain, and left the lodge.'

'When we were—when we found Grandfather the next morning,' admitted Philip, 'she looked for the will.'

'That doesn't look very much like heart-broken remorse, does it?' said Cockrill sourly. 'And then things began to go wrong; poor Edward was believed guilty, and then Ellen was accused and that upset Philip— and also made Philip turn to his wife with a renewal of his old affection for her. But Edward came to her room that night and told her his theory about Brough; it all fitted nicely and, if only Brough was not alive to deny the story, she might be rid of all her fears. Perhaps she made up her mind then and there to kill him with the strychnine she'd taken "in case". Perhaps the idea only came to her when she saw him, at dawn, going across to the lodge. We know she was in Ellen's room that night, and from Ellen's room you can see down to the lodge; it was bright moonlight that night, and anyway, almost dawn. I suppose the siren woke her, as it woke him; or perhaps she hadn't been to sleep. What Brough was doing there we shall never know; but I have an idea that he thought it might be a good place in which to conceal the will he was holding. The police would never think of looking in a place they'd already examined and sealed up, but they were searching everywhere else—even digging up the grounds. Anyway, she took the strychnine and crept down after him. Her original plan had failed. The draft will had been signed and, whether or not it was found, the old will would no longer held. And, in the meantime, Philip was going back to his first love. She saw Brough, then, and she crept down after him. It was a terrible risk; but no doubt she watched my man go round to the back of the house and knew she had a chance; and now not her happiness but her safety was at stake.'

'I think she did it for Edward,' said Peta. 'I think it was the only way that she could tell him—and tell us all—that he wasn't a murderer; that he needn't be mad—of course without giving herself away.'

'That's what I say,' said Cockrill. 'She was afraid for herself.'

It didn't matter. It didn't matter very much, thought Peta, what Cockie thought. Claire was dead. She had tricked and deceived them all. She had killed poor Grandfather, had taken advantage of his trust, to murder him; had killed Brough, and while, in agony, he died, had blotted his name with the onus of her own crime; she had left Ellen to ignominy and fear; she had let Edward suffer pain untold—but she was dead. She had given her life deliberately knowing what she did. And now Edward was free altogether of the fear that had hung over him long before Claire had fixed it there; he could go into the Air Force and be a real person and play no more tricks with his ego; and Philip had Ellen and the baby, and she, Peta, was in Stephen's arms and not a poor little rich girl any more. And Swanswater was gone and Bella no longer a prisoner there; she could go off to 'the Riviera and

Miami and places like that'; she could have a bijou house with frilly net curtains, a yellow front door, and geraniums in little pots. Swanswater was gone and the memory of Serafita and the worship of Serafita were cleansed away by fire—and the memory of Claire also, should be cleansed by fire. It didn't really matter what Cockie thought . . .

There was a signal from the house. Two men came down and carried Edward's stretcher up to the ambulance. 'They've found the young lady, sir. They're bringing her out.' The family stumbled up painfully to the terrace and there stood waiting, a little apart from the toiling men. Only Philip went forward when at last the moment came. A little procession made its way to the ambulance; the doors were slammed and it drove away. Philip came back, terribly white, terribly weary, infinitely sad. He said: 'She's dead, of course,' and held something out to Cockrill. 'She was—she was clasping this in her arms.'

Cockrill took it from him—a small, oblong, battered object, black with smoke. 'It's a—a message. Well, thank God for that; at least she wanted us to know, she wanted to save poor Edward!' He turned it over and over in his hands. 'She must have got it when they were in the drawing-room; I saw her dragging Edward back into the hall, you know, just before we got through to him. Of course, she couldn't explain to him, couldn't tell him the truth; he was unconscious.'

They all stared at it. Peta said, 'But what is it?'

'It's the explanation,' said Cockrill. 'It's the answer to a question that none of you seem to have asked. How can she have walked up those paths that night, and left no mark that couldn't be covered next morning by her footsteps? It's the box from under Serafita's portrait in the drawing-room.'

He put down the little metal casket on a garden table and opened it. Inside was a sheaf of dusty pressed flowers, a faded theatre programme—and nothing more; the gloves which had lain there he himself had taken out earlier in the evening and shown to them all, on the terrace, down by the river. He said: 'We

all thought that Claire could not have covered up her
own footsteps in the sand; but that's just what she did.
She made two lines of footprints, up to the french
window and away from it; but they were tiny prints
—so tiny that one normal print could easily cover two
of them at a time; and she took care, no doubt, to
keep them close together. She saw Brough come away
from the lodge, having surrounded it by sanded paths;
and in that moment, I think, she made up her mind.'
He plunged his hands into the shabby side-pockets of
his old tweed coat and chucked down two small objects
to lie on the table, beside the box. A pair of tiny, pale
pink, satin ballet-shoes—the block toes still embedded
with infinitesimal grains of sand.

Only Claire had inherited Serafita's little feet.

ABOUT THE AUTHOR

CHRISTIANNA BRAND was born in Malaya and lived there and in India until she went to England to attend a convent school. She wrote the first chapters of DEATH IN HIGH HEELS in 1941 and although she had never before written a book for publication, the novel was critically acclaimed at once.

She is the author of a number of mystery or suspense stories and novels, among them HEADS YOU LOSE, SUDDENLY AT HIS RESIDENCE, GREEN FOR DANGER, CAT AND MOUSE, A RING OF ROSES and THE ROSE IN DARKNESS. She lives in London.